The Egyptian Midwife

by
Naomi Munts

Published in 2022 by Amazon KDP Publishing
© 2022 Naomi Munts.

All rights reserved. No part of this publication may be reproduced, copied, stored in a retrieval system, or transmitted, in any form or by any means, without the prior written consent of the copyright holder, nor be otherwise circulated in any form of binding or cover other than that in which it is published and without a similar condition being imposed on the subsequent purchaser.

Cover image by zkorejo. © Naomi Munts.

Northern Egypt in the Middle Kingdom

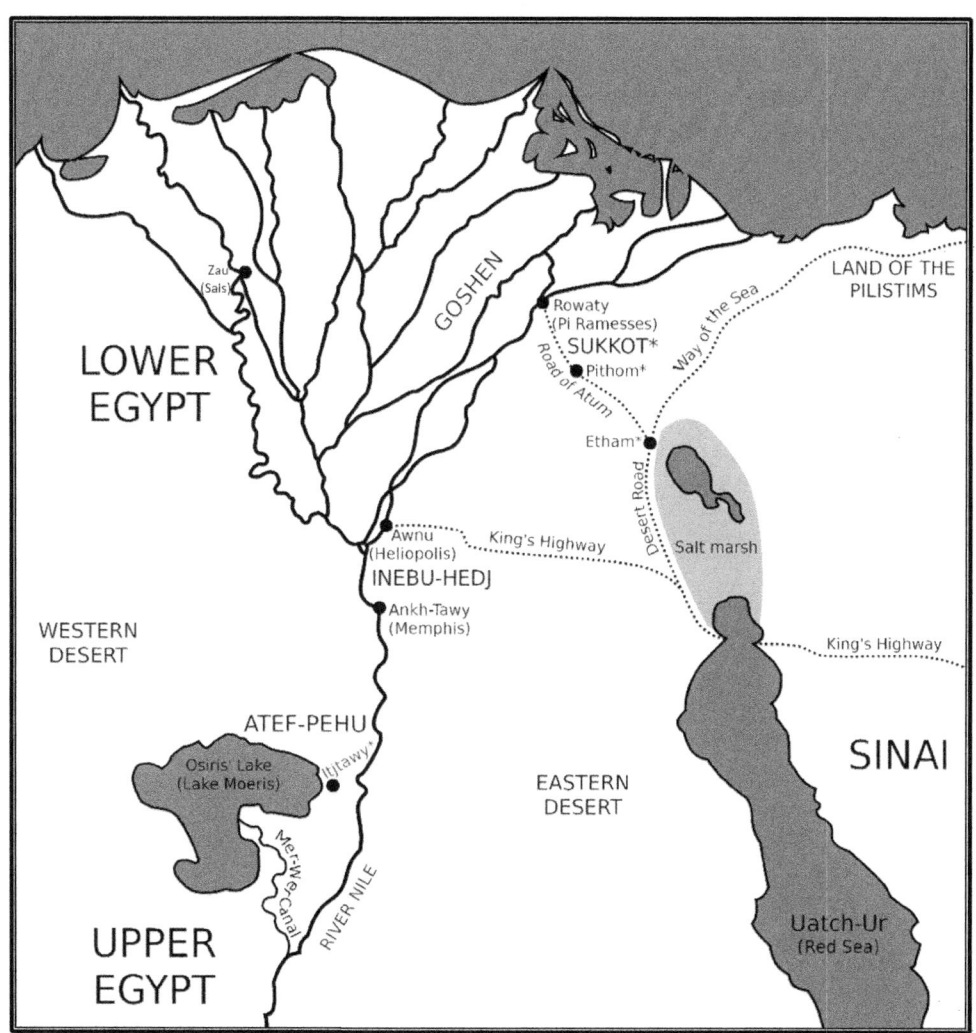

Locations marked with * are unknown/uncertain.
Where locations are better known by later names, these are given in brackets.
The name "Road of Atum" is conjectural, but it follows the course of a known trade route, today called the Wadi Tumilat.

Sources:
https://commons.wikimedia.org/wiki/File:Ancient_Egypt_map-hiero.svg
www.thebiblejourney.org
upload.wikimedia.org/wikipedia/commons/5/5c/Lake_Moeris.jpg
en.wikipedia.org/wiki/Via_Maris

Kings of the Late Thirteenth Dynasty of Egypt

Khaneferre Sobekhotep
(Reign length: Unknown[*])

Merhotepre Sobekhotep
(Reign length: Unknown[*])

Khahotepre Sobekhotep
(Reign length: 4 years, 8 months and 29 days)

Wahibre Ibiau
(Reign length: 10 years, 8 months and 29 days)

↓

Merneferre Ay
(Reign length: 23/33[*] years, 8 months and 18 days)

As his parentage is not mentioned in any of his attestations, this suggests that he was not the son of the previous king and may have usurped the throne from his predecessor.[†]

---

[*] The Turin King List, which records the order of the kings and the length of their reigns, is damaged in several places. The lengths of reigns for Khaneferre and Merhotepre Sobekhotep are lost, while the figure for Merneferre Ay is partially preserved; the damaged first numeral could be either a twenty or a thirty. (Source: K.S.B. Ryholt, *The Political Situation in Egypt during the Second Intermediate Period, c.1800–1550 BC*, Carsten Niebuhr Institute Publications, vol. 20. Copenhagen: Museum Tusculanum Press, 1997, p. 233.)
[†] Source: ibid.

Foreword

Many authors have written about the life of Moses, and there's no doubt that he was a remarkable man. But Moses owed his very existence to a whole series of remarkable women.

There was his mother Yokheved, of course, who knew from the start that he was "no ordinary child", and who had the courage and faith to protect him. There was Miryam, his sister, who, though only a young girl, possessed extraordinary wisdom – wisdom that enabled her to ensure Moses was raised by his own mother and knew his Hebrew roots.

Then there were the 'outsiders' – women who were not Israelites, but who nonetheless played an essential part in Moses' story. The princess who defied her own family to take him in and raise him as her own. His wife, Zipporah the Midianite, who saved his life at least once (Exodus 4:24–26), despite never being fully accepted into the Hebrew community.

There are some other key women, however, who entered the story even before Moses was born. Their names are Shiphrah and Puah, and they get seven verses devoted to them in Exodus 1. There's some debate as to whether they should rightly be described as "Hebrew midwives" or just "midwives to the Hebrews"; they are given Hebrew names, yet they were of high enough status to have had a personal audience with the King, which seems unlikely for slaves. I like to think that they were Egyptians who rejected not only the King's decree but the very gods and culture of Egypt, and who thus were given new names and integrated into the Hebrew community.

One thing is certain: without these compassionate and courageous women, there would have been no story to tell.

Prologue

Water. Source of all life. Bringer of violent death.

With a mighty rumble, the torrent crashes down from both sides of the causeway, meeting in the middle with a thunderclap that shakes the earth and sends fountains of boiling foam crashing upward to the heavens. For those caught between its watery jaws, death is sudden and instantaneous.

On the far side of the sea, the ragtag horde of men, women and children, who moments before had been fleeing in disarray, turn as one, mouths gaping wide in awe as wind-borne droplets of spray fall like rain onto their upturned faces, soaking them to the skin.

The multitude is loosely formed into a rough marching column, snaking away into the desert. Those at the rear, close enough to witness the full force of the cataclysm, are the stragglers: the sick, the elderly, and mothers with young infants. Ill-suited to desert travel, many of these will fall by the wayside long before reaching their destination. Yet any thoughts of turning back have been drowned with their enemies, washed away by the force of the deluge.

Gradually, the seething water grows calm. Gentle waves lap at the sandy shore as one by one the emigrants move on, their backs to the devastation they have just witnessed, their faces set to the challenge ahead. Lads with willow switches dart here and there, rounding up the sheep and goats that have been allowed to stray, driving them, with a flick of their canes, forward along the dusty road. Yet one old woman stands still gazing toward the sea, salt water running from her eyes over cheeks as cragged and weathered as crumpled papyrus. Whether the tears are of joy or sorrow, shock or relief, even she cannot tell.

A sound breaks her reverie. Turning her head, she sees a little she-goat that has become separated from her flock. All alone and not knowing which way to turn, the creature tremulously holds up an injured front leg, then flickers its ears and bleats forlornly up at her. Common sense would tell her to leave it; a goat that can't keep up with its flock will be no more than a hindrance on this desert trek. Yet the ancient woman stoops and speaks softly to the animal; then, with a strength that belies her age, she lifts it in one swift movement, sets it on her shoulders above the bundle that already rests there, and turns to follow the retreating column, staggering slightly under the weight.

"Mother! Come on, Mother, you'll be left behind!"

Five figures have detached themselves from the rear of the column and move swiftly toward the old woman and her burden. The first is a man, grizzled but strong, and it is he who addresses her. He raises his eyebrows at the sight of the goat but makes no comment as he lifts it from her shoulders and places it on his own. The first of his companions, a woman with wisps of greying hair escaping from under a blue-green headscarf, rests her bulky linen-wrapped bundle on the ground as she embraces the older woman warmly, then takes it up again and falls back to walk beside her husband. Another woman, younger and wearing a yellow headscarf, balances a heavy kneading-trough on her shoulders as she turns her head this way and that in an attempt to keep track of her children, a boy and a girl. The boy, slim and dark-haired, strides ahead of the others with a swing in his step and a light in his eye, while his younger sister skips ahead for a few paces then, laughing, returns to pet the goat's head and run her hand over its silky ears.

The sun is setting behind the saltwater lake, its dying rays tinting the waters a deep crimson. The old woman allows herself one last moment to gaze at the sight; then, with a little shudder, she turns away, setting her face firmly outward toward the trackless desert ahead.

-PART I-

1

Puah

It's quiet out here by the banks of the Nile. Apart from our own footfalls, the only things that disturb the stillness of the evening are the rushing of the water, the buzz of insects, the low croak of an ibis. And the sound of sobbing.

A glance at my granddaughter's face tells me she hears it, too. Slowing our steps, we follow our ears to a tall stand of papyrus reeds growing at the very edge of the water. Huddled in their shade we find a pitiful figure. A boy, no more than twelve years of age, crouches half-submerged in the muddy shallows, hugging his knees to his chest. His tunic, frayed and soiled, lies discarded on the bank, and though his face is hidden by his arms, there is no doubt that it is from him that the sobs are emanating. Drawing closer, we see the reason for them: the bony arch of his back is criss-crossed with angry red weals.

At the sound of our approach, he springs up, in the same movement reaching for his garment, though the action draws an involuntarily cry of pain from his lips. His tear-streaked cheeks redden beneath their patina of dirt as he clasps the tunic protectively in front of him to cover his modesty.

"It's OK," says Hana, her brown eyes registering sympathy and concern. "We're healers. If you let us have a look at your back, we might be able to help ease the pain."

Technically, of course, my granddaughter is not being entirely truthful; we wouldn't be officially classed as healers in the strict sense of the word.

But as midwives, we're well used to stitching wounds and applying healing poultices and tonics. And with my eight decades of experience, there's not one of my family or neighbours who wouldn't sooner come to me than to any physician. Anyway, her words have the desired effect. The lad relaxes; the tension eases from his shoulders and he kneels on the ground, allowing us to examine his wounds.

It's not hard to guess how he came about them, but I ask anyway: "What happened?"

His eyes fill with tears again, and the boyish treble of his voice quavers as he replies: "The slavemaster in the brickfield down yonder." He points and winces. "My dad's sick, and I've been trying to make his quota as well as my own all this week…" He needn't say more. The red welts are testimony to the futility of such an undertaking. My eyes harden a moment – is there not one *deben* of compassion in that slavemaster's cold heart? – but then I sigh. The slavemasters aren't concerned about exhausted children or sick fathers; they only care that enough bricks are produced to fulfil the regular shipments upriver to the building projects at Atef-Pehu.

Hana catches my eye then glances at the sun, which is nearing the horizon; the sky around it is already blushing orange. I sense her dilemma: she wants to help this lad, but there's also a woman in labour who is counting on us.

"You go on ahead," I say. "You'll get there much quicker without my rickety old legs slowing you down. Leave me some aloe and bandages, and I'll soon have the lad sorted. Then I'll come after you."

Hana hesitates. "The light will be fading soon…"

"How often have I walked these paths? I'll be fine," I tell her reassuringly.

She looks once more from me to the boy to the setting sun, then makes up her mind. Rummaging in her heavy papyrus-woven basket, she pulls out the items I asked for and bids me follow soon. Then she hurries away. I straighten and watch a moment as she hastens along the path, glancing back over her shoulder every now and then until she is out of sight.

Of all my grandchildren, Hana is the most like me. Tall and olive-skinned, her dark-brown eyes framed by long lashes, she reminds me of the woman I was forty or fifty years ago. She wears a green headcloth over her straight, dark hair, and in her simple linen tunic she looks no different from any other Hebrew slave-woman; but in truth, between my blood and her father's, there is more Egyptian than Hebrew in her. Not only that, she has also inherited my calling. I started taking her along with me on my midwifery visits when she was nine or ten; now it's more a case of her taking me along.

I break from my musings as the lad beside me shifts position, causing a sharp intake of air through his teeth as he stretches his wounded back. Turning my attention back to my charge, I speak reassuringly to him as I bathe his wounds then crush the aloe leaves into a poultice and bind them in place with the strips of coarse linen.

"They're not deep," I tell him, "though I can see they're painful. This should help soothe and cool them. Just keep them clean and keep the flies away, and they'll be healed in no time."

In my head, I add: *though there's no healing for a system that beats a child because his father is too sick to work.*

By the time I'm done, the boy is clearly feeling more comfortable, and he thanks me repeatedly before limping off south-westward toward the town of Rowaty. I watch him go, his small figure outlined briefly against the dying rays of the sun before it is swallowed by the dark hulking mass of the city. Then I turn and continue my journey in the other direction, toward the small riverside settlement that is my destination. I might not be able to walk too fast, these days, and my eyes may not see so well in the fading light, but what I said to Hana is true – my feet know every stone and rut, and I don't stumble once as I pick my way along the narrow raised path, the great river on my right and the dark, fertile floodplains on my left.

Well before the last rosy glow of daylight has faded, I find the house I am looking for and call out a greeting as I push open the door to the wood-pillared courtyard. The men, of course, have remained downstairs, and they greet me respectfully and exchange a few words before I start to laboriously climb the mudbrick staircase, wincing a little from the pain in my joints.

Up on the flat roof it is blissfully cool, breezes from the Nile blowing between the vine-covered pillars and providing a welcome respite from the sultry warmth of the evening. A cheap tallow lamp splutters and smokes, its flickering flame illuminating the shapes of four women. The young mother-to-be crouches near the centre of the birth-arbour, moaning softly in the throes of a contraction, while Hana stands behind her, supporting her and massaging her back. Next to them stands the girl's mother, murmuring words of encouragement to her daughter. The fourth figure rises from a stool a little distance away and comes to greet me.

"Puah, my old friend!" she exclaims, clasping my hands in hers. "Your granddaughter said you were coming. You look as youthful as ever!"

"You old flatterer, Miryam," I snort. "That staircase of yours makes me feel every one of my ninety-five years."

"You really are amazing, and it was good of you to make the journey. Hana told us about the boy you helped. A sad state of affairs." She shakes her head, her eyes solemn. "Still, the Lord sent the right people to help him. I wasn't sure if you'd still come, after such a delay, or if you'd want to return home; but here you are."

"Well, I wasn't missing this," I say. "Who'd have thought we'd both live to be great-great-grandmothers! How is Zilpah doing?"

"Hana says she has a while to go yet," replies Miryam. "Come, sit with me. We have much to talk about!"

I follow Miryam across the arbour and sink gratefully onto a stool beside her.

"Hi, Ghila!" Miryam calls to a girl of about twelve, who emerges from the shadows in the far corner. "Fetch a drink for our guest!" The girl hurries down the stairs and reappears moments later with a cup of thin beer.

As I sip my drink and answer Miryam's questions about the health and doings of my family, I keep one eye on Zilpah and Hana. The labour seems to be progressing normally, and I know that Hana is more than capable, but old habits die hard, and it's all I can do to stop myself from going and taking over. Although Hana has been delivering babies for many years and has even helped to train up the next generation of young midwives, it is one of the faults of the elderly that we tend to live in the past, and part of me still sees her as the nervous young trainee I used to take out with me. Then my mind wanders back still further, to the days of my own apprenticeship, and I close my eyes for a moment, remembering.

82 YEARS EARLIER

ANI

"But why do the slave women need us, anyway?" I protested, my lips forming into a pout. "Can't they deliver their own children?"

"Put that lip away, Ani, and start behaving more like a young lady of fourteen and less like a little child," replied Aunt Hasina calmly, packing her herbs and potions into her basket. "The Hebrew women are not permitted to study or train – only Egyptians may be admitted to the midwifery schools. The King wants all the Hebrews for his taskforce: the men to make bricks and build temples and tombs, the women to spin and weave, and then all together to bring in the harvest. They have their wise women, yes, but none with any medical training. And you know as well as I do that not every birth is straightforward. Any woman, slave or free, deserves help with a difficult labour."

"But they won't let us help them anyway," I objected. "Nanu says they won't use our spells, and they won't pray to Meskhenet or Taweret or even to Hathor."

"If you think there's no more to midwifery than spells and prayers, then you've got a lot still to learn," said Aunt Hasina with a slight frown. "You've been out several times with your Aunt Sera and assisted with plenty of Egyptian births; now it's time for you to see some Hebrew births too. Besides, Sera has Nanu to help her, and I have no-one. I need you."

"But the Hebrews stink!" I burst out finally. "They hardly ever bathe, and they don't shave – I might catch lice, or fleas!"

"Adah doesn't stink, does she?" said my aunt.

"Only because I make her wash," I muttered under my breath, but I didn't say it aloud. Adah was my own slave-girl, bought for me by my father when I was first old enough to wear a kalasiris. Small, skinny, and nervous, at first she could barely reach to pull the tight linen garment over my head, even when I was seated, and her childish hands fumbled clumsily over the brooches that clasped it at the front. But we'd grown together and now she was deft and adept, robing me each morning with practised skill, fastening the heavy gold jewellery around my neck and wrists, arranging and styling the hairpiece on my close-shaven head. And my aunt was right; she didn't smell.

Unable to think of any more objections, I sighed and picked up the basket. "Where are we off to, then?" I asked.

"The other side of town. Come on, you've wasted enough time already."

Hoisting the basket onto my shoulder, I followed my aunt through the dusty streets. At this early hour, they were fairly quiet: a maidservant hurried past on some errand for her mistress; a couple of young children tumbled out of an open doorway in pursuit of a ball, followed by the scolding voice of their mother; a schoolboy yawned and kicked at stones as he slouched his way to his lessons. We turned one corner and then another, passing row after row of mudbrick houses, following the slope downward toward the dry channel where the waters of the Nile would pass through the city in the inundation season.

Once we had crossed over by a wide wooden bridge and begun to walk uphill toward the western side of the city, the streets became narrower but more regular. The houses here were smaller and simply built in the Canaanite style, with a small courtyard surrounded by three rooms providing storage and overnight stabling for the sheep and goats. The cramped living quarters were built above this, with one or two rooms around a central hearth. As in Egyptian homes, each had a flat roof section, either adjoining the living quarters or, in larger houses, above them, accessed by a further steep staircase. A raised parapet around the edge made these areas a safe and comfortable place to sleep on hot nights.

Aunt Hasina navigated the narrow streets with long, purposeful strides, so that I had a hard time keeping up with her, burdened as I was with the heavy basket. There was more movement and bustle on this side of town, as slaves hurried past on their way to the fields, fearful of the slavemasters' whips if they were late. While house slaves in wealthy Egyptian homes could be of many nationalities, from dark-skinned Kushites taken in battle to lowborn Egyptians, the residents here were slaves of the state, and every one of them was Hebrew. Despite the hot sun, even the men were covered from the shoulder to below the knees in a heavy garment of flax, though they'd take this off to work once they reached the fields. They were bearded and wore their dark hair trimmed and shaped into mushroom-shaped coifs. The women's hair was hidden from view beneath headcloths dyed in shades of green, yellow, or russet; to my cultured Egyptian eyes, the variety of colours appeared quaint and rustic. Like my own Adah, they were modest in their dress, tunics of coarse linen covering them from neck to calf.

Thankfully, the house we were seeking was only in the second row. It wasn't hard to find; the anxious father-to-be was standing by the door waiting for us. He bowed his head and lowered his eyes respectfully, murmuring, "Thank you for coming. She's upstairs; her sister is with her."

At the top of the stairs, I saw that wooden pillars had been erected, wound about with vines and supporting a roof of matted reeds: just such a birth arbour as Egyptian women build when they are near their time. However, there were no shrines or images of the gods, and the birthing bricks upon which the mother-to-be squatted were plain and unadorned rather than inscribed with spells and depictions of Meskhenet.

The labour was a long one and delivery was complicated by the mother's small size and the baby's position, entering the world face-upward. I had witnessed a similar scenario with my Aunt Sera and it had resulted in a stillbirth, so I didn't rate this baby's chances very highly, unprotected as it was by any of the gods of childbirth. Aunt Hasina's face was grim as she bent over the exhausted mother, rubbing her belly with one of her herbal concoctions, while the sister continually muttered something in her own tongue, presumably a prayer to their Hebrew god. Around mid-afternoon, however, greatly to my surprise, I found myself attending to a worn-out but elated new mother, while my aunt presented the grateful father with a healthy baby girl.

On the way home, I walked in silence for a while, lost in my thoughts. Eventually, just as we were approaching our own street, I turned to my aunt.

"Aunt Hasina?"

"Yes, Ani?"

"Why would Hathor and the rest of the gods and goddesses spare that baby, born to slaves and infidels, and yet not save the child of Egyptian parents?"

Aunt Hasina didn't reply straight away but continued along the street, past the house I shared with my father and brother, to the entrance of her own house next door. Pausing with one hand on the front door, she turned and looked at me; her face was tired and worn.

"Childbirth is a risky business, Ani. Egyptian babies die, Hebrew babies die, and sometimes the mothers die too. Your mother was as devout as anyone, as is your father, but it didn't save her, or your baby brother either."

She stopped, and her jaw worked for a moment before she muttered, more to herself than to me, "If I'd known ten years ago what I know now, maybe… maybe things would have been different. I tried… the gods know, I tried my best. So did Sera. Every spell, every tonic, every amulet and incantation… Your father didn't leave his shrine, and no food or drink passed his lips those three days."

She swallowed. I felt a tightness in my own throat and realised my eyes were wet. I'd only been a child, barely four years of age, but what I remembered now was the crushing loneliness. My father hadn't wanted to see me. The slaves tiptoed around the house with long faces, and none of them would play with me or tell me what was going on. Both my aunts were there, but they were too busy to talk to me. Only Nanu would hold my hand, and she was as scared and bewildered as I was when we were driven from the birth arbour and sent downstairs out of the way. We held each other and listened to the muffled sounds from above. Murmurs. Groans. The groans grew fainter and the murmurs louder, more urgent. Both Nanu and I had seen births before, and we waited for the shrill cry of the newborn, but it never came. The light faded, the lamps guttered and went out, and still we sat, forgotten in the dark, clasping each other's hands. Time passed. We must have dozed. And when the new day came and I was finally allowed to see my mother, she was cold and pale as a corpse. I clung to her and begged her to talk to me, to sing me a song like she always did when I was scared, but though her lashes had fluttered and bloodshot eyes had met mine, she'd answered not a word. And then she was gone.

Now even the memory of her face had faded. I blinked hard, trying to summon an image of her brown eyes, tender with love as she rocked me and crooned a lullaby, but her features were fuzzy and blurry. I opened my eyes. She was gone. There was only my Aunt Hasina, and her eyes, too, were wet.

"There was nothing you could have done," I told her, trying to keep my voice level and not let it hitch and falter like a little child. "Father says that when the gods decide it's someone's time to meet Osiris, there's nothing anyone can do to stop it, any more than you can stop the sun from going down into the Underworld every evening."

My aunt was silent for a moment. "Maybe," she said at last, with a sigh. "But I've come to believe the life or death of a mother and child has more to do with the skill of the midwife – skill that I lacked." She blinked several times. "Of course, a fair amount of luck comes into it as well. But if the gods answered prayers, your mother would still be alive. Either they don't care for prayers" – she dropped her voice – "or they simply don't have the power."

Her grim expression eased, and a half-smile traced itself upon her lips.
"But don't tell your father I said that."

2

Puah

The tallow lamp flickers and gutters, and Miryam sends young Ghila to refill it before it goes out. Through the gaps in the screening vines, I can see cold pinpricks of starlight. The moon is on the wane, and it will be a while yet before it rises. A few feet away from me, Zilpah squats low on the birthing bricks, panting; it won't be long now before the baby arrives. Miryam and I watch for a moment, but Hana has everything well under control, so we return to our conversation, keeping our voices low so as not to distract the young mother from her efforts.

"How are your grandchildren?" I ask. "And your other great-grandchildren?"

"Oh, not so bad. Hareph has been sick, but he seems to be on the road to recovery now. Hadaccah is expecting again. Young Bezalel is growing into a fine young man, and very gifted – I could see him having a great future, if he weren't stuck here making mudbricks every day." She sighs.

"You have told me many times that the God of Israel will one day free his people and lead them back to the land of your ancestors," I remind her. "Have faith! Maybe it will happen soon."

"Sometimes it's hard to keep believing after so many years of slavery," says Miryam, "but you are right, my friend. My brother's life was preserved by the grace of God and by your God-given wisdom and courage, and I know of others who, like him, survived beyond hope in the days of that cruel decree. I cannot believe that they were saved only to make bricks for the King!"

I smile to hear the conviction growing in my friend's voice and see the spark returning to her eyes. As for her compliment, however, I feel that I hardly deserve it. The day I heard of the King's command will be forever etched on my memory, and as I recall it, my initial response contained very little of either wisdom or courage.

Ani

The shadows were starting to lengthen as I walked with Aunt Hasina back through the grimy streets, and the air was cool enough to make me glad of my woollen shawl. Street traders were packing up their wares; some of them optimistically dangled strings of beads or clusters of slightly withered figs in front of us as we passed. Mosquitoes whined irritatingly around our heads, and I swatted at them with my free hand while toting the heavy basket in the other.

It had not been a good day. Our first callout had been to a young mother who was miscarrying her child; there was nothing we could do, but we had stayed with her and dealt with the distressing but necessary business of ensuring everything was delivered and nothing was retained to bring sickness to the mother. We left satisfied that she was going to be physically OK, but knowing that nothing can fully heal that empty place in a mother's heart. We'd arrived home only to find another woman anxiously waiting for us; her daughter had been labouring all day with no progress. We attended and managed to deliver a live baby boy, but he was premature and very tiny, struggling for every breath, and I doubted whether he would make it through the night. All I wanted to do now was to get home, crawl into bed, and descend into blissful oblivion.

We approached my house and I made to walk past as usual, to see Aunt Hasina home and return her basket. However, just as we were passing the door, it opened and the tall figure of my father appeared.

"Ani, Hasina, I've been waiting for you. Step inside a moment."

Surprised, I glanced at my aunt as we followed my father into the house and across the courtyard. Between his job as a scribe and his priestly duties, my father was a busy man, and although I would dine with him in the evenings, it was unusual for him to send for me at other times. As for Aunt Hasina, although she was his sister and they were always polite to each other, I got the impression that they didn't quite see eye to eye. I think we were both wondering what could have happened for him to be personally watching out for our return.

"Wait here," my father commanded, pausing outside his own room. Stepping inside, he quickly returned carrying a small papyrus roll with an impressive-looking seal.

The papyrus was of the best quality, white and fine-textured. My aunt leant closer to see, and I heard her gasp.

"The seal of the King himself!"

"Indeed," said my father flatly. "And addressed to you, Hasina." His voice betrayed no emotion, but I wondered if he was somewhat peeved that the King had sent a message to his sister rather than to him. "Hasina, midwife to the Hebrews," he read, breaking open the seal and unrolling the papyrus.

My aunt and I leant closer. I had had some schooling, befitting a young lady of my position and the daughter of a scribe, but I had found it extremely dull and had not progressed beyond learning the simplest elements of the script. Aunt Hasina could read and write fairly well, I knew, as she always wrote out her own labels for the various jars of potions and herbs she prepared at her home. However, my father was obviously the best placed to interpret the beautifully formed hieratic characters, so it was he who read aloud:

By order of Khaneferre Sobekhotep, Majesty of the Horus, Ruler of the Two Lands, Wearer of the Red and White Crowns, granted life, stability and dominion like Ra forever.

To our loyal subjects, the midwives to the Hebrews, greetings.

Owing to the greatness of multitude of the said Hebrews and in consideration of the threat thereby caused to the peace and stability of the realm of Lower Egypt, it is our royal decree and command that the following measure should be taken for the security and prosperity of the Two Lands of Upper and Lower Egypt.

This shall be the decree and ordinance for every midwife who shall assist a Hebrew woman in childbirth and observe her on the birthing bricks: that, should she bring forth a male child, you are to take it and cause it to be put to death; yet if she brings forth a female child, you shall let it live.

This ordinance shall stand by the pleasure of the King, Khaneferre Sobekhotep, Majesty of the Horus, until such time as he shall see fit to repeal it.

Life, prosperity, and health to you our loyal subjects.

As my father read these words, I felt at first shocked, then angry, and then giddy with fear. To kill innocent babies! It was against every instinct and inclination of my heart; yet what fate would await me if I were to disobey a direct command from the King?

I glanced at my aunt and opened my mouth, but she silenced me with a look. She had blanched slightly as my father read, but now she looked perfectly composed, save that something was smouldering deep in her eyes.

My father, too, was watching my aunt. "The messenger arrived around midday," he said. "I trust you will do what the King requires of you?" There was a hint of a plea in his voice.

"The King's word is law," replied Aunt Hasina, "and Ani and I will do what is necessary. Come, Ani, I need your help with my basket."

My father continued to watch his sister with troubled eyes as I shouldered the basket and the two of us crossed the courtyard.

Aunt Hasina said nothing more to me as we left the house, walked down the street, and entered her own front door. As she closed the door and took the basket from me, I felt I could stay silent no longer.

"What are we going to do?" I burst out.

"What do you think is right?"

"I don't know!" I wailed. "It can't be right to kill babies, but to go against the King's decree..." I trailed off.

"Listen to me, Ani," said my aunt. Her voice was low and urgent, far removed from her usual serene tone. "The aim of our profession is to save babies' lives wherever possible, not to take them. As for the King" – she dropped her voice even lower – "whatever some may say of him, I believe he is only a man. Kings and kingdoms rise and fall.

"I won't bore you with too much politics," she went on, "but you know that for several decades now, we have had our own king here in Rowaty, separate from the powers that rule from Itjtawy. The kings in the south didn't like it, but they tolerated it, having bigger matters on their minds. Then last year, when our young King Nehesy died so suddenly, the king in Itjtawy set his sights northward, and to avoid a war that we couldn't win, King Nehesy's sister and heir was pledged in marriage to the southern king Khaneferre, bringing our own kingdom under his reign. For us ordinary folks, the change in rulership hasn't affected us too much, so far. But if this new king starts throwing his weight around, the Hebrews aren't the only ones who won't like it.

"Yes, the King is a man like any other man, and he is capable of making mistakes. 'Threat to the peace and stability of the realm'! Can you think of anything that is more likely to make slaves rise up against their masters than slaughtering their children?"

"But if the King finds out we've disobeyed him..." Suddenly I had a flash of inspiration. "I've got it! We can stop attending the Hebrew women, work as midwives to the Egyptians instead. That way we don't have to kill any babies, but we're not directly disobeying the command either."

"You can do that if you like, Ani, but as for me, I will keep on doing what I've been doing. Without a midwife to tend to the more difficult births, many of those babies, and many of the mothers too, will die just the same as if I'd killed them. But I'll understand if you want to go back to working with your Aunt Sera."

Seeing Aunt Hasina's courage, I felt ashamed of my own cowardice; yet I couldn't quite summon the resolve to commit myself as she had done.

"Give me some time," I said. "I need to make up my mind."

"Of course," said my aunt. "It's not a decision to take lightly." She smiled. "You're shaping up to be a good midwife, whether to Egyptians or Hebrews. Whichever you choose, I'm proud of you, Ani."

Which left me feeling worse than ever.

3

Puah

All conversation has ceased in the birth-arbour, and every pair of eyes is turned to young Zilpah as she concentrates all her effort into an enormous push. Hana is there, crouching low beside the birthing bricks to support the baby's head, then expertly manoeuvring the shoulders as Zilpah gives one more push and the new little life enters the world. Zilpah's mother is on hand with cloths and blankets, and Hana reaches into her basket for twine to tie the cord and a knife to cut it. Miryam and I rise and come over to offer our congratulations.

"Well done, Zilpah," says Hana, "you barely needed me there!"

Everyone is beaming, laughing and chatting, with mingled joy and relief. While childbirth could never be described as 'easy', a straightforward birth with no complications is always something to celebrate. All of us in the room, and none more than I, know that things can sometimes end very differently.

ANI

"Twins!" declared Aunt Hasina, with a certain amount of satisfaction in her voice. "Come, Ani, and see."

I crouched beside my aunt and gently palpated the stomach of the labouring mother, while Aunt Hasina talked me through what I was feeling. "Here is the head of the first one, see, and here's the other one's bottom – the head's up here. The first one is head down, which is good. The second one might turn before it's born, or we might need to deliver it feet first. We'll need to watch the cord, too, because sometimes it can slip out after the first twin is born."

Although I was listening, a part of my mind was still elsewhere. I had agreed to accompany my aunt today, but as to the future, I was still undecided. It was as if my heart were telling me one thing and my head another. While I admired my aunt's courage and longed to follow her example, the instinct of self-preservation (or was it cowardice?) was an equally strong force in the opposite direction.

A sudden hammering on the door jolted me out of my thoughts and set my heart beating fast. *We haven't delivered any male children yet,* I told myself firmly. *We haven't disobeyed the decree. It must be about something else.*

The start of the winter rains had forced us off the roof and into one of the small first-floor rooms for this labour, so I could clearly hear as the door was opened and a male voice called out urgently, "Please, I need the midwife; is she here?"

"Stay here, Ani, and call me if anything happens," instructed Aunt Hasina, rising and hastening down the short flight of stairs to meet the newcomer. Taking her place next to the labouring woman, I strained my ears to catch every word of the conversation happening in the courtyard below.

"It's my wife. She's in labour. Please, will you come?"

"Is it her first?" asked my aunt. "How often are the pains coming?"

"I don't know, it seems to be all the time." The stranger's voice sounded young, and close to tears. "Yes, it's our first. Please..."

"When did it start? If it's her first, it is likely to be many hours, sometimes even days. I'm with a woman now and I can't leave her, but I can come to see your wife afterwards."

"But we have no-one, and she won't stop bleeding..."

"She's bleeding? How heavily?"

Just then, the woman next to me groaned. Swiftly I checked her, then called down the stairs, "Aunt Hasina! I think the first one is starting to come!"

"Just a moment." I heard Aunt Hasina's solid footfalls on the stairs; when her face came into view, I could see she was frowning. She strode across to the labouring woman and stooped to check her, then straightened up and spoke to me in a low but urgent voice.

"Ani, this man says his wife is in labour and is bleeding. I don't dare leave; these twins will be arriving soon, and I'll be needed. Besides, it may well be that everything is fine with this man's wife – men can sometimes get a bit hysterical when it comes to childbirth! But all the same, someone ought to be there, just in case. Will you go?"

"Me?" I stuttered. "But I've never done it on my own before!"

"You've delivered plenty of babies with me over the past seven months. You're a good midwife, Ani. I trust you."

The King's decree, the bleeding woman, my own inexperience – all were eclipsed for a moment by a sudden surge of pride. Aunt Hasina trusted me; she had called me a good midwife! Then all my worries came rushing back, but with them was a new resolve. I was the midwife and a woman needed me.

"Yes, I'll go."

"Excellent!" My aunt's voice was brisk and businesslike again. Propelling me in front of her, she leant down the stairwell and addressed the young man waiting anxiously at the bottom. "Ani here will go with you." She must have detected a trace of doubt in his eyes, for she added, "She may be young, but she's fully capable, I assure you."

"Thank you," said the man. He couldn't have been more than twenty, his beard not yet grown, his hair bedraggled by the rain. I hurried after him, three paces across the small pillared courtyard and out of the door, calling out a "Goodbye!" to my aunt as we left the house.

The rain was refreshingly cool at first after the humid stuffiness of the house, but it wasn't long before I was wet through and starting to shiver.

As we hastened through the narrow streets, I tried to find out a little more about the man I was following and the situation I would face when we arrived.

"What's your name?" I called over the pounding of the raindrops.

He seemed surprised by the question but answered, "Achyan."

"And your wife's name?"

"Keshet."

"Is anyone with her? Her mother, or yours?"

"They're both dead. My sister is with her, but she's only a child. There is no-one else."

"No aunts, or cousins?" I pressed. Used to the family support system when a woman was giving birth, it seemed incredible to me that someone could really have nobody.

"No, there is no-one. I have a male cousin only, and unmarried. My aunt passed away some time ago, and my wife has no family."

"And you say she's bleeding? How heavily?"

"It's soaked through all the rags we have." His voice cracked with worry. "Please, hurry!"

We increased our pace, my mind racing with everything Aunt Hasina had ever told me about bleeding in labour. It didn't sound good, but I still held out hope that Achyan might have been exaggerating in his description of the problem, as my aunt had predicted.

It wasn't much longer before we reached the house we were heading for. The door was opened by a child of about eight, wide-eyed and seemingly terrified. Wordlessly, she led us to the corner, where a girl barely older than me lay groaning on a bloodstained blanket.

"Keshet..." moaned Achyan. He sank down beside her and turned his eyes to me in mute appeal.

Aunt Hasina would no doubt have taken charge and made Achyan wait outside, but Keshet had reached out and grasped his hand, and I felt that it would be callous to ask him to leave. Instead, I crouched down next to him and pressed her other hand between mine.

"Keshet, can you hear me? It's going to be OK; I'm a midwife."

My words sounded empty and hollow in my own ears. I could see that her blood loss had been considerable; her face was pale, and I doubted whether she would have the strength to push when it came to it.

"When did the pains start?"

Her voice was weak and she seemed to have difficulty speaking. "This morning... I was working... I tripped... fell on my stomach..."

"And that's when the bleeding started too?"

She nodded, her face clenched with pain.

"I didn't know what to do," broke in Achyan, his face mirroring his wife's pain. "I took her home. Then I went for the midwife, but no-one was there. I went round the town, asking everyone if they knew where the midwife was..." His eyes started to well up, and he turned hastily away.

"It's OK, you've done all the right things," I reassured him. Then I turned back to Keshet. "I'm just going to examine you to see how far along you are."

She nodded again, but suddenly her face contorted. "I – I think I need to push!"

"OK," I said as calmly as I could, while I desperately tried to recall everything I had been taught. "Roll onto your side, if you can; it's easier for the baby to be born that way."

As I helped Keshet onto her side, I called to the little girl, who was hovering near, "Get her something to drink!" I didn't have any of Aunt Hasina's herbs to mix with it, but it had occurred to me that, with all that blood loss, Keshet ought to be drinking something.

"Can I do anything?" asked Achyan in a fraught voice.

"Pray to your God," I muttered to him so that Keshet wouldn't hear. He closed his eyes a moment in despair. Then he turned his face away, but I could see him mouthing Hebrew words in supplication to their invisible God.

Keshet groaned and pushed with all her strength. I crouched beside her, murmuring whatever words of encouragement I could summon, and making her take sips of weak wine in between contractions. Her face was drained of all colour and she looked as if she might pass out at any moment, but somehow she kept pushing, and eventually a head, then a little body, slipped out into my arms. Yet it was blue and lifeless, and however much I rubbed and chafed, it lay limp and still without taking a breath.

Although I had not really expected any different, still I found my eyes filling with tears and my voice breaking as I told Achyan, "I'm so sorry, your son didn't make it." I passed him the tiny lifeless bundle, wrapped in a blanket, and saw him bow his head with grief as his tears fell on the little head. Keshet, with no strength left even to weep, closed her eyes and lay back on her blankets. Yet my work wasn't over yet, and I forced myself back into the moment; there was nothing I could do for the child, but I couldn't lose the mother as well.

"Listen to me, Keshet." My voice sounded harsh in my own ears, a grating intrusion on the girl's grief and exhaustion. "I need you to push one more time. We still have to deliver the afterbirth."

I wasn't sure whether she had heard me or not, but her body responded, the muscles tensing and contracting. There was a sudden crimson rush and the cord went slack. Achyan paled and swayed on his feet. I understood his horror – my own stomach turned at the scarlet torrent that had gushed forth along with the placenta. Keshet had lost so much blood already, I wondered how there could be any left in her body. Yet somehow, a pulse still throbbed weakly at her throat. Long black lashes, like a scribe's pen-strokes on the bleached parchment of her face, fluttered open, deep brown eyes locked on Achyan's tear-jewelled hazel ones.

"Achyan," I began tentatively. He flicked his gaze toward me for a fraction of a second before fixing it once again on his wife. I pressed on, a tremor in my voice. "I need you to go and tell my Aunt Hasina – that's the other midwife – what has happened. If she can come herself, she will. If not, please ask her for one of her sleeping draughts. Keshet is very weak, and she needs to sleep in order to recover."

I saw Achyan pull himself together with an effort. Gazing one last time at the still little form of his son, he laid it tenderly beside Keshet, stooped to kiss her forehead, then pulled on his cloak. I could see that, for him, having something to do was the best remedy for grief; so I called to the little girl, who stood nearby with head bowed, shedding silent tears, "Please bring another drink for Keshet, and some rags and water for washing."

As I crouched beside Keshet, encouraging her to take sips of watered wine, I gazed at the tiny bundle beside her and realised my mind was made up. Powerful the King may be, but who was he to decide that lives such as these had no value and could be snuffed out at his whim? Seeing the grief of Keshet, Achyan, and his little sister, I determined that I would do all that was in my power to keep other families from experiencing that same grief, even if it meant acting in direct defiance of the King and his decree.

4

Puah

Hana needs to attend to the new mother, so once she has finished cutting the cord she passes the new baby to me. I look down and smile. "It's a boy! Miryam, you have a great-great-grandson!"

I rub the baby down and swaddle him, such familiar actions that my hands can perform them automatically, leaving my mind free to wander. Zilpah's mother has gone to inform her son-in-law of the good news, and I hear the sounds of celebration from down in the living quarters. Life may be hard for the Hebrews under this king, but the occasions for joy and festivity are all the sweeter for it: the weddings, the comings-of-age, the births. Yet, as I remember all too clearly, there was a time, under a previous king, when what should have been the happiest of all events was robbed of all its joy.

Ani

"It's a boy!" announced Aunt Hasina. Yet her tone was hushed, and every face in the birth-arbour was etched with worry, from the new mother to the aunts and cousins – even the child of six who hovered anxiously by the stairs.

"You have nothing to fear from Ani or me," said my aunt softly, passing the baby to his mother. "But I think it's best if the men join us up here, so we can discuss what should be done."

The mother nodded, so I helped her into a clean tunic, and Aunt Hasina went to summon the men. Once the father, his brother, and their father had joined us upstairs, we held council, keeping our voices low, while the little girl parted the screening vines with her hands and kept watch to ensure we couldn't be overheard.

"As I said, you needn't fear us," continued my aunt. "We're midwives, not murderers. Yet I think it would be wise to take precautions. Once the King realises his decree is not being effective, he may well decide to take matters into his own hands – or rather, the hands of his soldiers." The young mother shuddered and clasped her baby closer to her, causing it to start crying, a thin wail that reflected the fear on the faces all around.

"Please, do you have a suggestion?" asked the father, fixing desperate eyes on my aunt.

"Well, it's not easy to hide a baby," said Aunt Hasina, gesturing to the infant, whose wails were getting steadily louder, "but you can disguise the fact that it's a boy. All babies look much the same when swaddled. Call him by a girl's name for now, and let it be put about that you have had a girl. So long as you don't forget yourselves, he should be safe."

"And as he grows?"

"Who knows what the future holds? Kings come and go; it may well be that we have a new king in a year or two, who forgets all about this decree."

"We will do as you say. May God bless you for your kindness."

As we left the house, I glanced at my aunt and couldn't help but notice how tired and careworn she looked. It dawned on me that I probably didn't look much better myself. On top of all the anxiety and fear caused by the decree, we had both been busier than ever over the last couple of weeks. Even with me now taking many of the callouts by myself so that the work was divided between us, the sudden increase in the number of times our services were required meant that both of us were working pretty much all hours, missing meals and snatching a few hours of sleep as and when we could.

"We can't go on like this indefinitely," Aunt Hasina muttered to me, as if she had been reading my thoughts. "We've been getting called out far beyond the bounds of Rowaty, to every settlement along this branch of the Nile, and even eastward as far as Pithom – areas that should have their own midwives."

"Do you think the midwives are refusing to work with the Hebrews?"

"Either that, or the Hebrews don't trust them so are coming to us instead. Word about us has spread, it seems; let's hope that it has only spread within the Hebrew community."

I mentally filed this away as something to worry about later. I simply didn't have the time now. Besides, I had chosen my path and was determined to walk it.

"I can't think that any midwife would agree to deliberately kill a baby," I said. "Maybe we can talk to them, persuade them to help?"

"I don't know," said my aunt slowly. "To many people, even those who work among the Hebrews, slaves are only slaves and not worth taking such a risk for. There may even be those who would consider it less of an evil to kill a Hebrew baby than to disobey the King."

"Couldn't we at least try?"

"I think we'll have to. We can't keep on doing this alone." She stifled a yawn. "No sleep for us today, then – we'd better get going if we want to reach Pithom by nightfall."

Before undertaking the journey eastward along the Road of Atum, we decided to call in on my Aunt Sera, who worked as a midwife for Egyptian ladies. She lived about half a mile from us, near the temple of Amun, where her husband served as a lay priest along with my father. On reaching her house, we were admitted by her Hebrew serving-girl, who showed us to the garden where Aunt Sera reclined in a leafy bower, laconically flicking at flies with her white lotus fan. My cousin Nanu was with her, and both of them rose to greet us.

"My dear Hasina, and Ani too, what brings you out in this abysmally muggy weather? You must be parched! Ilana, go and fetch some wine for our guests."

The day wasn't hot, but it was humid, and the shade of the woven palm screens was inviting. I sank down beside Nanu, grateful for the chance of a brief rest before beginning our journey. Aunt Hasina, however, remained standing.

"This is only a brief visit, Sera. Ani and I are off to Pithom this afternoon."

"To Pithom!" repeated Aunt Sera incredulously. "Why would you need to go all the way to Pithom – and in this weather? Surely it can't be for a delivery?"

"As a matter of fact, I was in Pithom for a delivery a couple of days ago. But today is merely a – shall we say – social call. I wanted to ask if you and Nanu can cover us if we get any callouts while we're away."

"You mean to Hebrew women?" spoke up Nanu; there was fear in her voice. "Oh, no... I'm not sure if we can..." She trailed off.

"We have our own work to attend to, you see," Aunt Sera broke in. "And the Hebrews, well, you know as well as I do, they probably won't be keen to see any midwives anyway, not after that decree..."

"Ani and I have been run off our feet since the decree came out," countered Aunt Hasina. "They're crying out for midwives – midwives who will fulfil their calling to preserve life, to protect babies and guide them into this world, not snatch them out of it."

Aunt Sera looked uncomfortable. "Of course we have no more desire than you do to harm any children, but the King is bound to find out if his orders aren't being carried out, and I for one have no desire to face his wrath, or to expose my daughter to it. I'm surprised you're encouraging Ani to put herself at risk, Hasina."

"Ani is old enough to make up her own mind, and to know that the easier path isn't always the right one."

"I have wondered," said Nanu slowly, "whether the gods and goddesses approve of this decree. I mean, every day we're asking Hathor to watch over women in labour and to bring the child safely into the world; we're calling on Taweret to nurture and protect the baby, Meskhenet to breathe life into them, and Ptah to drive all evil from them. Isn't this calling down curses on ourselves if we then harm the child, or even if we refuse to help the mother in her need?"

"But these are the children of slaves who do not acknowledge our gods," said Aunt Sera. "I don't think Hathor is going to concern herself with those who won't call on her name."

"What about the God of the Hebrews?" I put in. Three sets of eyes turned to look at me, and I felt myself going hot. "I just mean – well, they're slaves, as you say, and they don't pray to our gods, but I've attended births where I didn't expect the child to live, and it did. If that happened to an Egyptian, wouldn't we say that the gods must be protecting them? And more than that; their lives are hard, yet nothing seems to stop them multiplying and spreading across this whole land. That's the whole reason why the King wants to get rid of them. But doesn't it show that there's some powerful force behind them? The Hebrew God sounds like a God I wouldn't want to anger."

My cousin and both of my aunts were still staring at me; even I felt a little taken aback by the speech I had just made. Aunt Hasina was wearing her slightly cynical smile. Aunt Sera seemed rather put out; but Nanu looked thoughtful, as if my reasoning had impressed her.

"Well, we'd better get going," said Aunt Hasina after a moment, draining her cup. "I suppose it's down to your own consciences what you'll do if someone calls for us. Thanks for the wine, Sera. We'll see ourselves out."

We left Rowaty by the lower gate and soon found ourselves walking down the Road of Atum in a south-easterly direction. This being Peret, the season of growing, the usually dry and dusty wadi bottom was coated with a layer of silty black mud, deposited by the inundation and moistened by the recent rain. A couple of months earlier it would have been impassable, the overflow of the Nile cascading down the valley in a brown torrent to drain into the brackish marshes north of the Uatch-Ur, the Great Green Water. Now, though, the banks were dry and firm, though any sheep or goat that strayed from the green pastures on either side would find itself mired and unable to move, bleating for help from the herdsboys who lazed in the shade of bushes as their flocks browsed on the spiky grass clumps.

The journey took us a good five hours in total. We plodded on as the shadows gradually lengthened, mile after mile. The band of green narrowed the further we walked, until only a thin belt separated us from the desert on the far side, its red-brown dusty starkness commencing abruptly just beyond the acacia-lined slopes of the shallow gully. As we walked, I reflected that it must take real desperation for a labouring woman's husband or relative to trek all this way and back again, just to find a midwife who was willing to help them.

I had never ventured this far east before, and my aunt filled me in on some of the history as we went along.

"Pithom was built by the Hebrews, like Rowaty, only more recently," she told me. "Pithom is their name for the town; it's officially called Pi-Atum, after the temple of Atum that stands there, but since three-fourths of the residents are Hebrew and they won't take our gods' names on their lips, Pithom is the name that's stuck.

"Rowaty was where the Hebrews first settled when they came to Egypt long ago, at the time of the Great Famine. Successive rulers, with the memory of the Famine still fresh in their minds, set them to building storehouses, where grain could be stockpiled against future want. The administrative building in Rowaty was one, and more were built away to the east, in what we now call Pithom. Of course, we've had many years of prosperity since then, and the original purpose of the buildings has been mostly forgotten, at least in Rowaty; the grain stores rotted or were spoiled by vermin and were never replaced. The storerooms beneath the administrative building are used as cells now. Pithom has been rebuilt as a fortified guard town, so maybe the granaries there are still maintained as a defence against siege."

"Who are the midwives in Pithom?" I asked as we paused to drink from our waterskins and eat the dates we had purchased from a street vendor in Rowaty. "Do you know them?"

"When your Aunt Sera and I were studying midwifery at the temple of Neith in Zau, one of the other students was from Pithom. Her name is Thiti, and it's her house we're going to. I believe she has two daughters who are also midwives, and they attend to women of all ranks, including slaves – or at least they used to."

We finished our food and resumed walking in contemplative silence, wondering what sort of reception we would meet with at our journey's end.

The sun was just touching the horizon as we neared our destination, its blazing disc seeming to set the fields alight and casting the fortified walls of the town into silhouette. Positioned as it was close to Egypt's eastern boundary and on the trade route of the Road of Atum, Pithom functioned as part of Egypt's defence system and was built more like a fort than a town. The guards stationed on the watchtower may have wondered what had brought two women, one middle-aged and one barely past childhood, along the wadi alone in the fading light; however, I knew that the main focus of their attention would have been eastward toward the desert, where the setting sun might glint on the spear-tips of Midianite or Canaanite invaders.

The banks of the wadi had been growing steeper the further east we came; by now it had become a gorge, spanned by a wooden bridge. We hurried over, anxious to be within the gates before they were shut for the night. The gatekeepers looked curiously at us, but as we were clearly not a threat, they held off from closing and barring the heavy gates until we were safely through.

Once inside, I followed Aunt Hasina through the winding streets, stumbling a little from fatigue. Through the growing haze of weariness, I reflected that this town was not really so different from Rowaty. Although it now functioned as a military outpost, and a fair proportion of its population consisted of soldiers and their families, even soldiers needed a place to worship, so there was a temple with a full complement of priests; there were merchants to supply the people with food and wares; scribes so that messages could be sent and received; and of course all of these needed slaves: slaves to see to their personal needs, slaves to care for their livestock, slaves to make mudbricks and quarry limestone to build dwellings for the living and the dead. Many of the houses we passed were built in the Hebrew style, with rooms surrounding three sides of a pillared courtyard. My aunt led me past all of these houses, however, to a larger Egyptian-style house near the centre of the town. She knocked on the door.

We were admitted by a slave girl who went to fetch her mistress, a pleasant-looking woman in her late thirties. When she saw who her visitors were, an odd mixture of emotions flitted across her face: surprise, fear, and a hint of shame. Yet she welcomed us in, called for meat and wine to be set in front of us, and bustled off to see about beds for us to stay the night.

Aunt Hasina and I spoke little as we ate; both of us were too exhausted after our long journey following weeks of inadequate sleep. When we had finished, however, my aunt rose at once with a look of determination.

"Thank you for your hospitality, Thiti; Ani and I are much obliged to you. Before we take to our beds, however, we should like some time to speak with you in private. We have important matters to discuss."

That same mixture of fear and shame flushed across the face of our hostess once again, followed by a look of resignation. "Very well, Hasina. If you come into my parlour, I will give orders that we are not to be disturbed."

We followed Thiti to a comfortable and well-furnished room and seated ourselves on two of the carved wooden chairs. Thiti, however, remained standing, twiddling a few strands of long black hair between her finger and thumb like a nervous teenager. As Aunt Hasina opened her mouth to speak, she cut in before my aunt had had the chance to utter a word.

"I know why you're here, of course. I've heard the rumours that the Hebrews are going all the way to Rowaty to find a midwife who will attend them, and I knew it must be you, Hasina. You always were one to know your own mind and stick to your principles, no matter who might tell you otherwise – even the King." She lowered her voice as she said this, and there was a trace of admiration in her tone. Yet she carried on: "I know what you are going to ask me, and the answer is no. It's just too dangerous, and I have my family to think of."

Although I knew how important the outcome of this conversation would be, by now I was fighting a losing battle to keep my eyes open. The good food and wine, on top of my fatigue, had fuddled my wits, and although I was aware of my aunt answering Thiti, her voice now seemed to be coming from far away and I couldn't keep track of her words. My head nodded lower and lower onto my chest as I slouched in my chair.

Suddenly, my aunt was beside me. "My apologies, Ani," she said. "I have asked too much of you today, and every day for the last two weeks. Get yourself to bed now. Thiti and I will continue talking, as two old friends who haven't seen each other in a while, and I will tell you everything in the morning."

I wanted to argue, but I simply didn't have the energy, so I allowed myself to be led away to a makeshift bed composed of straw pallets covered with soft blankets.

The following morning, I had no recollection of having undressed or of laying myself down. However, there was one event that I remembered even through my stupor. It must have been some time around midnight, and in the pitch darkness I felt my aunt shaking me, her breath warm on my cheek as she whispered in my ear:

"Thiti has agreed to help us. I thought you would want to know now, rather than waiting until morning."

I gave no answer but smiled with relief as I drifted back into blissful sleep.

5

Puah

The first golden rays burst over the horizon into the grey dawn sky as the birds chorus their welcome to the new day. Stretching my aching limbs, I ease myself into a sitting position, taking care not to disturb the others.

I am the first one awake; my body seems to need less sleep these days, and I rarely lie past dawn, even after a late night. Downstairs, the men will soon be rising to go to work, but for now all is silent. The women have been given the benefit of sleeping on the flat roof, where the night air is cooled by the breezes from the Nile. Next to me, Hana is still fast asleep; Miryam is snoring a short way away. I smile to myself and briefly wonder whether I had been snoring as loudly; it seems to be another of the inevitable effects of ageing! Over in the birth-arbour, even the new baby is sleeping, snuggled next to his mother.

Hana and I had accepted the offer of beds for the night, but we will soon be making our way back to our homes in Rowaty. From our position on the rooftop, I can look out eastward to where the town stands illumined by the sun's early rays, elevated on its two turtlebacks of sand to protect it from the annual inundation of the Nile. On the crest of the nearer turtleback, the town's principal buildings can be seen rising above the encircling wall: the administrative offices, the temples, and, towering above everything else, the palace where the King and his retinue stay on their visits to the delta region. Even at this distance it is an imposing sight, with its shining white walls burnished by the rays of the sun. As I look at it, I can picture the many-pillared courtyard, featuring the beautifully tiled pool with its impressive system of water channels; the leisure garden laid out like a huge senet board, on which live people would serve as playing pieces for the amusement of the dignitaries; the grand courtroom in which the King himself would sit in judgement upon a majestic throne of Lebanese cedar overlaid with gold and adorned with emeralds and lapis lazuli. I had caught no more than a glimpse of it, many years ago, yet that single look was enough to inspire awe and terror even now, eight decades later.

Ani

"A summons," said Aunt Hasina, her face blanching as she read the parchment handed to her by the messenger.

"A summons?" I repeated blankly, staring uncomprehendingly at my aunt.

"From the King." She showed me the broken seal, on which the King's mark was still clearly visible.

"Seven days from today," said the messenger impassively, "at the palace in Rowaty."

"Thank you," said Aunt Hasina, "you may go."

"And the answer?" the messenger asked.

"I am the King's obedient subject and will appear before him at the hour named." My aunt's face was still grey, but the familiar steely glint was back in her eyes.

"Very good," said the messenger, turning to go.

We watched him silently until he was out of earshot. Then I took a deep breath.

"I'm coming with you."

"Ani, there's no need..."

My heart was hammering in my chest like a caged bird trying to break free, but I stood firm. "You can't go alone. I'm coming with you."

Aunt Hasina looked hard at me. Then she shook her head slightly.

"You are a stubborn, wilful, disobedient child, Ani," she said with a trace of pride, the corners of her mouth turning ever so slightly upward.

One week later, I stood with my aunt outside the palace gates. My heart felt as if it were somewhere in the region of my throat, and I inwardly beseeched any gods who might be listening that I wouldn't be sick or otherwise embarrass myself.

Three days prior to this, I had joined the crowds lining the banks of the Nile to watch as the royal barge arrived, bright-painted timbers gleaming in the sunlight, the gold-covered falcon-heads on prow and stern dazzling the onlookers. In the middle of the deck, slender pillars of polished cedar, banded with gold, supported a canopy of blue and scarlet cloth. Behind the royal vessel came others, lacking the gold falcon-heads but still lavishly decorated, bearing the courtiers, servants, and all the King's retinue. Rows of oars flashed in unison, silver droplets cascading downward from them as they rose, then dipped back down to ripple the shimmering surface.

The coxswain shouted an order and hauled on the heavy steering oar; the rowers on the right pulled backward and the boat turned gracefully, resting with a gentle bump against the temple's landing stage. As the helmsman leapt ashore and hitched it to the moorings, the blue-and-scarlet hangings twitched aside and a regal figure, resplendent in snow-white pleated shendyt and jewel-studded golden belt, stepped elegantly out onto the dock.

This was my first glimpse of King Khaneferre Sobekhotep, come north from his capital of Itjtawy for the first time since ascending to the throne last year. On his head, rather than the usual nemes headdress, he conspicuously wore the red-and-white pschent crown, emphasising his double rule over Upper and Lower Egypt. He strode forward from the landing stage and along the processional way, accompanied by the corpulent figure of the Royal Vizier and flanked by members of his personal guard in pure-white shendyts, armed with burnished spears. The crowds parted before him. Men and women waved palm branches and shouted his praise, strewing the path at his feet with garlands of papyrus reed flowers, while children gawped at the spectacle. Behind him came the royal guard, rank upon rank, then the courtiers and their wives and children, and finally an army of slaves, stooping beneath heavy wooden chests filled with fine linen garments, gold, and jewellery. Borne high on a litter in the midst of the courtiers was the queen, our own Princess Merris, born and raised here in Rowaty. She had travelled south for the wedding just months before, and now the royal couple were returning to spend some months in the palace in Rowaty, overseeing the administration of the agricultural and mining projects here in the delta. Seated on a scarlet-draped seat borne aloft on golden poles, the queen was opulently dressed in linen so fine it was almost transparent, the dark skin of her arms and neck adorned with gold and precious stones that caught the sunlight and made it hard to look at her without being dazzled.

The parade was certainly an awe-inspiring spectacle, but I hadn't come here to stare at the glamour and glitz. Slim enough to squeeze through the crowds, dodging elbows and shifting feet, I manoeuvred my body to the front of the throng so that I could study faces. Perhaps it was simply because of his decree, but I thought that the King's countenance was hard and cold, his eyes lacking any gentleness of compassion. A smile curved around his lips as he received the homage of his subjects, yet far from softening his expression, it only emphasised the appearance of ruthlessness and pride. At his right hand walked the vizier, Neferkare Iymeru, and while he was shorter, his face broad and bulbous next to the aquiline features of the King, both pairs of eyes glinted with that same icy austerity. Although neither man was looking in my direction, I suddenly felt a childish urge to hide myself, so I ducked my head and allowed myself to slip backward as the crowd pressed around me, swallowing me.

That was three days ago, and now as I stood with Aunt Hasina waiting for the gates of the palace to swing open and admit us, the image of the King's hard, arrogant face kept forcing its way into my head. He obviously knew we had been disobeying him, and he had the power to end our lives with a word. Why had I been so foolish as to volunteer myself to come? The summons was in my aunt's name, not mine; I had no obligation to be here. There was still time for me to leave; I could slip quietly away now and no-one would even know I had been there. I could keep my head down, go back to my original plan of only attending Egyptian mothers... but even as I thought this, my conscience reproached me and I thought of my Aunt Hasina, who could not escape this meeting even if she had wanted to; of Achyan and Keshet and their tiny, stillborn baby; of all the other Hebrew mothers and how much more they would suffer if no-one were prepared to make a stand.

Stubborn, Aunt Hasina had called me, and I truly believe it was stubbornness rather than courage that kept me from running away. My legs were trembling, my tongue felt as dry as old papyrus, and my stomach physically ached.

"Have mercy on us and protect us," I muttered under my breath, hoping that Taweret or one of the other gods might be listening. Then I remembered what Aunt Sera had said. The gods would be on the King's side. We had disobeyed the King; and why would the gods reward us for helping those who did not worship them? Our only hope was that the God of the Hebrews might defend us who had tried to defend his people. "Protect us," I whispered again, appealing this time to the Hebrew deity. Though I found it hard to pray to an invisible God with no image to set before my eyes, I did feel a little better when I had done so. Someone was on our side; we wouldn't be standing alone.

I jumped as the heavy wooden gate began to open. Soon the figure of the gate warden appeared before us, armed and stern. He examined the summons my aunt handed to him, then passed it back and gestured for us to follow him.

Had I been there for any other reason, the opulence of the palace would have been a source of admiration and wonder to me. We followed our guide through the entrance building, decorated with gorgeously painted columns and frescoes, into a wide courtyard lined with decorative pillars. Passing several open doorways, I caught glimpses of the extensive network of gardens, all laid out for the pleasure and relaxation of the royal family. Perhaps the women of the court, together with the princes and princesses, would be resting in the shade, walking among the flowers, or entertaining themselves with a game of senet. The King himself, however, would not be with them. He would be seated in the throne room, ready to judge the cases that were brought before him, ours among them.

As we approached the huge door that must lead us to the throne room, I couldn't keep my legs from trembling. Aunt Hasina, however, walked as she always did, calmly and with dignity. A couple of paces from the door, she stopped and turned to me, speaking in a low voice.

"Wait here, Ani."

"But..." I began to protest.

"No arguing; wait here."

Feeling a mixture of relief and disappointment, I inclined my head in submission and fell back, watching as the warden exchanged words with the guard at the door and then ushered my aunt through. A moment or two later, both the warden and the guard exited the chamber and returned to their posts.

With the guard once again stationed outside the throne room, there was no hope of trying to listen at the door, so I stood where I was, feeling rather foolish and wondering again why I had come. The guard kept his eyes fixed forward and paid me no more attention than if I had been one of the serving-girls who bustled in and out of the other doors around the courtyard. My eyes drifted around the room, taking in the panoply of brightly coloured wall reliefs. Gilded images of the gods were interspersed with depictions of previous kings. My father could no doubt have named each king from his representation, as well as interpreting the hieroglyph characters with which they were surrounded, but I, poor scholar that I was, knew little more than to recognise the royal status of the figures as denoted by their crowns and the oval cartouches surrounding their names.

As my gaze continued to travel over this array of royalty, something made me stop and furrow my brow. The image that had caught my attention was not that of a king; he was bare-headed and lacked a cartouche or any of the regalia of royalty. It was obviously a person of great importance, however, as he held a staff of office and wore a long garment painted in red and blue. The detail that had caught my attention, however, was his hair: picked out in bright red paint, it was gathered on top of his head in a characteristic coif, emphasising his undeniably foreign features. There could be little doubt that the figure was a Hebrew.

How had a Hebrew man come to be featured on the wall relief of the royal palace? And why was he represented with a splendour equalling that of the royal figure beside him? My curiosity overcame my inhibitions, and I decided to approach a serving-girl who was sweeping the floor not far from the relief in question. She looked up in surprise.

"I heard that it's an image of the official who first built this palace, a great many years ago," she said in answer to my question. "Before this was a royal residence, it belonged to him. They say there was a statue of him, too – a splendid one, as high as this ceiling, and set with gold and precious stones. But it hasn't been seen in hundreds of years – buried with him, most likely, if it ever existed. Maybe it's just a legend."

My brow furrowed still further. As far as I knew, the Hebrews had always been slaves; how could one of them have risen to such a high position that he was able to build palaces and commission colossal statues of himself? I was itching to find out more, but then I noticed that the guard's eyes had followed me across the room and he was looking at me suspiciously, so I merely thanked the girl and reassumed what I hoped was a casual and disinterested pose.

The time dragged by. How long my aunt spent in the King's presence I couldn't have said, but it seemed to me that the god Ra, who had been riding high in his sun-boat when we had entered the palace, must by now have completed that voyage and embarked upon the night-boat for his journey through the underworld. The more time passed, the more anxious I became; I tried hard to focus on keeping my breathing regular, and I chewed on my lower lip until it bled.

Just as I felt I could stand it no longer, I saw the guard snap to attention as the throne-room door began to open. On the verge of leaping forward, I stopped myself just in time. The figure that emerged was not Aunt Hasina but a man, short and corpulent, carrying a staff of office and garbed in a rich robe and striped headdress. I recognised him at once as the hard-eyed figure who had walked beside the King as they disembarked the royal barge: Neferkare Iymeru, vizier, second only to the King himself in influence and status.

"Asim," he addressed the guard. "A word in your ear."

The vizier's cold gaze swept over the courtyard, taking in the various servants and officials; it lingered on me for a moment and I held my breath, but he must have decided that I was only a serving-girl, for he turned back to Asim and leaned in closer, murmuring something in his ear.

Once again, my curiosity was stronger than my fear. Instinct told me that this conversation had something to do with my aunt; so, holding my breath and feeling my heart thumping against my ribs, I edged a little closer.

The vizier's voice was soft, barely more than a whisper, and he cupped his hands around the ear of the guard, who had to bend his knees and stoop his head to bring it to the right level. Much to my frustration, I could hear nothing of the vizier's words. Asim, however, had a gruff voice and was clearly more used to barking orders than whispering secrets. His half of the conversation carried quite clearly to my ears.

"Every Hebrew household?" I heard. "Then you will need to assign me more men. We will have to go in pairs, in case they resist."

Neferkare Iymeru murmured something inaudible, and a look of satisfaction crossed the guard's face, only to be replaced by a frown.

"But how can we tell if such a young infant is a girl or a boy?" he asked.

The vizier's brow darkened with frustration at the apparent density of the guard. "Check them," he mouthed, not taking the time to hide his mouth this time; I clearly saw his lips form the words.

Suddenly he glanced up, looking straight into my eyes. I froze, my heart standing still in my chest as his features creased into a frown.

At that precise moment, the door to the throne room opened again, causing both men to start and look round. Released from the spell of the vizier's gaze, I breathed again as the figure of my aunt appeared in the opening. With a slight nod in my direction, she strode forward through the courtyard toward the exit; the guard hesitated momentarily then stepped forward to escort her, while I scurried along in their wake.

Not until we were safely out of the palace and several minutes' walk away did Aunt Hasina speak. Although I was desperate to know what had happened and what the King had said, I knew better than to ask. Eventually, just a couple of streets away from our own homes, she stopped and turned to me.

"Well, that went as well as could be expected."

"What did you say to him?" I asked.

"I told him that Hebrew women are like the cattle and goats of the hills – they are strong and vigorous and have already given birth before we arrive to assist them." My indignation must have shown on my face, because she added, "I know, I know; but it was the only thing I could think of that the King and his court might believe. That's how they see their slaves, anyway – as just another form of livestock, no more human than a beast of burden – so when I used that image to the King, he seemed to accept it."

"Was that it, then?" I asked. "You must have been in there for hours!"

"Less than an hour, actually," she replied, pointing at the golden disc of the sun. To my surprise, it was still high overhead, and I realised that the shadows had barely lengthened since we had first stood outside the palace gates.

"After I had spoken my piece, I was sent to another room to wait," my aunt continued. "The King wanted to consult with his vizier, it seems. Either way, I was kept waiting for quite some time, and when I was summoned again, the vizier had gone. The King dismissed me, so I left immediately."

"I saw the vizier," I said, suddenly remembering. "He talked to the guard – said something about checking the babies. I think he knows the Hebrews are passing off boys as girls!"

Aunt Hasina's face darkened. "I don't like that vizier – he's too clever," she muttered. "I'll try to spread the word among the Hebrews, but what can they do? It's not easy to hide a baby, and the parents will be risking their own lives if they try. Besides, I have a feeling the vizier saw through my words, too. I wouldn't be surprised if he has me followed from now on and sends his soldiers round to any Hebrew house I call at."

I shuddered, recognising the truth of her words and also their implication. If it was no longer safe for Aunt Hasina to visit the Hebrews, that left them with only one midwife they could call on: me.

-PART II-

6

Puah

Sunrise and sunset are my favourite times of day. As a habitual early riser, I will almost always spare a few moments before the day's hustle and bustle begins, just to watch as the first hints of orange gild the grey dawn sky directly above the horizon, ahead of the sun's dazzling white-gold circle that bursts suddenly upward into sight as the birds of the air trill a joyful welcome. While I no longer believe that it represents the god Ra born afresh each morning, it still feels like a moment of new birth, with the whole of creation joining together to celebrate the new-born light.

The setting of the sun is a quieter occasion, filled with a solemn majesty. As a final gift before it sinks out of sight, the blazing disc paints sky, water, trees, and buildings with hues of regal splendour, which linger on even after its topmost edge has hidden itself behind the distant skyline.

I stand, as I am accustomed to do, on the flat roof section outside the living quarters of my house, watching in silence as the colours gradually fade to blueish black and the first faint glimmers of stars become visible. Then I sigh and walk back away from the parapet, passing the stairway to the storerooms below, and enter the dim lamplit space of the living chamber, where my daughter-in-law Chenya is waiting.

"Echud is late tonight," I observe.

Chenya's sigh echoes my own. "I knew he would be. He has been worried about not fulfilling his quota for the week."

"Surely he will be home soon," I say with a hint of uncertainty. "He can't make bricks in the dark!"

"He is getting older," Chenya replies. "The work wearies him, and the journey home from the plains takes him longer than it used to."

We sit in silence for a while, watching the lamplight stutter and flicker on the walls. Above us, on the upper roof section, I hear the soft tones of Echud and Chenya's youngest daughter, Reena, settling her children to sleep with a story.

At last, the front door creaks open and we hear a heavy tread on the stairs. Chenya rises quickly and hurries to get food ready. I stand to embrace my son as he trudges wearily through the open doorway to the living quarters and sinks onto one of the stools. With a grunt of thanks, he accepts a loaf of bread and a cup of beer from his wife, then he says nothing more until he has drained the last drop and scooped the final fragments of bread into his mouth. Chenya comes and stands behind him, gently massaging his broad shoulders, and he relaxes at her touch, leaning into her with a tired sigh.

"Thank you, my love," he murmurs gratefully. "I needed that."

"Did you succeed today?" Chenya asks him anxiously. "Did you make your quota?"

"Just about," answers Echud. "The light was fading as I finished the last bricks. Any later, and I wouldn't have been able to finish. Still, I've escaped the slavemaster's rod, for this week at least. Tobit and Asher helped – I couldn't have done it without them."

"They are good nephews," Chenya murmurs.

The conversation lapses into silence. Echud leans heavily on Chenya, his eyes half-closed. I study the lines on his face, the slump of his once-powerful shoulders, and realise that he is indeed getting on in years. As a mother, it seems strange to think of my son as old, but he is well into his seventies now, and the daily toil of the brickfields is taking its toll on him. What's more, I know that his patched and worn tunic hides the scars of beatings from the times when he didn't manage to meet his quota. The first time he dragged himself home, stumbling and bleeding, it nearly broke my heart.

I think of the others. Of Reena's husband, carried to an early grave by disease worsened through poor nutrition and hard labour. Of the grandchildren and great-grandchildren born too soon, too small, or too sick, who despite my best efforts I hadn't been able to save.

Not for the first time, I find myself wondering if things could have been different. Was it my fault? Was it the choices I had made that had condemned my children to a life of hard servitude? Had I chosen and acted differently, I could have raised my children in a life of privilege as free-born Egyptians. I think back to the opportunities I had in the past. Given the choice to go back, would I act any differently?

ANI

I was humming to myself as I pushed open the door of my house – not an Egyptian song, but one of the haunting Hebrew melodies taught to me by Achyan and Keshet. I had been to visit them that morning, as I often did, and the Hebrew music had a way of getting under my skin, working its way deep into my consciousness so that, having heard a song once, it would play itself round and round in my head all day. Besides, this music seemed entirely appropriate considering the way I was currently dressed.

Carefully setting down the bundle of cloths in which my potions and midwifery instruments were disguised, I reached up to my throat and unknotted the yellow headscarf, replacing it with a hairpiece of straight, dark locks. I took up my polished bronze mirror and checked my reflection. Puah the Hebrew slave-girl was gone; I was Ani the Egyptian once again.

My own serving-girl, Adah, entered the room at that moment and grinned at the sight of me.

"Have you had a good day?" she asked, as she helped me change out of the rough linen tunic and into my usual undergarments and long beaded kalasiris.

"Yes, thank you, Adah." I returned her smile. "Just the one delivery today – a fairly straightforward one, as it turned out – and no bother at all with the guards. In fact, I walked right past a pair of them who were patrolling the street in the Hebrew quarter, but they paid me no attention whatsoever. Your idea was a stroke of genius – no-one takes any notice of a slave just going about her masters' business, or of a Hebrew girl entering a Hebrew house!"

Adah's grin broadened at the compliment. She finished fastening my earrings, then took up my heavy neck-collar of brightly coloured beads.

"And how is Keshet?" she enquired.

"She is well," I answered. To Achyan's relief, and mine, Keshet had not been required to return to work in the fields after recovering from the birth. A local merchant to whom she had sold some finely spun flaxen yarn during her recuperation period had recognised her skill and purchased her as his assistant. This meant that she was permitted to stay at home with her spindle and distaff rather than labouring outside under the hot sun; and her health, while it would always be delicate, was much the better for it.

This arrangement also meant that I could go to visit her regularly, in my guise as Puah the slave-girl. Any Hebrew families needing help with a difficult labour would send to Keshet, and if I was not already sat beside her, keeping her company as she spun, then she would always find a way of getting the message through to me.

It was Keshet who had come up with the name of my Hebrew persona.

"In your Egyptian custom, you are named for the splendour of the sun's light, and indeed, to our nation you have been a ray of hope in the midst of darkness. Your name should be Puah, meaning radiance. Long may you continue to shine!"

In the evenings when he finished in the brickfields, Achyan would join us, and he would tell me marvellous tales from the history of the Hebrew people. I was fascinated to learn that his own ancestor, a man called Yosef, had come to Egypt as a slave many generations ago, yet had risen from these humble beginnings to become the vizier over all Egypt.

"Though it seemed that everyone had deserted and betrayed him, even his own family," Achyan said, "he was loved by our God, who gave him the power of telling the future through the dreams of the King. In his God-given wisdom, he led Egypt safely through the time of the Great Famine and earned the gratitude of the King and all the Egyptian people. Afterwards, he was reunited with his family and they settled here, in this very town of Rowaty. The great imperial palace here was once his house."

I remembered the image I had seen on the wall relief in the King's palace, and the statue spoken of by the servant girl.

"So what happened?" I asked. "How did your people end up as slaves?" Achyan shook his head.

"Rulers and dynasties rise and fall," he said. "That king and all of his line are no more; a new king came to power, who did not remember Yosef and all he had done for Egypt. To him, the Hebrews were no more than foreigners, and thus a threat to be dealt with." Achyan's brow creased, and his eyes hardened.

"As you say, kings rise and fall," Keshet interjected softly. "Before he died, Yosef prophesied that his people would one day return to their homeland. It may not happen in our lifetime, but the power of this king will not last forever."

"Hush," Achyan had murmured then, looking nervously toward the house's open windows.

Now, back at home, I pondered this conversation while Adah put the finishing touches to my attire. This Yosef had clearly been a man of great wisdom, and one who could see into the future – Achyan's story was corroborated by the wall stela I had seen in the palace. If his God had told him of the famine and shown him how he and all Egypt could survive it, then his prophecy of the Hebrew nation leaving Egypt was not to be taken lightly. But how could it come about? And what would happen to Egypt if the Hebrews were to leave – if a culture so dependent on its labour force were to suddenly lose it?

My thoughts were interrupted by a knock on my chamber door, followed by the appearance of my father. His eyes rested on the discarded Hebrew tunic and headscarf, then on the bundle from which my medicines and tools protruded, and his brow momentarily creased into a frown. The next moment, however, he turned to me with a smile.

"Well, my Ani, you have grown into a beautiful young woman," he said. "To think that you will soon be sixteen years of age!"

"Not for another three months," I replied, surprised. It was not like my father to give out compliments, and I wondered where this conversation was going.

"I fear that I have neglected you of late," my father continued, as if he could tell what I was thinking. "Between my duties and your, er, calling," his eyes flicked back to my bundle on the floor, "I have seen so little of you in recent months. You have become a woman, and I have missed it."

"It's OK," I said rather awkwardly. Much as I loved my father, I had no real desire for him to take a greater interest in my doings. Our relationship, I felt, worked best with a bit of distance.

"However, I mean to remedy that," my father ploughed on as if he hadn't heard me. "There is one fatherly duty in particular that I mean to fulfil. I won't be around forever, and it's up to me to make sure that you will be well provided for after I am gone."

"I can look after myself," I muttered, not liking where this was leading.

"I know you can, Ani, but your midwifery skills will not be enough to support you financially. Especially since…"

He trailed off, but I had seen his meaning. Neither Aunt Hasina nor I charged any money to the Hebrew women we helped; even had we done so, they would hardly be able to afford to pay enough to maintain us in the lifestyles of wealthy Egyptians, were that our only means of support.

Taking my silence as an acknowledgement of his point, my father smiled again.

"Hathor favours you, my daughter. You will have no trouble finding a suitable husband. In fact, when you have finished getting ready, perhaps you could join us in the courtyard. There's someone I'd like you to meet."

With that, he exited my chamber, leaving my thoughts in a turmoil. On the one hand, my pride had been touched; I was proud of my independence and resented the fact that he had apparently picked out a future husband for me and invited him over without even consulting me first! However, I realised that his argument did make sense. One day, I would need to find financial support from somewhere. On top of this, I had to admit to myself that I was intrigued to find out who this suitor was. I had never before given serious thought to the idea of marriage, but my father's compliments, and the thought that there was someone seeking my hand, gave me a warm feeling inside.

Adah put the last of my rings on my fingers, applied kohl to my eyes and ochre to my lips, and arranged my headpiece, fastening it with ribbons and beads. I spent rather longer than usual checking my reflection in the bronze hand-mirror; then, with my insides fluttering, I made my way down to the courtyard.

Having had no idea what to expect, I felt my stomach do a back-flip at the sight of my prospective husband. He was young – no more than twenty-five – with darkish skin and a brilliantly white smile, which lit up his face as I came into view. He was simply dressed in a belted white shendyt skirt, displaying his muscular torso. Unlike some men, however, he didn't seem affected or flaunting of his appearance but had kept it low-key with minimal jewellery and a plain khat head-cloth.

"Er... hi," I muttered, my face burning, feeling intensely foolish.

"Peace be with you," he replied formally. Unlike me, he had remembered his manners; however, I noticed a slight quaver in his voice, and it made me feel a bit better.

My father rose to make the introductions. "Tothi, this is Ani, my daughter. Ani, Tothi works alongside me in the administrative building."

He was a scribe, then, meaning that he was intelligent as well as handsome. I thought of my own pitiful attempts to learn to read and felt even more inadequate.

"Well, I'll just, er..." My father gestured vaguely toward the house. "Shem and Adah will be around if you need anything." And he hurried off, casting backward looks over his shoulder.

For a while I stood with my eyes cast down, trying to look demure and respectable. When the silence had stretched on longer than I could bear, I risked sneaking a look at Tothi, only to catch him glancing at me at the exact same moment. Our eyes met for a second, then I hastily looked away.

Trying to cover my embarrassment, I felt I ought to be the first to speak, since he was, after, all, a guest in my house.

"Erm... shall we sit down?" I suggested, far too formally.

"Thanks," he replied quickly.

He lowered himself to the ground, but immediately he sprung up with a cry. In our courtyard were a number of acacia trees; I often collected their leaves and resin for use in my tonics. A broken-off branch from one of these lay on the ground, and Tothi had managed to sit right on one of its long thorns.

I suppose it was nerves; either way, I couldn't help myself. A sudden, loud giggle escaped me. Horrified, I clapped a hand over my mouth. What must Tothi think of me? But the next moment, he had thrown back his head and let out a peal of laughter. Before I knew it, both of us were clutching our sides in mirth as all the tension and nervousness flowed out of us in fits of hilarity.

Tothi, I thought, was all right.

7

Puah

The night is drawing in now, the deep purple-blue of the dusk sky darkening to almost total blackness, save in the west where a pale corona surrounds the moon's silvery crescent. The tallow lamp is burning low in our dimly lit living chamber, and Echud yawns. My eyelids, too, are starting to droop. It's time to go to bed.

I cross the room to the bed I used to share with my husband. It's been more than ten years, but I still miss the comforting feel of his body next to mine. Still, I can't complain; he lived to a good old age and died peacefully in his sleep. When my own time comes, which can't be too far away, I believe that I will see him again.

A drowsy quiet has settled over the house, punctuated only by the occasional faint bleat from the small flock of sheep and goats stabled in the room below us. Chenya reaches out to extinguish the lamp; but just then, the peace is broken by a sudden knock at the door.

"Who could be calling at this hour?" mumbles Echud sleepily from his bed. "It had better be important."

He drags himself into a sitting position, then he rises clumsily and pulls his tunic back over his head before taking the lamp from Chenya and stumping down the stairs to the door.

Lying in the dark, I strain my ears, trying to pick out individual voices from the faint murmur of sound below. However, I don't have long to wait.

The door bangs shut again, and Echud's footsteps hurry up the stairs, accompanied by his heavy breathing.

"Who was it, Echud?" Chenya beats me to it.

"It was Shimeon," says Echud, naming his eldest grandson. "He's just come from Yared's house, and you'll never guess what Yared heard from Ithamar!"

Shimeon's wife, Abiyah, is a sister of Yared, who in turn is a son-in-law of Ithamar, Miryam's brother's son; so you could say that Miryam and I are now distantly related. Mind you, thanks to the complex network of marriages and family ties, you could probably say the same about most of the Hebrew community in Rowaty.

"So what did Ithamar tell Yared?" Chenya asks, her tone a mixture of amusement and curiosity. Whatever Shimeon's news was, it has certainly woken Echud up; his face in the lamplight is more animated than I have seen it in a long time.

"Mosheh is back!" Echud announces. "And he is going to the King to demand our freedom!"

It's hard to describe the effect these words have on our little household. Chenya leaps from her bed as though she were a maid of fifteen years of age rather than a matron of sixty. A fire I have never seen before blazes in her eyes. Roused from their beds by our raised voices, Reena and her two children appear in the doorway that leads to the rooftop, seven-year-old Amana peering curiously from behind her mother, while Baruch, a lad of ten, stands with his head held high, an expression of fierce joy on his face. As for myself, the tide of emotions that sweeps through me forces me to sit back down hastily upon my bed.

Freedom! As an Egyptian girl I had not fully known the meaning of the word. Now, it means not having to watch my children and grandchildren suffer under the slave-master's rod. Not watching my great-grandchildren grow up with no better prospects than a life of labour under the hot sun. But is it possible? Could such a thing ever truly come to pass? Or is it no more than a false hope, fading only to bitter disappointment and a life yet more hopeless than it had been before?

"Are you sure of this, Father?" Reena asks Echud softly, her face reflecting my own doubts. "Has Ithamar seen Mosheh himself?"

"Four nights ago, Shimeon told me, Ithamar's father Aharon had a dream that he would find his brother Mosheh if he crossed the border and travelled two days' journey into the wilderness, to a certain mountain. He believed that the dream was given to him from heaven, so he risked everything and went."

"Quite a journey for a man of eighty-three," Chenya commented.

"Indeed; but he is strong and healthy, despite his years, and he trusted our God to see him through. Anyway, when he reached the place of his dream, there was Mosheh! They returned to Rowaty together, arriving just this evening at Aharon's house. Ithamar has seen him, and they're calling all the elders to meet there at daybreak. That's why he went to Yared, and Yared sent Shimeon to fetch me."

I felt a rush of pride that my son should be counted among the elders of the Hebrews, but this was followed by a pang of anxiety.

"But if you attend this meeting tomorrow, will you not be punished for missing your work?"

"Don't you see, Mother?" It was Chenya who answered. "This is the fulfilment of the promise our God gave to Yosef all those years ago! Why should we fear the slavemasters any more, or even the King? In a few days, we'll be on our way back to our homeland!"

"Shimeon told me," Echud began slowly, but with growing conviction, "that Mosheh met with the Lord God Himself out in the wilderness."

Everyone in the room fell silent, hanging on Echud's every word.

"He saw an acacia bush that was on fire, but no matter how fiercely the flames burned, the leaves did not wither – they stayed fresh and green! Then the Lord spoke to Mosheh from the bush and gave him powerful signs to perform in front of the King. When the King sees them, he and all his court will have no choice but to acknowledge that our God is greater than him, greater than any of the gods of the Egyptians! His heart will be struck with fear, and he will have to let us go!"

Echud is shouting now, and in a sudden rush of memories I am forcibly reminded of his father – so quiet most of the time, so gentle, slow to speak and slow to put himself forward, but with a passion that, once roused, burns with an unquenchable flame. It's an infectious passion, and I find my doubts melting away in its heat. He must be right. After all, hadn't it been clear, right from the beginning, that Mosheh had been set aside for some special purpose? Even from the first day of his life, hadn't our God had His hand on him? There was no-one alive who knew that better than I.

ANI

It had been a long day. I had been woken in the early hours of the morning for an emergency call-out and hadn't been home since. I had at least had the chance to eat – each family I had visited had been generous in providing me with the best food and drink they had to offer – but it was now three hours past noon, and tiredness was creeping up on me.

What's more, I missed Tothi. He came to visit most afternoons after he had finished his work, and I tried to be home for him whenever possible. Today would be only the second time that I had missed him, and I felt a pang as I pictured his disappointment.

I had known Tothi for just under a month now, but it seemed much longer. Once we had both got over our initial awkwardness, the conversation just seemed to flow. He had a great sense of humour – his whole face would light up with the sparkle in his dark eyes and that dazzling smile that sprung so readily to his lips. And he thought I was beautiful! Unused to compliments, I wasn't sure how to handle them at first, but my confidence grew the more time we spent together. My father was overjoyed by our blossoming relationship, and a marriage date had been set for two months' time – just after my sixteenth birthday.

Nearly an hour had passed since Tothi's usual arrival time. Would he wait for me? My father would have invited him in, I was sure; but would he still be there when I returned? Or would he have turned away, disappointed? Maybe there was still time; if this birth happened soon, I could be home before the sun was low in the sky…

The birth; I had to concentrate on the birth first. Giving my head a little shake, I wrenched my full attention back to the labouring mother. That was the reason I was here; this woman needed me. She had been in labour since yesterday morning, her pains now frequent and intense but with nothing to show for them; if I was tired after my broken night's sleep, I couldn't imagine how she must be feeling. The strange thing was that this wasn't her first baby. Normally, births get easier with each successive labour, yet I had seen a child of about three years old downstairs, playing with a pebble, and a solemn-eyed girl of six or seven was hovering anxiously near her mother.

"Did you have difficult births with your other children?" I asked the woman, searching for some clue that might help me to diagnose the problem.

She did not answer straight away. Her face twisted as a contraction mounted, and for a long moment her whole body writhed in the throes of the pain; then it eased and she let her head flop back onto the bed, exhaustion written in her features.

"No," she replied at last, her voice faint. "Aharon was a quick birth. Miryam took longer, but nothing like this."

"And how long ago did your waters break?"

"Yesterday evening. About the tenth hour."

She closed her eyes, and I saw her body tense as another contraction mounted. They were coming thick and fast, and had been for some time now; why had the labour not progressed to the pushing stage? And for how much longer could she withstand such punishment?

"I'm going to examine you to see if I can work out what the problem is," I said, with as much confidence as I could muster. "Are you still feeling the baby's movements?"

She nodded.

"That's good." At least the child was alive, then. Often a drawn-out labour such as this one resulted only in a dead baby.

I placed my hands on the mother's belly, pressing gently at first, then more firmly as I moved them around, trying to feel how the baby was lying. I frowned; it didn't feel right at all. The baby's head wasn't where it should be; in fact, it felt as if it was over to one side. An internal examination confirmed my fears; instead of the usual head-first presentation, I could feel what was undeniably a shoulder.

My blood began to pound in my ears. I closed my eyes for a second and it was as if I were a child again, clinging to Nanu in the dark, words I didn't understand filtering down from the roof above:

The child is transverse; this is its shoulder…

What are we to do? She can't deliver like this, and I've never heard of a transverse child being turned successfully…

It would be better if the child were dead; then at least we might try removing it to save her…

What will we tell Sapthah? And little Ani?

Despite the hot sun, the room felt cold; I found that I was shaking. I couldn't do this. The little girl was watching me, and I saw my four-year-old self reflected in her pale face and wide eyes. I licked my dry lips; I had to make a decision.

"Can you call your father?" I asked, my voice thin and tremulous in my own ears.

She nodded and disappeared down the stairs. A moment later, the father appeared, anxiety written on his face.

"I need you to send immediately for my aunt Hasina," I told him without preamble. "I can't deliver this baby without her help."

The father looked panicked. "I was told it's not safe to call for her; that the King's guards are watching her."

Keeping my voice down so that the labouring mother couldn't hear, I told him, "The baby is lying sideways in the womb, and my aunt is the only person I know with the skill to deliver it. Without her help, you will lose not only your child, but also your wife."

The father's eyes widened and his face blanched. "I will fetch her right away." He hurried off, taking the stairs two at a time.

Feeling somewhat stronger now that I knew I'd be able to pass responsibility to my aunt, I returned to the mother's side. Her face, too, was pale and her eyes were bloodshot; she looked completely done in from the effort of labouring for so long. My job now was to keep her alive and as strong as possible while waiting for help. I only hoped that my aunt would arrive in time.

"Help is on its way," I told her. "In the meantime, roll onto your side and take deep breaths when the pains come. It's important that you don't try to push; your baby is in the wrong position, and we need to turn it before it's possible for it to be born."

She nodded weakly. I doubted if she had the energy to push anyway; the big question was whether she would be able to summon the strength when the time came.

For now, there was nothing to do but wait. I found myself pacing the birth-arbour compulsively, sometimes checking the mother to reassure myself of her condition, sometimes joining the little group of female relations who were peering anxiously through the screen of foliage. It would take the husband a quarter of an hour to get to my aunt's house, if he hurried. Then she would have to pack her bag up before following him back here. I had no doubt that she would come as quickly as she could; but would it be quick enough? I didn't even dare to think of the possibility that she might not be home.

Finally, to my immense relief, one of the aunts called out that the midwife was coming. Sure enough, a moment or two later, I heard the brisk tones of Aunt Hasina's voice, firing questions at the men, followed by the welcome tread of her feet on the stairway. I had never been so glad to see her.

My aunt wasted no time on greetings. Going straight to the labouring woman, she passed her hands over her belly, palpating and feeling. I saw her face tighten, the ghost of that day from eleven years ago passing over her features. Then she set her jaw and beckoned me over.

"You were right, Ani. The baby's shoulder is lodged in the birth canal, and its head is over to the right. It will be difficult to turn it, especially at this late stage."

The mother turned her face toward her with a look of despair. My face must have mirrored hers, because Aunt Hasina's next words were addressed to both of us.

"Difficult isn't the same as impossible. I've made a special study of transverse babies, and there's a technique we can use to try to turn it within the womb. What's your name?" she asked the mother.

"Yokheved," came the weak response.

"OK, Yokheved, I need you to roll onto your back and do your very best not to push for a while. I'm going to find the baby's feet and draw them downward, so that we can deliver in the breech position. Ani, you can help guide the baby from the outside. I'll talk you through what to do."

I nodded and took up my position. The birth-arbour was filled with a tense silence. Little Miryam and the three aunts stood huddled together, all eyes on us.

Aunt Hasina's face was a mask of concentration, her brow furrowed deeply as she felt around for what seemed like ages; then she gave a little grunt of victory.

"Aha! There's the first foot. Now where's the other one got to?" Another anxious moment; then the baby gave a kick, and my aunt exclaimed, "Got it! Now we're getting somewhere."

Yokheved gasped and set her teeth as my aunt began to draw the feet gently downward, while I helped to guide the little body into a breech position, following my aunt's instructions.

"There! Now I'm going to keep hold of the feet. When you feel the urge to push, Yokheved, you can – not too hard at first, just a gentle push to help deliver the body."

We waited. Two more contractions rose and fell, Yokheved's face pale and tense with pain. My heartbeat mounted with each one, trailing off into an irregular patter as nothing seemed to happen. A third time I felt her belly tighten beneath my hands, and this time she gave a deep groan and bore down. A buzz of excitement rippled through the little cluster of spectators as first the feet and legs, then a little body slid into view.

"It's a boy, anyway," said Aunt Hasina after a quick check. "Don't celebrate just yet, though – we still have to deliver the head, and that's the hardest…"

She broke off. Echoing up the stairs came a violent banging sound. Someone was pounding on the front door.

"Guards," muttered one of the aunts, her eyes wide.

I felt as though my stomach had plunged to my feet. The King's guards! They must have followed Aunt Hasina, which meant that it was all my fault. If I had just been a better midwife, I could have delivered this child myself. Now his life would be stolen from him before it had even begun.

Aunt Hasina, however, had the familiar steely glint in her eye. Her voice was calm, yet she instantly took charge of the situation and none dreamt of questioning her.

"Tell them they'll have to wait," she directed the most senior of the aunts. "Be courteous, but inform them that the child hasn't been born yet. We can't have men bursting in here in the middle of a birth."

The woman nodded, visibly pulled herself together, and disappeared down the stairs.

My aunt now addressed me. "Ani – or rather, Puah – stand over there with the other relations. There's no need for them to start following you all around Rowaty, like they do me. They'll just assume you're a sister or a niece – but keep your mouth shut, we don't want your accent giving you away." Seeing the look on my face, she added more gently, "It's not your fault, Ani. Plenty of midwives with far more experience than you would still not have known how to deliver this baby. At the very least, we've saved the mother's life."

All the time my aunt had been talking, her hands had continued to work, supporting the baby's body and turning it this way and that to help ease the arms out. Now Yokheved gave a tremendous push, followed by another and another, and finally the baby's head was out and he lay in Aunt Hasina's arms. Yet it seemed we were too late. The little body was limp and lifeless, and a blue pallor seemed to creep over him even as we watched. Yokheved took one look at her tiny son and let out a cry of exhaustion and despair.

At that very moment, the senior aunt burst back into the birth-arbour, wide-eyed and breathless.

"They wouldn't be stayed," she panted. "They're coming up!"

Even then, Aunt Hasina didn't lose her cool. First, she covered Yokheved's dignity with a blanket; then she set about tying and cutting the cord. By the time the guards made their appearance, she was busy wrapping the still little body in a clean cloth.

"Show us the child," demanded the older of the two guards. His face was grim, and the afternoon sunlight glinted off the sharp copper head of his spear.

"Very well," replied my aunt, "but you needn't trouble yourselves about him. He was stillborn."

She rose, holding out the pitiful little bundle. The guard hesitated. He looked around the birth-arbour, at the wailing aunts, at Yokheved's silent tears, then finally at the child's still body. He seemed reluctant to touch it.

"We should check it," said the other guard, with a trace of uncertainty.

"No need," muttered the first guard. He seemed unable to tear his eyes away from the baby, and as he stared at it, his features seemed to soften. A rush of recognition washed over me; the man of bronze was gone and there was a human face, a face I knew. I couldn't recall his name, but he was a neighbour, living only one street away from me. Nanu had recently attended his wife; the child had been a boy, and it had not survived.

"Come." The guard motioned to his colleague. "We are not needed here. Let the slaves bury their dead in peace."

With that, both guards exited the birth-arbour, and we heard their heavy footsteps retreating down the stairs.

Aunt Hasina stood motionless for a moment until the last echoes had died away; then suddenly she sprang into action.

"Quick, Ani, fetch my basket! There may yet be time!"

Placing her mouth over the baby's nose and mouth, she blew gently into his nostrils, then set about rubbing and chafing him all over, first with a dry cloth, then with a rag soaked in a herbal concoction from her basket. Every few seconds she would stop, watch intently, then breathe into his nostrils again.

The aunts stopped their wailing and watched in fascination. I knew what she was doing, of course, having done it many times myself, but privately I thought she was offering no more than a false hope. It was too late; the child was undoubtedly dead.

Just as these thoughts passed through my mind, the baby's legs jerked. He gave a gasp, followed by a faint whimper.

"He lives!" exclaimed one of the aunts in a hushed tone.

"Praise the Lord," whispered Yokheved.

My aunt said nothing, but a satisfied smile crept over her face as she continued to massage the baby's hands, feet, and chest.

From this point, the child's progress was startlingly rapid. Within minutes he had lost his blue colour and was a healthy pink all over; a short while later he was suckling vigorously while Yokheved, looking remarkably restored herself, thanked us again and again.

"The danger is far from over," warned my aunt. "The bigger and stronger he grows, the harder it will be to hide him."

"I know," answered Yokheved, "but our God has preserved him so far – both through birth and from the guards. His life is a double miracle, which means he is no ordinary child. I name him Mosheh – "drawn out" – for just as your hands drew him out from my womb, the hand of our God is on him and will draw him onward. I don't know what his future holds, but I believe it will be something remarkable."

As she spoke, her voice grew ever stronger, and a light shone in her eyes.

"As for the two of you," she continued, "Egyptians you may be, but our God's hand is on you, too. He has already used you for the saving of many lives, and whatever He goes on to accomplish through this child, you are part of that. He will surely bless you and reward you with families of your own."

I smiled rather shyly, thinking of Tothi; but my aunt made a noise that sounded something like, "Hmph!"

Yokheved looked questioningly toward her. "You doubt this?"

"I have been married now for nearly thirty years," my aunt replied, "and it hasn't happened yet. Am I to conceive a child now, just as I approach the age where it becomes impossible?"

"With our God, even the impossible is possible," Yokheved answered with confidence. "Sarah, who became the mother of all our race, was barren until her ninetieth year."

I had heard the story before, from Keshet, and had not known then what to make of it. However, today's events had served to strengthen my growing conviction of the power of this Hebrew God.

Aunt Hasina said nothing, but the cynical smile playing around the corners of her lips told me that she remained unconvinced.

8

Puah

I awake early, as usual, but today I am not the first one up. Though the sun has not yet risen, the room is illuminated by the orange flame of the tallow lamp over in the corner. Chenya has not placed it on its lampstand but on the floor at the far side of the room, presumably so as not to disturb me. In the pre-dawn darkness, the little flame seems brighter than usual, making the shadows flicker and dance on the mudbrick walls.

Both Echud and Chenya are already dressed. Echud is biting into a loaf of coarse brown bread, while Chenya busies herself arranging the bedclothes. As I pull myself into a sitting position, she smiles at me and brings the lamp over to place it on the stand in the centre of the room.

"Good morning, Mother," she greets me.

"A good morning indeed," adds Echud, wiping crumbs from his mouth. "And who knows how many more mornings we will spend in this house!"

He rises from his seat and kisses Chenya full on the lips, making her blush and giggle like a little girl.

"While you're at the meeting, I'll make bundles of all our possessions," she declares. "We can be ready to leave at a day's notice!"

Our chamber door creaks open and young Baruch appears, excitement and eagerness written in every line of his body.

"Can I come with you, Grandfather? Please?"

"Sorry, my child," says Echud gently, "the meeting is only for those elders who have been invited. If we all brought our families, there would be no room! Besides," he adds, "no matter how great the occasion, the flock still needs to be taken to pasture."

Baruch's face falls. Normally he enjoys going out with the goats, relishing the responsibility and the sense of freedom it entails, but today is different.

"Can't someone else take them, just this once?" he begs. "If I'm out with the flock, I'll be the last to hear all the news."

"I doubt there will be any news today," I tell him realistically. "Even if Mosheh goes to the King this same afternoon, no-one will hear anything until nightfall at the very earliest. But if by some chance there is anything to report, your mother or sister will go to find you. Don't worry, you won't be left out!"

"I suppose so," says Baruch gloomily, kicking at the floor. He slouches slowly from the room, his shoulders drooped.

"Nevertheless," I say, once he is out of hearing distance, "I may call on Miryam today. I'd rather not rely on rumours, and no doubt she will be able to fill me in on everything that's going on."

"Take Reena with you," Chenya suggests. "She shouldn't be out working on such a day as this."

So it is that, an hour or so later, Reena and I arrive at Miryam's door just as the sun completes its emergence above the hazy outline of the horizon. Echud had accompanied us most of the way, Aharon's house being next door to Miryam's, and as we said goodbye to him at Aharon's door, I saw Reena straining to catch a glimpse of the famous Mosheh. I can't blame her; after all, she hadn't even been born when he went into exile forty years ago after killing an Egyptian slavemaster. To her, the Prince of Slaves is little more than legend.

Miryam greets us with an enthusiasm that belies her years, and she ushers us into her already-crowded house. The wives of several of the elders are here, together with numerous other friends and relations; it strikes me that the King's taskforce will be noticeably under-strength today.

A couple of Miryam's granddaughters bustle around fetching drinks for everyone, while her great-granddaughter Zilpah rises from the stool on which she had been sitting nursing her baby and offers the seat to me. I accept gratefully and take the baby into my arms for a cuddle. Already his little body is starting to fill out, and he gazes curiously up at me with bright, alert eyes. He is a fine, healthy little boy, and again I think how wonderful it will be if he can grow up free and unoppressed.

Casting my eyes around the packed room, I notice an unfamiliar face. In the corner, not far from where I am sitting, is a woman, around fifty years of age, who stands out from the rest of the Hebrew guests due to her darker skin. While most of the women are chatting animatedly among themselves, she stands mutely, as if overwhelmed by the flood of humanity that throngs around her. I feel a rush of sympathy for her, and, catching her eye, I beckon her over.

Her name, it transpires, is Zipporah, and she is Mosheh's wife, married to him during his exile in the desert of Midian. Full of curiosity, I open my mouth to question her further; but at that moment, Miryam rises to her feet, and an expectant hush falls over the room.

Miryam, as I had guessed, knows every detail of Mosheh's encounter with the Lord in the wilderness; she must have sat late into the night talking with her brothers. She relates the tale to her houseful of guests as we listen, entranced: the miracle of the bush that burned but was not consumed; the promise that our God has heard his people's cry and will deliver us; the powerful signs given to Mosheh as proof.

"What's more," Miryam continues, "The Lord even revealed His own most holy Name to Mosheh."

A buzz goes around the room. While the Egyptians give many names to their deities – as do the Kushites, the Greeks, and every other civilization I know of – the Hebrews refer to their God simply as "our God" or "the Lord". If anything more specific is needed, they may say "the God of our fathers" or "the God of Avraham", or sometimes even *El Shaddai*, "the Lord Almighty". Yet even Avraham himself, who I am told walked and talked with the Lord, was not entrusted with His Name, which is the very essence of His being.

Miryam waits until the room has fallen so silent that a solitary fly buzzing near the window sounds unnaturally loud. Every face is lifted toward her.

"Yahweh," she says in an awed tone. "I AM WHO I AM. That is what He told my brother. The God who was, and is, and will be. He who was, before time began. He who was, in the time of Avraham, and who swore by His own self that he would give the land to his descendants. He who has been, all through the years of our oppression, and has heard every cry, even when we thought He had forgotten us. He who will be, and will keep his promise, and will lead us out of this land with dancing – yes, even taking the very riches of Egypt with us!"

It is as if Miryam has been touched by a spirit from heaven itself; her words are like holy fire, and every soul in the room is kindled. Miryam and some of the other women produce tambourines; although her house is so full there is barely space to move, somehow we are all dancing and singing for sheer joy. Anyone passing the house must have thought we were mad, or drunk; such a display of exuberance can't have been seen before in this community of downtrodden slaves. At this moment, I don't think there's a single person who doubts that by this time tomorrow, we will all be free.

Ani

"Our God keeps his promises," said Keshet earnestly. "One day there will be an end to this oppression. One day we will be free."

Achyan wouldn't meet her gaze. He stared fixedly down at his lap, his head cradled in his hands, his back hunched.

I knew how he felt. Keshet and I had been enjoying a chat and a catch-up when he had returned early from the fields, weighed down with some terrible news. Good friends of theirs, whom a couple of months ago I had delivered of a healthy baby boy, had been visited by the guards. The family had tried to hide their infant son by passing him off as a girl, but the guards had seen through the deception, and he had been snatched from his mother's arms and murdered.

At such a time, it was hard to have faith in anyone or anything. Achyan felt as I did; but Keshet, although she was deeply distressed by the news and had shed many tears, was unshakeable in her conviction. Somehow, however black the storm-clouds, she never lost faith that the sun still shone above them and would one day break through in glorious light.

I had no callouts that day, which was a good thing as I would have found it hard to concentrate on my work. Not only was I weighed down with grief and anger over the fate of that innocent little child, but as I made my way homeward, my head downcast and my shoulders stooped, there was another worry that preyed on my mind.

Before Achyan had returned with the tragic report that had driven all else from my head, Keshet had been sitting spinning while I filled her in on all my news: the health of my family, the births I had attended, the time I had spent with Tothi. She had listened quietly until I had finished, occasionally nodding or making a brief comment; but then she turned to me with a bashful smile.

"Puah," she began, addressing me as always by my Hebrew name, "do you know if there is any way for a woman to check whether she is with child?"

I stared at her. "You don't mean…"

"My cycle is two weeks late," she said with a slight blush. "It may be nothing, but if there's a way of telling…"

There was a shy sort of glow to her face that made me swallow down the thoughts that had first rushed into my head. Instead, I returned her smile, and said as lightly as I could manage, "Well, it will be too early for me to tell by feeling your belly, but there is a test you can try. Take a small cloth bag and fill it with wheat, and fill a similar bag with barley. Water them with your urine and wait to see if they sprout. If the barley grows, you're expecting a boy. The wheat will grow if it's a girl, and if none of the seeds sprout, then you're probably not pregnant."

Which would be a good thing, I wanted to add. Keshet's health was still so delicate, and her body needed more time to heal after the trauma of the last birth. Aunt Hasina and I had barely been able to save her last time; how would she cope now with the demands of another pregnancy and labour? But I could see how much she wanted to be a mother, so I kept all my misgivings bottled up where they wouldn't show. Now, however, as I walked back home, their weight was added to the burden that pressed upon my shoulders.

I reached my front door, arriving at just the same time as Tothi. He smiled down at me.

"Well well, it's the little slave-girl! And here I was hoping to find my beautiful Ani!"

Although I had been looking forward to seeing him, I wasn't in the mood for his teasing today.

"I'll just go and get changed," I muttered, fleeing past him to my chamber.

Adah, thankfully, asked no questions as she helped me out of my Hebrew attire and bathed my tear-stained face for me. I would tell her later, but right now I had to face Tothi, and the last thing I needed was to start crying again.

"Ah, there she is!" Tothi exclaimed as I joined him in the courtyard half an hour later. "And so much the prettier now that you've got rid of those Hebrew rags. Well, at least you won't have to wear them much longer."

"What do you mean?" I frowned up at him.

"Our marriage, of course, silly! Once you're my wife, there will be no need for you to go dressing up and waiting on the slave-women. My salary is more than enough to support us both."

"But I don't want to stop being a midwife," I protested. "I love my work."

"Well, you didn't seem too happy when you got home today," said Tothi, his brow creasing. "In fact, I've never seen you so downcast. Did something happen?"

I swallowed, chewing on my lower lip. Somehow, it didn't seem right talking to Tothi about what had happened today; but how else was I to make him understand what being a midwife meant to me? Besides, if we were to be husband and wife, surely we should share our burdens as well as our joys.

"I just... I had some bad news today," I blurted, and before I knew it, I was sobbing into his chest, pouring everything out: how I had delivered this little boy two months ago, the chill of fear that marred the birth of every healthy male child, and how I had thought the danger had passed for this particular family, only for hope, life, and innocence to be snatched so suddenly away.

Tothi said nothing for a while, just stroked my hair and let me sob myself into silence. Then he took me gently by the shoulders, kissed my tear-swollen eyes, and smoothed my hair back from my face.

"Don't you see?" he said gently. "This is exactly why you can't go on doing this. The burden's too great for you. You can't take responsibility for the life of every Hebrew baby. Besides, what if you're caught? What if you're arrested for going against the King's decree?"

I sniffed. Maybe he was right; maybe I was foolish to think that I could take this on, all by myself.

"You have a compassionate heart," Tothi went on, "and I love that about you. But at the end of the day, they're only slaves."

I pulled away from him. "They're people. They're my friends."

"They're slaves, Ani," he repeated, "and you are a high-born Egyptian. How can they class you as a friend? It's against every law of society."

I stiffened and scowled at him, opening my mouth to argue, but once started, he wasn't about to let me break his flow; it felt as if he'd been wanting to say this for some time. His voice rose, drowning out my counter-arguments as he continued: "Besides, they have a different culture, different gods. What will people say of me, if my wife spends all her time among uneducated, unwashed, impious slaves? You're angering the King, angering the gods."

My temper flared. "What about you, Tothi? Am I angering you?"

"Well, yes!" He was shouting now. "Yes, you are, actually!" He took a few deep breaths, then went on more calmly, "If you are to be my wife, you need to try to see things from my perspective. Your stubbornness hurts not only yourself, but me too – not only because I care about you and don't want to see you in trouble, but also because it will affect my reputation, my career. Please try not to be selfish."

This stung me far more than his shouting had done.

"Me, selfish? When you would let babies and their mothers die, just to advance your career?" It was as if I were seeing him through new eyes, and I didn't like what I saw.

"Ani, how many times do I have to say it? They are *slaves*. A slave is his master's property, just as an ox or a sheep or a donkey is. You don't cry over every baby lamb that's slaughtered, do you? Besides, it's not like they don't breed fast enough."

I couldn't even bring myself to answer this.

"Goodbye, Tothi," I said coldly, walking toward the door. "Don't bother calling again."

"Hey, where are you going? Ani! Ani, come back, let's talk this over!"

I didn't look back. I didn't want to give him the satisfaction of seeing the tears that were streaming down my face.

9

Puah

It is early afternoon, the time when the cattle in the fields retreat to whatever shade they can find and conserve their strength by moving as little as possible, save for flicking their tails to deter the ever-persistent flies. All sensible humans, too, take refuge from the beating sun and the oppressive humidity; even the slaves are allowed a rest. There's no profit in killing off a workforce through dehydration and heatstroke.

In Miryam's house, conditions have become almost unbearably stuffy. There are simply too many bodies in too close a proximity to each other. Yet, even if there were an alternative that did not involve exposing ourselves to the full force of the sun, I doubt that any of us would take it. Shortly before noon, Aharon's youngest son Ithamar was sent to tell us that Aharon and Mosheh, along with all the elders, were on their way to the palace to demand an audience with the King. At Miryam's, we will be sure to hear the news first.

The claustrophobic atmosphere is making me breathless and a little faint. I decide to make my way up to the rooftop to get some air, but as I rise from the low stool, my vision clouds over and I sway on the spot. Instantly, Reena is there at my elbow, steadying and supporting me.

"Are you OK, Grandmother? You've gone very pale."

"I'll be fine in a moment," I murmur. "Just need some air."

Gripping my arm, Reena steers me through the throng of guests, heading for the stairs. I lean rather heavily on her as we climb, grateful to have somebody to look out for me. My family are more precious than all the jewels of Egypt; what would I do without them?

On the flat roof, the interwoven vines of the birth-arbour are still in place, providing welcome shade from the sun's force while allowing the feeble breeze to sigh through. We are not the only ones to have sought recourse up here; Zilpah paces up and down with her baby boy, talking softly to him to soothe his fractious cries, while six or seven other women of varying ages stand around, sipping drinks or peering anxiously through the screening foliage in the direction of the palace. Among them I notice Aharon's wife Elisheba, and also Zipporah, the dark-skinned Midianite woman. It is she who now releases the vines she had been parting with her hand and turns toward us with a cry.

"They're coming! Mosheh is coming back!"

There is a general scramble as everyone rushes to push back the leaves and see for ourselves. Zipporah is right; a little procession is heading along the road from Rowaty, and while my diminishing sight cannot make out faces at such a distance, there is little doubt as to who it must be.

Zipporah's shout must have been heard in the room below us; soon the rooftop is a press of bodies, all competing for a view. Miryam takes just one glance; then, sprightly as ever, she hurries back down the stairs, and soon I see her retreating back heading eastward along the road. I shake my head in admiration; for a woman of eighty-seven years, she is making quite a pace, notwithstanding the punishing heat. Nonetheless, the path is long, and the minutes seem to stretch on and on until her receding form finally reaches the grasshopper-sized figures of Mosheh and the elders.

The little party continues to draw nearer, Miryam now among them, but they are moving frustratingly slowly. I remind myself that the day is hot; several of the elders, including my Echud, are quite advanced in years, and not everyone has Miryam's energy. Yes, that must be the reason.

As the column draws nearer, however, I begin to sense that all is not well. Where is the celebration, the singing and dancing? Where are the raised hands and the shouts of praise? The closer they get, the more my misgivings grow. Even my rheumy eyes can now make out the bowed heads, the slumped shoulders and shuffling feet. This is not the victory parade we were all hoping to see.

Miryam detaches herself from the contingent and slowly makes her way back home. It is with heavy footsteps that I descend the stairs, leaning once again on Reena's arm; I am loth to have Miryam confirm what my heart already knows, but I need to hear it from her anyway.

"The King refuses to let us go."

The words fall heavily on my ears, and whatever flicker of hope remained in my soul gutters and dies like a lamp that has run out of oil. Around me, every face reflects my own disillusionment and desolation; it seems that the burden of slavery crushes us with a greater weight than ever, having mocked us for a while with the illusion of relief.

"Don't despair!" Miryam urges us. "This was foretold; it is all part of Yahweh's design. He Himself has hardened the King's heart so that He can display still greater signs and wonders. We will yet be free, and all of Egypt will see that our God is a God of miracles!"

I raise my eyes from the floor and fix them upon Miryam's, taking heart from her conviction, clinging desperately to the faint light of hope that her words have awoken in me. Others, too, look up, longing and timid hopefulness and fear of disappointment chasing one another across their features. Yet to the majority of the women in the room, Miryam's words are not enough to quell the bitter sense of letdown caused by the shattering of our expectations. I see some drawn into themselves, heads buried in their hands, unreachable by any attempts at encouragement, while others stand around in groups of two or three, muttering darkly among themselves. Our unity of spirit, for all it seemed unquenchable an hour or so before, has evaporated like the morning dew. Yet in my own heart, that tiny spark of faith still glimmers, almost extinguished by the sudden cold torrent of disappointment, but rekindled by Miryam's assurance. I can't see how our deliverance can now be achieved, but over the long years of my life, I have learnt that even the impossible is not necessarily so.

ANI

"Here you go, Ani," said my Aunt Hasina, handing me a simple green linen dress, a brown headscarf, and a pair of leather sandals. "Now you can be Puah the slave-girl again."

"Thanks," I murmured as I undid the clasp of my heavy beaded neck-collar and let it fall to the floor, followed by my rings and bangles. Abandoning the constricting tightness of my kalasiris and stepping instead into the looser, lighter Hebrew tunic, I felt a huge sense of freedom: I was finally back to being me.

The last few weeks had been excruciating. Tothi had called daily, begging to speak with me, but I had refused to see him. I couldn't deny to myself that I missed him, but every time I started to weaken, I would hear his words echo in my head – *You don't cry over every baby lamb that's slaughtered, do you?* – and I'd remember the beautiful, healthy little boy that had been snatched from his mother's breast; I'd recall that dreadful moment at Yokheved's house when the guards' knock pounded on the door; I'd think of Achyan and Keshet, weeping over the lifeless form of their tiny son.

My father had begged, cajoled, shouted, and threatened, to no avail. Eventually, in a fit of rage, he had seized my Hebrew garments, together with my precious bundle of midwifery tools, and hurled the whole lot into the fire. I shrieked and made a grab for them, singeing my hand in the process, but he caught me by the shoulders and held on grimly while I fought like a cat, kicking and struggling, my breath coming in sobs as I watched the instruments of my calling disintegrate into smoke and ash. Finally, when there was nothing left to save, he allowed me to slump to the floor and weep silently into the dust, my body aching and my eyes stinging from smoke and tears.

Later that evening, when my father had gone to bed, I crept out of the house and down the street to Aunt Hasina's door. Taking one look at my filthy, tear-streaked face, she had drawn me inside, wrapped her own cloak around me, and set about making up a bed for me. That was two nights ago; I hadn't been back to my father's house since, and I had no intention of doing so. Nor had he come looking for me, though he must surely have guessed where I would have gone.

"Not bad," said Aunt Hasina critically, straightening my headdress and stepping back to take in my appearance. "Now, assuming you want to continue in your calling…"

"Of course I do!" I broke in quickly.

"…then I think it's safest if you remain as Puah, in private as well as in public. We know this house is under observation, and it won't do to have your disguise uncovered."

I nodded, seeing the common sense in her words.

"Now, I have one more gift for you," my aunt continued in her businesslike tone. "After all, it is your sixteenth birthday tomorrow, and that is no small occasion." She hesitated a second, then she lifted her own basket of midwifery tools and passed it across to me.

"Really?" I breathed, reverently fingering each immaculate instrument, all beautifully crafted and some of her own invention, and the row of gleaming crystal phials containing her hand-brewed potions, neatly labelled in her meticulous writing.

"Really." Aunt Hasina smiled. "I can't attend the Hebrew women myself – you saw what happened when I did – and the Egyptians have no real need of me, between Sera and Nanu and the other midwives. Besides…"

Something about the uncharacteristic way she had left that last sentence hanging made me look up from my examination of the tools. She sat with her eyes averted, a half-smile playing about her lips and the faintest suggestion of colour about her cheeks – most unlike her usual forthright demeanour.

"Besides what?" I asked with some concern. "Is anything the matter?"

In answer, she rose and silently beckoned for me to follow. We passed from the women's quarters through the entrance hall and the vestibule, then descended the steps toward the underground storage area. There, my aunt moved some sacking aside and pulled out a small linen bag. She opened it and showed me the contents. It was full of sprouting barley seeds. I opened my eyes wide in comprehension.

"I haven't told your uncle yet," she said in a low tone, "because I wanted to be quite sure. In fact – would you mind examining me?" The blush was unmistakeable this time.

We returned to my aunt's chamber, and she lay on the bed while I pressed gently on her belly. While there was nothing yet to see from the outside, on palpation I could clearly feel the raised bulge of the womb.

"I'd say you're around three months, or just over," I ventured.

She nodded. "The first time I missed my flow, I put it down to my age. But by the second month, there were other signs, too, and I felt bold enough to try the wheat and barley test. Though even when I saw the seeds start to sprout, I didn't quite dare to believe… the test has been known to give false results…"

"But surely you don't still doubt it now?" I demanded. "Three months… that's how long it's been since we visited Yokheved! Do you remember what she told you?"

"I do, Ani, and I don't deny it any more. I know I'm an old cynic. When your uncle and I were first married, my hopes would rise every month, only to be dashed time after time. Months turned into years, and I prayed to every god in Egypt, bringing sacrifices, incense, and tears. In my desperation, I tried calling on other gods too – those of the Greeks, the Kushites, the Canaanites, and yes, even the God of the Hebrews – but still I remained childless. I started to think that if any of the gods even exist, they must not care, and so it was pointless to petition them any further."

"I get the feeling," I said thoughtfully, "that the Hebrews' God is exclusive. I mean, if He had answered your prayers back then, you might have put it down to Hathor or Taweret, or to one of the other gods you had prayed to – and He wanted you to know it was Him."

"I think you're right, Ani," said Aunt Hasina. "When you next see your friends Achyan and Keshet, will you ask them how I can make a thanks-offering to their God? He's done what all the other gods together were powerless to do – and made a cynical old woman very happy."

10

Puah

How different this morning is from the bright expectancy of yesterday's dawn! Today, the beauty of the sunrise seems only to mock at the death of our hopes. Echud and Chenya eat their meagre breakfast in silence. Reena tries to lift her children's spirits with a song, but her voice cracks and fails after the first few lines, and she makes no further attempt. Little Amana glances from downcast face to downcast face, then hides her own face in her mother's lap. Young Baruch, meanwhile, is sullen and angry. He speaks not a word to any of us, but as he drives the flocks out of the stable I hear him beating them with his willow switch, venting his frustration on any beast that is wayward or slow.

For myself, I try to hold on to Miryam's words from yesterday, but it is hard. Just as yesterday's optimism had spread with the rapidity and intensity of an inferno, so today the bitter disillusionment of those around me is like the cold and heavy floodwaters that rise yearly from the river, spreading inexorably outward to drown and quench each smouldering ember of hope.

Echud swallows the last mouthful of bread, then he rises from his stool.

"Well, I'd better get to work," he says in a dull, flat tone.

I understand the implications behind his statement. Yesterday, there had been no need to think of such matters as taskmasters and quotas. Today, such thoughts rise back to prominence – especially with a whole day's worth of missed work behind us.

Chenya sighs deeply and gazes after her husband's stooped form as he trudges wearily from the house. With another sigh, she begins to clear away the dishes.

"Here, let me do that," I offer.

"Thanks, Mother. Reena and I had better be off, too."

Chenya and Reena work as house-slaves for the family of my cousin Nanu's son. Unlike most of my relatives, Nanu did not disown me all those years ago when I turned my back on the gods of Egypt and publicly embraced the Hebrew faith and lifestyle. She even called on me to attend the birth of her first grandchild, having stopped practising midwifery herself when her own son was born. Rather than taking payment for this service, I begged her son and daughter-in-law to purchase Chenya, who had recently married Echud and was expecting their first child. Not only did this free Chenya from hard physical labour in the fields as a slave of the realm, but it also meant that every child born to her would also be the property of Nanu's family. Alim and his wife Sekhet are good masters; they treat Chenya and Reena well, allow them to return home every evening before sunset, and never require them to cook unclean meat or prepare offerings for the Egyptian gods. Still, I always feel a certain awkwardness over the fact that my family are slaves to my cousin's family.

When Chenya and Reena have left, I potter around for a while cleaning the house, then sink down on my stool with a sigh and take up my spindle and distaff. My failing eyesight, coupled with the fact that I never learnt to spin as a child, means that the yarn I produce is of indifferent quality, but it will help to clothe the family nevertheless. Young Amana comes to sit at my feet with her own little spindle. Some days she goes with her brother to take the flocks to pasture, but, sensitive to his foul mood this morning, she has chosen to remain with me. As we work, I tell her stories of the births I have attended. In a few years' time, she will be old enough to go out with her Aunt Hana occasionally and pick up some midwifery skills herself. Today I once again relate the tale of Mosheh's birth. It does me good to recall it, and by the time Baruch returns in the late afternoon, I am feeling somewhat more positive.

Baruch's mood, too, seems to have been improved by the quiet tranquillity of the pastures with only the sheep and goats for company. He fetches us each a bowlful of warm goats' milk, and we are sat sipping them when Chenya and Reena also arrive back home.

The news that they bring raises our spirits still further. It seems that Mosheh's fame has spread beyond the Hebrew community. Alim and Sekhet spoke of rumours that the power of the gods is in Mosheh, or even that he may himself be an incarnation of one of the gods. The mighty signs shown to Echud and the other elders yesterday morning – the staff that turned into a snake, then back into a staff again when Aharon seized it by its tail; the water that turned blood-red when poured upon the ground; the hand that became snow-white and leprous, only to be restored to healthy skin again – these signs may not have impressed the King, but word has clearly spread, and the tale has been exaggerated with each retelling, until some are apparently saying that Mosheh himself will turn into a monstrous serpent and swallow up the King and all his court in one mouthful. I can't help but smile when I think what my Aunt Hasina would have had to say about such stories.

We talk for half an hour or more; then Chenya says that she should start preparing dinner, and she goes downstairs to fetch a bag of flour from the storeroom. A few moments later, I hear the front door open, followed by a scream and a crash. We all scramble to our feet; Reena is the first to reach the top of the stairs.

"Father!"

The anguish in Reena's cry sends ice-cold daggers into my chest. I stumble out to join her, dreading what I am about to see.

My grandsons Tobit and Asher are half carrying, half dragging Echud up the stairs. He is naked, and his back is a bloody mass of torn flesh. He is unconscious, which is a mercy; I can't begin to imagine what pain he must have suffered.

I stand for a moment paralysed by the shock and horror of the sight; then the medical part of my brain takes over, and I begin issuing orders.

"Put him on my bed, it's nearest. On his front, and gently! Reena, fetch me some oil and wine, the best we have, and a clean garment to make into bandages. Baruch, run to Hana's house, as swiftly as you can. I need honey for his wounds, and frankincense for the pain, and she's the only person I can think of who might have them." As Reena and Baruch dash away, I turn to my two grandsons. "Tell me what happened."

"When we arrived at the brickfields this morning, there was no straw to use in the brick-making. We had to spend the best part of the day gathering straw wherever we could find it, and then of course we couldn't meet our quota. All of us were beaten" – I notice for the first time that Tobit and Asher also have bloody stripes staining the backs of their tunics – "but Uncle Echud spoke out, blaming the taskmasters for not providing us with straw, so he was punished the most severely."

"They must have realised that he was with Mosheh and Aharon yesterday." I had been so focused on Echud that I hadn't heard Chenya re-enter the room; her voice quavers, and her hands shake as she holds out a jar of oil. "It's the last jar; I dropped one earlier when I saw him come in."

Reena has also returned with the wine and bandages, and I soak one of the linen strips in wine and use it to gently clean the ragged piece of raw flesh that is my son's back. Unfortunately, he regains consciousness as I am doing so; he howls with pain and his body jerks convulsively as the stinging alcohol touches his wounds. As quickly as I can, I soak the rest of the bandages in oil and bind them around him; the oil will soothe the agony somewhat, as well as protecting his back from the flies that have already started to swarm around.

As my hands work to fasten the bandages, I think about what Chenya said. Is this the King's revenge on those who dared to defy him yesterday? More than that, is it mere coincidence that the workers were given no straw today? Then and there, I make a decision. Tomorrow I will go myself to the King's palace and beg him to treat the people fairly. Right now, I feel no fear of him – after all, what can he do to a woman of my age? – but only a smouldering anger. Over my lifetime, I have seen no less than five kings rise and fall, yet the persecution of the Hebrews is unrelenting. And whatever my birth, the Hebrews are my people now – my lot lies with them, for better or worse.

ANI

It was dark, and I held my torch aloft as I hurried back toward my aunt's house as quickly as I could. I felt vulnerable out on these streets alone at night-time.

Just around the next corner, the light of my little flame picked out a group of Egyptian peasant men, clearly fresh from one of the taverns that stayed open late into the night. Seeing me, one of them made a lewd remark; his friends sniggered, and all three stumbled toward me, their breath reeking of cheap beer. Luckily, in their inebriated state it wasn't too hard to give them the slip; I merely ducked under the groping hands of the nearest man and stuck out a foot for good measure, sending him sprawling face-down in the dust while his companions guffawed loudly.

My heart beating a little faster than usual, I picked up my pace still further, taking a more roundabout route to avoid any further taverns. Of course, had I been dressed as Ani the high-born Egyptian, there's no way those men would have dared approach me; but all they saw was Puah the slave-girl, who was fair game. I made up my mind not to mention this incident to my aunt.

At last I reached the relative safety of my own street, though, as always, I kept an eye open for any sign of my father. It was highly unlikely that he would be out at this time of night, but I was keen to avoid any uncomfortable encounters. I had almost bumped into Tothi the other day, and although I didn't think he had recognised me, the rush of emotions that I had felt on seeing his face had left me unable to think clearly for some time afterwards.

Tonight, however, I reached Aunt Hasina's door without further incident and pushed it open. I was looking forward to telling her about the evening's work; I had safely delivered a pair of twin girls, both in the breech position, and felt like I had the right to a bit of bragging. However, when I entered the women's quarters, I saw that my aunt had company. Two Egyptian women stood with their backs to me, facing my aunt; their hair was short and unadorned, and their clothing was that of the peasantry. They turned around as I entered, and it struck me that the older woman's face was somewhat familiar; where had I seen her before?

"Ani, you remember Thiti," said my aunt with a smile. "And this is her youngest daughter, Nailah."

Of course! This was Aunt Hasina's friend, the midwife who we had visited in Pithom; but why was she now dressed as a peasant?

"Pleased to meet you, Ani," said Nailah. She was a couple of years older than me and took after her mother in looks, with a pleasant face and a ready smile. Thiti wasn't smiling now, however. She looked pale and wan, with shadows under her eyes suggesting she hadn't slept in a long while.

"Thiti and Nailah arrived here about half an hour before you, Ani," Aunt Hasina told me. "They have had a long journey, so I insisted that they ate and drank before embarking on any lengthy explanations. Thiti had just started to tell me their tale, but I think it would be best if you hear it as well – if you have no objection, of course," she added to Thiti.

Thiti glanced at me nervously. "I take it Ani can be completely trusted?" she said hesitantly.

"Of course," answered my aunt immediately. She lowered her voice. "Ani is living with me at present. Her family situation has become rather… difficult, and it has seemed prudent for her to disguise herself as a Hebrew slave-girl. So you see, she is in somewhat the same situation as yourselves."

Thiti relaxed a little and sat down gingerly on the stool my aunt offered her. Her eyes continued to dart fearfully about the room, and she jumped at every slight sound.

"It began a week ago," she began, twiddling her fingers together as she spoke. "I delivered a Hebrew baby – a boy. Everything seemed fine, but a few days later I received a summons to court. There, as a witness, was the baby's father. I found out afterwards that the guards had promised to let his child live if he would testify against me."

"Don't judge him too harshly, Mother," said Nailah softly.

"I don't. I know a father, or a mother, would do anything to save their child. Anyway, it didn't work.

"After the trial, I was taken to a cell." She shuddered. "I don't want to talk about that part. But the next day, I was released. It seems the guards, having got what they wanted, had taken the baby and killed him anyway." She looked down into her lap and blinked a few times, before continuing, "The father, mad with grief, came back and told the courts it had all been a lie. He said that the guards had fabricated the whole thing because they had a grudge against me. As it turns out, that part was true. You know my husband was a guardsman before he passed away? Well, one of the guards used to work with him, and he had never forgiven him for being promoted above him. I didn't even know about it, but it all came out in the retrial. The baby's father was beaten for having lied to the court the first time, but they let him live. I don't think he cared whether he lived or died. The baby that was taken had been his only surviving child – his wife had had several stillbirths previously."

We sat in silence for a long moment. Eventually, Nailah took up the story.

"Mother was afraid that the guards would speak to other families, would find someone else to testify against her. If this happens, she is certain she won't escape a second time. So we left Pithom. We disguised ourselves as peasants to avoid being followed, and we sneaked out of the house at night-time. We spent the night sleeping in the temple and set out as soon as the city gates had opened. We had taken money, but we didn't dare to stop and buy food, so it was a hungry and weary journey. Every time we heard feet approaching, Mother would panic, and we had to hide until they had gone by. We were lucky to reach Rowaty before the gates had closed, but then Mother couldn't remember where you lived, and we were too afraid to ask anyone. Eventually, by some miracle, we found this street, and she recognised your house."

"So here you are," my aunt concluded, "and you are very welcome." She frowned suddenly. "Don't you have two daughters, Thiti? Where is your eldest?"

"She wouldn't come," said Thiti, her voice cracking. "She said that if she left Pithom, there would be no midwives left in the town, and women would suffer. She means to carry on looking after both Egyptians and slaves, just as before." Thiti bit her lip so hard it drew blood, then buried her head in her hands.

"She'll be OK, Mother," said Nailah soothingly. "Her husband's house is quite a distance from ours, and they won't make the connection. She merely has to say that she attends only Egyptian women."

"But what if she is betrayed, as I was?"

"You know how word spreads in the Hebrew community. After what happened to the father who witnessed against you, no family is going to be deceived again."

Thiti seemed somewhat comforted. She stopped twiddling her fingers and sipped at the wine my aunt had given her.

"You can stay here as long as you like," said Aunt Hasina. "If you wish, you may help me attend to the Egyptian women in Rowaty. I will be glad of the help." For a brief moment, her hand rested lightly on her own waist.

"But what of the Hebrew women here?" asked Nailah. "Is there no midwife who still helps them?"

"That's my job," I announced proudly. "That's why I'm dressed as a Hebrew girl. I won't let them down."

"I'm not sure, Ani," said my aunt slowly. "Things are getting more and more dangerous. The guards clearly know that there are midwives helping the Hebrews, and I wouldn't want you to go through what Thiti has suffered."

"Now you're talking just like Aunt Sera," I said hotly. "The Hebrews need us. If our positions were reversed, would you really be thinking of abandoning them?"

Aunt Hasina gave one of her half-smiles. "No, I suppose not," she conceded.

"Then let me help, too," said Nailah suddenly. "Find me a headdress, and I'll be a slave-girl like you. I saw earlier how many Hebrew houses there are in Rowaty – far too many for just one midwife." Thiti and my aunt both opened their mouths to argue, but Nailah cut them off. "No-one here knows me, and I'll be dressed as a slave. How risky can it be?"

Thiti buried her face in her hands once more, but she said nothing. My aunt glanced at her, then at Nailah's determined face.

"I'm sure you're right, Nailah," she said aloud; but anxiety and doubt still lingered in her eyes.

11

Puah

The night is not a restful one. Chenya, Hana, and I take it in turns to nurse Echud, who alternates between periods of fitful sleep and hours of agonized moaning and writhing. Despite the frankincense Hana gave him, his pain must be unbearable, and every one of his groans is echoed by my own heart.

Chenya, I know, does not sleep at all but sits and holds Echud's hand, talking softly to him as her tears fall into her lap. For myself, when Hana is taking a turn to watch, I join Reena and the children outside on the rooftop and try to get some sleep. I don't want my mind to be fogged by weariness when I go before the King in the morning. Sleep does not come easily, however, and even from outside I can hear Echud's groans drifting on the still night air. By the time the sky begins to lighten from blue-black to pinkish-grey, I must have had half an hour's sleep at most.

Before I leave, I help Hana to change Echud's bandages. The wine and the honey have done their work, at least, as the swelling has gone down somewhat and the flesh looks pink and healthy with no sign of necrosis. It is still very raw, however, and removing the old bandages causes the wounds to open up and bleed again. I hate to leave him, but I know he is in excellent hands with Hana, and I feel that this is something I must do.

As golden sunlight seeps across the sky, I make my way through the streets of Rowaty alone. Reena would have come with me, as would Tobit and Asher, but I won't let any of them miss their work today; no more of my family must risk such a punishment. Chenya, of course, won't leave Echud's side, and I don't insist. Alim and Sekhet will understand.

As I approach the palace, I realise that I am not the only one seeking an audience with the King today. Several elders of the tribes are there, moving stiffly and painfully, their tunics striped with dried blood. The oldest among them are missing, and I wonder how many are in as bad a way as Echud: how many will be permanently crippled or even die from their wounds. I push this thought away. Echud will not die, not with Hana to nurse him.

The elders greet me respectfully, as one of their own number, even though I am a woman and an Egyptian by birth. One of them asks after Echud; I answer as levelly as I can, trying hard to keep my voice steady. We wait for an hour or so, our group gradually expanding as we are joined by more of the elders and their sons and relatives. A couple of the elders' wives also arrive, making me feel slightly less self-conscious.

There are now around twenty of us, all told, and the time has come for action. The guard at the palace doors eyes us insolently and levels his spear at us as he asks what we want, but he permits us to enter on the condition that all weapons of any kind are left outside. I am allowed to keep my staff; clearly an old woman leaning on a stick is not seen as a threat.

As we pass through the opulent passageways and splendid courtyard, some of my companions gaze around in wonder at the extravagance of our surroundings. The elders, of course, were here only two days ago with Mosheh and Aharon, but the women and some of the younger men are visibly awestruck and cowed by the majesty of it all. For myself, it takes me back to that day as a girl with my Aunt Hasina, and some of the apprehension I felt then seems to infect me across the intervening years. Until now, my anger and my anxiety for Echud have masked any fear, but now I feel like a child again, overwhelmed by the magnificence of the King's presence. I remind myself that, under all the trappings and paraphernalia of royalty, the King is only a man, whereas we have the immortal God on our side.

After being made to wait in the courtyard for nearly an hour – for no other reason, I am sure, than another chance for the King to demonstrate his superiority and authority over us – we are finally shown through to the throne-room. King Merneferre Ay is seated on a throne of gilded cedar, resplendent with jewels. He clasps the animal-headed *was*-sceptre, the symbol of his kingship and power, and on his head he wears the double crown of red and white, with its twin motifs of rearing cobra and vulture's head. He glares at us with disdain.

"Why do you slaves abandon your work yet again? Have you not yet learnt the consequences of your laziness?"

"O King," one of the elders speaks up boldly, "the fault is not with us, but with the taskmasters you have set over us. They refuse to provide us with straw, yet they expect us to produce just as many bricks as when we were given straw. We labour and sweat all day, yet such a thing is impossible. Why should we be beaten for the taskmasters' negligence?"

The King's eyes glint; he leans forward and points his sceptre at the elder who has spoken.

"Laziness!" he hisses. "Indolence, idleness! That's what's wrong with you, all of you! You spend all day idling instead of doing your work. How else do your heads get filled with such idle thoughts?

"'O King, please let us go and sacrifice to our God!'" he says in a high, mocking tone. "Do you think I'm stupid? I know what you're planning, you and that Moses vagabond! My grandfather took him in, treated him like a son, and how did he reward him? By murdering one of his servants and running away like a coward, only to return with this talk of leading my entire workforce off into the wilderness! And in a pathetic attempt to justify his actions, he spouts some fairy tale about his God – as if the gods of Egypt aren't enough for him!"

The King has risen from his throne, and now he advances toward us, his face livid, eyes blazing and sceptre outstretched. As one body, we shrink backward in the face of his wrath.

"There is only one cure for this nonsense," he breathes, his voice soft and dangerous once again. "Good honest work! If you spent more time working and less time daydreaming, you wouldn't have the time to fill your minds with such fairy stories. That's why I've ordered my taskmasters not to provide you with straw – not today, nor tomorrow, nor any day from now on. You can gather the straw yourselves, and you can meet your quotas every day or be beaten, just as before. That should put an end to such laziness and idle thoughts."

"B-but…" stutters the elder who had spoken.

The King's voice rises to a shout again. "Now begone from my presence, and get back to your work!"

At his shout, the guards who line the edges of the throne-room advance on us with their spears lowered. Retreating before them, we have no choice but to fall back, leave the throne-room, and withdraw from the palace in disarray. My head pounds, and there is a lump in my throat. *No straw – not today, nor tomorrow, nor any day from now on.* Must my Echud, then, be beaten every day? Will my grandchildren, too, suffer this for the rest of their lives – lives that will surely be cut short, for no-one can survive such barbaric treatment for long! Where is our God? He told Mosheh that he had heard our cries – why has he now forsaken us?

ANI

O God of the Hebrews, I have given up home, family, and friends for You and for Your people. Why have you forsaken me now?

It was a prayer of desperation, born of grief, betrayal, and fear. Never had I felt so alone, so helpless and friendless.

The day had started out promisingly enough. In the morning I had introduced Nailah to Keshet, and they had hit it off straight away. As a matter of fact, it would have been hard not to like Nailah, with her unquenchable good humour and constant willingness to help. Having someone to share the burden of the midwifery work was also a welcome novelty; when a callout had come at mid-morning, Nailah had been eager to take it, leaving me more time just to relax and catch up with Keshet.

Like my Aunt Hasina, Keshet was now a little over three months into her pregnancy, and she simply glowed. Achyan, too, had been over the moon when she had told him the news, which made me think that maybe my worries over Keshet's health were ungrounded. In fact, I had never seen her looking so well; she had had little to no sickness, and everything was going about as well as a pregnancy could go.

I confided my aunt's news to Keshet, and she rejoiced with us, giving praise to her God for the miracle. She held Aunt Hasina in high regard, having a deep debt of gratitude to her for the expert care she had given her when her life had hung in the balance. When I told her that my aunt, like myself, had put aside her doubts and placed her faith in the God of the Hebrews, Keshet was delighted.

"The two of you may be Egyptians by birth, but the Lord has drawn you to Himself, blessed you, and counted you among His own people. Your aunt should be given a Hebrew name, just like you. You are Puah, radiant like the sun; and Hasina in Egyptian means 'pretty'. I name her Shiphrah, 'beautiful and shining'. Our God has filled you both with His light, and you shine like beacons of hope to our people."

I nodded in agreement. It was perfect. This last week or so, my aunt had indeed seemed to become more and more radiant, her delight over the gift she had been given reflected in her appearance and her whole demeanour. Her face had seemed to soften, hard lines of cynicism giving way to creases of joy and laughter, and even Thiti had commented on the sparkle in her eyes. Smiling at Keshet, I sipped my drink as I watched her deft hands twirling the spindle to draw out the smooth, even thread, reflecting on how two such different women, both dear to me, were united by that same glow of joy stemming from the wonder of new life that grew inside them.

My reverie was broken by a knock at the door.

"Don't get up, I'll get it," I said to Keshet. Rising quickly, I descended the stairs, passed through the small storeroom, and pulled open the front door.

An Israelite girl of eleven or twelve stood there, twiddling nervously with the folds of her headscarf. I had seen that anxious look many times before, and even before she spoke, I knew it was me she had come for.

Sure enough, the first words out of her mouth were, "Is the midwife here?"

I nodded. "That's me."

"Thank goodness," she sighed. "It's my sister. This will be her first child, and she's having difficulty."

Yet again, I felt a surge of gratitude to Nailah. Had she not taken the earlier call herself, I would have been in a difficult position, having to try to work out whose need was greatest. Nailah had made things so much easier.

"I'll be there as soon as I can," I told the girl. "You go back to your sister and wait with her. Where does she live?"

The girl gave me the details, and I said goodbye to Keshet and headed off. Before I could see to the patient, I would have to go back to Aunt Hasina's home for some spare midwifery supplies; Nailah had borrowed the ones I'd had with me. This done, I set off once again, potions and instruments hidden in a bundle of cloths to make them less conspicuous.

Despite my good spirits on leaving Keshet's house, an inexplicable sense of discomfort seemed to steal over me as I left my aunt's house and walked toward the street the girl had named. I was jumpy, startling at the smallest sounds, and often caught myself looking back over my shoulder as if I were expecting to see someone following me. *That's nonsense,* I told myself firmly. *All anyone will see is a slave-girl going about her master's business. It's just Thiti's story that's giving me ideas – and if Nailah can get over that, so can I.* However, I was relieved when I had arrived at the house and the door had shut firmly behind me.

The girl I had met at Keshet's showed me up to the birth-arbour and introduced me to her sister, who was young – about my own age – and clearly distressed. I examined her and found that labour was well underway, but she was suffering particularly intense pains in her lower back and, having no previous experience, had got herself into rather a state, convinced that something was wrong and she was going to die. Once I had calmed her down with lots of reassurance and one of my aunt's herbal tonics, I helped her into a more comfortable position and began to massage her back to help ease the pain. Her progress from then on was rapid, and before too long I was being showered with thanks as I placed a beautiful baby boy in her arms.

"Please could you take him to show my husband?" she asked me once I had dealt with the afterbirth and given both mother and baby a wash. "He's been so worried."

"Of course," I smiled. Aside from the actual delivery, one of the most rewarding parts of my job was seeing the expression on a father's face when I presented him with a healthy baby and the news that his wife was doing well.

Cradling the baby wrapped in a linen cloth, I descended the stairs to the living quarters below. I pushed open the door – and froze in horror.

The father was there all right, looking pale and terrified. Flanking him, spears in hands, stood two Egyptian guardsmen.

The first guardsman crossed the room in a couple of paces, his spear tilted threateningly toward me, a cruel smile playing about his lips. I could see at once that there was no hope of quarter here – this was a man who would thoroughly enjoy carrying out his allocated task.

"Boy or girl?" he asked brusquely, gesturing with his spear-tip.

"Girl," I replied automatically, my tongue dry and wooden.

"We'll soon see about that," responded the guard; and, before I could react, he had twitched the cloth aside. Then he grinned, slowly, humourlessly.

"Well, well, well," he smirked. "An odd-looking girl, indeed!"

Instinctively, my arms tightened around my precious bundle and I half-turned toward the door – but the other guard was already there, spear raised, blocking my exit. I was trapped.

"Hand it over," snapped the first guard, his eyes hard and cold as iron, all trace of his grin disappearing.

I backed away as far as I could, feeling the cool earthen surface of the wall at my back. The baby, protesting the tightness of my grip, began to cry, a thin, newborn wail. I heard footsteps on the stairs above, then the voices of the mother and her sister, calling out and hammering at the door – but the second guard held it shut with his weight; and besides, what could they do?

The first guard raised his spear menacingly; the father leapt forward with a cry, but the guard thrust the butt of the spear into his middle and he fell back, doubled over in pain. I tried to turn toward the wall, shielding the baby with my body, but the guard was too quick for me. I heard myself scream as the spear-tip flashed suddenly downward; then I sunk to the floor, sobbing with shock and horror, as the blood seeped across the front of my tunic.

The guard stooped low over me, pulled the tiny body from my unresisting hands, and flung it contemptuously onto the floor. Then he put his badly-shaven face so close to mine that I could feel his hot breath. Flecks of saliva peppered my face as he spoke.

"Now for you – Ani."

Even through the fog of grief and shock, an instinct of self-preservation kicked in.

"M-my name is Puah," I croaked.

"Ah, yes. Puah, the little Hebrew slave-girl." His eyes glittered maliciously; then, in a sudden movement, he snatched my headscarf from my head, exposing my hair – my short, black, undeniably Egyptian hair.

"Let's see if you remember your real name after a night in the cells," he snarled.

I was powerless to resist. Wrenching open the door, he dragged me forcefully across the threshold, past the ghost-white mother and sister, and down the steps to the front door, the other guard's spear-tip pricking at my back. One final glimpse of the scene stamped itself indelibly upon my mind – the weeping father hunched over the tiny form, the mother slumped insensible in the corner, while the sister's tears mingled with the bloodstains on the floor.

How I managed to sleep I will never know, but I awoke with a start from a nightmare filled with the glazed, lifeless stares of a multitude of dead babies. My head pounded and my body ached all over.

The cell floor was hard and bare; it stank of urine mixed with something else that I didn't like to contemplate. All was dark, and I had no idea what time it was.

My prison was a dank and airless basement underneath the main administrative building. In the morning I would be escorted to the temple of Amun for my trial. My stomach turned a backflip at the thought. I supposed I should be grateful that my case was being dealt with so quickly – I had heard of prisoners being left to languish in these cells for weeks or months before anyone got round to doing anything about them – but my thoughts were still in a turmoil and I had no idea how I would defend myself, even if I was given the opportunity to do so. Scenarios chased one another across my mind. I could hardly plead innocence; I had been caught red-handed, and no doubt the guard would testify against me. What would the punishment be? A flogging seemed the most likely outcome. My skin crawled at the thought, not just of the pain but the humiliation of being publicly stripped and beaten. I sat hugging my knees, staring blindly into the darkness, not daring to fall asleep again.

Eventually, slits of lamplight appeared around the edges of the heavy wooden door. I heard a series of clunks as bars were lifted and the pins in the lock were shifted upward; then I was forced to shield my eyes as the door swung open, a rectangle of light framing the burly figure of the prison warden.

"Here," he grunted, not unkindly, stooping to set a loaf of bread and a wooden water-bowl on the filthy cell floor. "Eat quickly, and wash. I'll be back for you in half an hour."

Then he was gone, leaving me blinking, blinder than ever in the renewed darkness of the cell.

Groping my way toward the door, my hands found the food, and I picked it up somewhat reluctantly. The bread was coarse and stale, and although I was hungry, I could barely manage to choke down a single mouthful. I drank greedily, though, and splashed the remaining water over my face, rubbing away the worst of the dirt and tearstains. There was nothing I could do about the bloodstain on my tunic, and even the thought of it threatened to bring my one mouthful of bread back up again.

A little later, the door opened again. Before motioning me through, the warden produced a length of rope and bound my hands behind my back – not that I was in any fit state to attempt escape.

Stiffly and awkwardly I climbed the stairs, the warden behind me. We passed through the administrative building and out of the door into the brilliant sunlight. The distance to the temple of Amun was not long, but nonetheless I had attracted quite a crowd of onlookers by the time I reached the temple gate. I felt my cheeks burning, and I cringed at the stares and the not-so-subtle comments that followed me as I walked, the warden keeping step with me, holding the rope firmly.

Trials were commonly held in the gateway of the temple, so that the sun-god Amun could preside over the administration of justice. Members of the public were free to watch the proceedings; a crowd had already gathered in front of the two colossal towers in anticipation of the morning's entertainment. They parted to make way for me, every eye taking in my appearance: my bare head, my filthy stained tunic. I walked with my gaze lowered, avoiding eye contact as best I could, while trying to subtly scan the crowds for any familiar face, but none of my family could be seen. They must not have been informed of my trial, for which I was vaguely grateful – my father would have been distraught and angry and disappointed and anxious all at once, and I didn't think I could have coped with his emotions on top of my own. A part of me childishly wished that my Aunt Hasina were there, to support me with her strong, kind yet imperturbable presence, but at the same time I realised the foolishness of this wish. She would undoubtedly have tried to defend me and ended up implicating herself in the process. No, it was best that she, together with Thiti and Nailah, remained safely unaware. Nonetheless, I felt very alone, very small and vulnerable, standing there under the weight of the condemnatory stares of so many strangers, some of whom cursed or physically spat at me as I passed. Above the heads of the people, carved stone figures of the ram-headed god stared balefully down at me, adding their condemnation to that of the mob.

As I reached the front of the crowd, four figures came into view, standing between the carven obelisks of the temple gate. Closest to me, clutching a wooden palette containing reed pens, ink, and papyrus, was a scribe who was obviously acting as court recorder. To his right, leering unpleasantly, stood the first of the two guards who had arrested me yesterday. To the scribe's left, directly in the centre of the pylon – my heart seemed to stop beating at the sight – it was the vizier himself! Smaller, pettier offences would be dealt with by lesser officials – Neferkare Iymeru would only personally officiate in the case of major crimes against the state, the crown, or the gods. It was at this point that I truly began to fear for my very life.

As the vizier turned his small, glittering eyes upon me, I was reminded forcefully of the way in which a snake stares into the eyes of a mouse. If I met his gaze, I felt sure, I would be paralysed, struck immobile and completely defenceless. By an instinct of self-preservation, I wrenched my eyes away and focused instead on the one other figure within the temple.

Standing with his back to me on the right-hand side of the pylon, seemingly studying the carvings on the obelisk, was a tall, muscular young man. Although I could see only his back and his white headcloth, there was something familiar about the way he stood, and a flicker of suspicion started to grow inside me. Just then, he turned his head quickly to glance over his shoulder at me – then hurriedly looked away. Our eyes had met for only a fraction of a second, but it was enough.

Tothi!

Suddenly everything seemed to fall into place. Tothi had known about my work, my attempts to save the Hebrew baby boys, my slave-girl disguise. He had known, or at least guessed, that I was now living with my Aunt Hasina. And as her house was already being watched, all he had to do was tell the guards to look out for a Hebrew slave-girl wearing a green tunic and brown headscarf, carrying a bundle of rags. I must have been followed from my aunt's house when I went to pick up my spare equipment. It was all I could do to keep from yelling "Traitor!" across the pylon at him.

Yes, I had ended our engagement; no doubt I had hurt him; but nonetheless, perhaps naively, I had thought that he still cared about me. Was it a desire for revenge that had led him to betray me to punishment, possibly even to death? Was it personal ambition? Again I heard his accusing voice: *It will affect my reputation, my career.* Or was it some misguided sense of loyalty to the King, or to the gods? Could it be that he honestly thought he was doing the right thing? As for the baby, the tiny, defenceless baby – he probably hadn't even given a thought to what his actions would have meant for him, for the family. *A slave is his master's property, just as an ox or a sheep or a donkey is.* No, the baby's death would leave no weight on Tothi's conscience.

I felt tears prickle behind my eyelids and had to exert every ounce of will I had not to let them fall. Grief, shock, and hatred vied for position in my chest, temporarily overwhelming my fear. I couldn't stand to look at Tothi any more, even from behind. Turning my gaze away, I found myself once again meeting those cold snake-eyes of the vizier; but they had lost their effect on me. Whatever doom he pronounced, I was ready to meet it.

Of the two of us, it was Neferkare Iymeru who looked away first. He turned to the scribe on his right and gave a slight nod; the scribe instantly squatted on the floor and took up his reed pen.

"I, Neferkare Iymeru, royal vizier and Priest of Ma'at, protector of the realm and administrator of justice, preside today over the case of Ani daughter of Sapthah, midwife to the Hebrews, accused of wilfully and knowingly subverting the decree of the King Khaneferre Sobekhotep, Majesty of the Horus, Wearer of the Red and White Crowns, regarding the threat posed by the Hebrews to the stability and security of the realm."

He turned his eyes once again toward me, and this time they glistened as coldly as marble.

"You are Ani, daughter of Sapthah?"

I could see no point in denying it. I nodded.

"And yesterday, around the ninth hour, you delivered a Hebrew woman of a male infant."

I nodded again, my own eyes hardening. This was the man who was responsible for the loss of so many innocent new lives. I would not give him the satisfaction of showing any fear before him.

"Are you aware of the King's decree that any male infant born to the Hebrews is to be slain?"

I hesitated, weighing my options. After all, the original decree had been addressed to my aunt, not to me. However, I quickly realised that to plead ignorance would be useless. The guard had no doubt testified that I had tried to pass the baby off as a girl. Besides, Tothi also knew the truth.

"Yes," I said, as defiantly as I dared.

The vizier smiled thinly.

"Yet instead of obeying the decree, you attempted to deceive those who would have fulfilled it – firstly by disguising yourself as a Hebrew slave, and secondly, by lying when asked whether the child was male."

I said nothing. My mouth was dry, my palms were sweating, and my heart threatened to burst out of my chest with every beat, yet I fought to keep my legs from shaking or my eyes from betraying any shadow of fear. The crowd had begun to mutter; I couldn't make out the words, but I sensed the growing wave of hostility toward me.

"Nor is this the first time," the vizier continued. "I have a testimony on record from this young man, Tothi son of Khaa, a respected scribe, that you have regularly been in the habit of defying the King's decree, and of speaking traitorous words against the King and against the gods."

The hum of the crowd rose to a loud buzz. I felt the blood run from my face. *Traitorous*? That word itself would seal my fate. There was only one sentence for treachery – death.

"Not traitorous, my lord."

I looked up quickly – it had been Tothi who had spoken.

"Not traitorous," he repeated, "merely foolish. Ani is little more than a child, and she is easily led. Her aunt –"

"My words and my opinions are mine alone," I interrupted, more bravely than I felt. I wouldn't let him bring Aunt Hasina into this.

"It seems we have a confession," said the vizier smoothly, with a humourless hint of a smile. His voice was not particularly loud, yet somehow it rose above the growing rumble of the crowd. "This will speed up the process. There is no need for any further witnesses."

"My lord –" Tothi began, his face blanching.

"Thank you for your testimony, Tothi. You may go."

For a moment Tothi hesitated; his eyes met mine and he gazed at me almost pleadingly. I met his gaze levelly, my eyes hard as iron. Perhaps someday, if I lived, I could forgive him for what he had done to me, but the image of the dead baby haunted me still, and for that there could be no forgiveness.

Tothi soon dropped his glance. His whole posture registering defeat and despair, he shuffled away into the crowd, who parted to absorb him.

"Now for the sentence," announced the vizier. He paused for effect, looking toward the scribe, who waited with his pen poised. I clenched my hands together, digging my nails into my palms until they drew blood. Whatever happened, I told myself, I must not cry, or faint, or show weakness in any way. Yet I felt so alone. Where was the Hebrew God? I had risked all for His people; why had He not come to my aid? Did He not care about me, an Egyptian? Or was it that He was unable to save me? Here, in the house of Amun himself, was the power of the vengeful sun-god too strong for Him?

Neferkare Iymeru looked directly at me, his eyes glinting maliciously. His swollen lips parted slightly; he wetted them with his tongue, then raised a hand to silence the crowd. I could do nothing but stand helplessly, watching those lips with a kind of morbid fascination, waiting for my doom to fall.

It never fell.

"I believe I can help with that."

The voice rang out from somewhere behind the crowds – a female voice, not particularly loud, yet carrying an unmistakeable note of authority. The vizier broke his gaze, distracted; released from his spell, I turned my head to see the crowds parting, shoving and elbowing one another, those who were further away craning to catch a glimpse of the speaker over the heads and shoulders of their neighbours, while those in her path pushed backward against the crush, making space for her to pass. As they did so, I could finally see who it was that had delayed my condemnation.

She was tall and dark-skinned, as her brother had been, traits inherited from their Kushite mother. Even without the fine garments and jewellery, she would have been instantly recognisable: Queen Merris, wife of Khaneferre Sobekhotep, daughter of Rowaty's own King Sheshi and sister to King Nehesy. I sank to my knees and bowed my head; beside me, the prison warden did the same.

"You honour the court by your presence, O Queen," said the vizier dryly, sounding anything but honoured. "However, as the Priest of Ma'at, I believe the responsibility for the sentencing of prisoners lies with me."

"That is so," returned the Queen. "However, as Queen, I have the privilege of selecting a retinue for myself. As you know, my maid Anku has recently left me to get married. I intend to take this young lady into my service as her replacement."

I lifted my head slightly, my heart fluttering at the faint ray of hope.

"But the girl is a confessed criminal!" protested the vizier, his usual composure slipping somewhat. "I could find you a dozen more suitable..."

"As I have said," the Queen cut in, "the selection of my attendants is my decision, not yours. Ani is a young lady of good family, and she will serve me well."

"The King, your husband..."

"...will not interfere with women's matters," finished the Queen smoothly. "Besides, I gather that your main charge against Ani is that, in the course of her employment as a midwife, she has somehow hindered the execution of the guards' duties? I can assure you that, as my handmaiden, she will have no cause to do so again. The problem is therefore solved, and there is no need for any further measures to be taken."

Perhaps for the first time in his career, Neferkare Iymeru was stymied. The Queen's authority outranked his own, and he could do nothing to gainsay her. He bowed his head in submission, shooting me a look of purest loathing from under his hooded eyelids as he did so. For myself, I felt quite giddy. The events of the past forty-eight hours had succeeded one another with such rapidity that I was losing track of reality. Was I truly going to be allowed to walk free?

"Warden, if you would release my new handmaiden," said the Queen, lightly but with enough authority to command immediate obedience. My gaoler produced a short knife and, with many a furtive glance at the vizier, began to cut my bonds. Soon my hands were free; I stretched them out in front of me in relief, rubbing at my chafed wrists.

"Your Highness, I..." I began, feeling that some words were necessary, but not knowing what to say. The Queen had saved my life; but why? She was the wife of the very king who had issued the fateful decree; why should she intervene on behalf of one who had broken it?

"Come, Ani," the Queen commanded, a hint of amusement twinkling in her eyes as she looked from my bemused face to the vizier's thunderous one. "I must introduce you to the rest of my retinue, who will teach you your new duties."

I bowed my head in gratitude and followed the Queen, the crowds parting respectfully to let us through.

Suddenly our progress was halted by the arrival onto the scene of Aunt Hasina, breathless and pale-faced, hastily dressed, her hairpiece askew.

"Ani!" she burst out. "I came as soon as I heard... What happened? Are you..."

"I'm fine," I assured her. "Queen Merris spoke for me and has taken me into her service."

My aunt seemed to notice the Queen for the first time; she started, then bowed her head low. "Thank you, Your Highness... if anything had happened to Ani, I could never have forgiven myself..."

"I'm fine, Aunt Hasina," I cut in, fearing that she would end up incriminating herself if she continued. "You should go home and get some rest," I added, with a pointed glance toward her belly. I knew she was willing to put her own life on the line for my sake and that of the Hebrews, but a careless word now could harm more than just herself. Nonetheless, I was touched by her obvious concern for me. Never before had I seen her usual unflappable composure slip so far.

Then again, to call today a day of strange happenings would have been a serious understatement. The world had turned topsy-turvy, and no-one was acting how they should. The day's events passed again in front of my mind's eye like a series of painted images on a wall relief. Tothi's betrayal... the Queen's inexplicable intervention... and the baby. I blinked hard, trying to get that last picture out of my head, but the harder I tried, the more vivid it became. I knew it would be a very long time before I could close my eyes without seeing that image, seared onto the inside of my eyelids as if with a branding iron.

12

Puah

The sun is about an hour from its zenith as we leave the palace, but it does little to warm our spirits. Many of our group, particularly the oldest and the youngest among us, seem struck dumb, temporarily concussed by the King's words and their implications for us and for those we love. Others of the men, however, have begun to mutter among themselves, their faces dark as the winter storm-clouds.

As we step out into the sunlight, I raise my head and see that quite a crowd has gathered outside the palace. Hope, then, has not completely died among the Hebrew community; many have yet dared to defy their taskmasters and leave their work for a second day, still holding on to the dream of freedom, the faint chance that the King may have reconsidered. I drop my eyes to the ground once again, not wanting to see that last forlorn light flicker and fade away once and for all.

"Mosheh!" Korah, one of the elders, calls out suddenly.

Quickly I lift my eyes again and look. I hadn't seen him before over the heads of the crowd, but indeed he is there, along with his brother Aharon; those around him are shifting aside to allow him to come forward.

Before Mosheh can say a word, however, Korah has stepped forward, his eyes flashing.

"Do you want to know what the King said? You, who didn't even bother to come with us today? You, who sat comfortably at home yesterday while the rest of us were being mercilessly flogged for bricks we were unable to make?" He pauses for a second, breathing heavily; Mosheh says nothing, seemingly taken aback by the venom in Korah's tone.

"He called us lazy! He said that we must meet the same quota of bricks, day after day, but we will be given no straw to make them with! And it's because of you! Your words, your actions – not just recently, but your crime from forty years ago – and we are the ones being punished for it! Just look around, Mosheh! Ask any of the elders here today, and they will show you the stripes of the overseers' sticks. Malakai, Hamuel, Echud – all of them lie at death's door from the beatings they received yesterday. And how many more will follow? How can we survive being beaten daily for failing to complete an impossible task? You promised us freedom from the King, but all you have done is put a sword in his hand to kill us! May the Lord judge you for what you have done to us, Mosheh!" Korah's voice cracks and he turns away.

I look at Mosheh, expecting him to give an answer, but I am disappointed. Throughout Korah's tirade, he has made no effort to speak but merely stood with his head bowed under the force of the bitter words, like a sapling bending before a fierce desert wind. Now he stands there still, wordless and impotent, and despite myself I wonder why our God has given us such a man as our leader. If he cannot give an answer to his own people, how can he speak for us before the King? Can a reed break down stone, or a blade of straw turn aside hardened bronze?

It is Aharon who finally speaks, and his voice is steady, though laden with pain.

"We will enquire of the Lord. It is He who hardens men's hearts, and He who humbles them. He has promised to lead us out of Egypt, and His word will not return empty. Take heart! He will yet overthrow the King and all the gods of Egypt."

I want to believe Aharon, truly I do. After all, I made my choice long ago, deserting the gods of Egypt and casting in my lot with the people of the Lord. Yet at this moment, my store of faith is at very low ebb, and, judging by the unquelled muttering from among the elders, I am not the only one.

ANI

Ani, daughter of Sapthah. Ani, midwife to the Hebrews. Puah, shining beacon of hope. Ani, criminal and traitor, deserving of death. Ani, privileged attendant to the Queen of Egypt.

Over the last few months, I have been many things to many people. But who am I really?

Such were the thoughts that ran through my head as I lay in the beautifully carved wooden bed in the palace of the King. My blanket and headrest lay discarded on the floor; I had no need of them, for I had no desire to sleep. I had become quite the philosopher these past few nights, pondering deep questions of existence, identity, and the gods themselves. By keeping my mind busy, I could put off for as long as possible the moment when I would finally lose the battle and succumb to sleep, to dreams.

The other handmaids with whom I shared a room had already become used to my wakings in the early hours, and most of them would barely stir now when I sat bolt upright with a cry, eyes wide and staring, hands twitching and shaking as sweat soaked my brow. One of the girls, Aahotep, would rise from her own bed and sit beside me, stroking my clammy forehead and talking soothingly to me until my tremors had subsided. I was grateful; she reminded me somehow of my Aunt Hasina, and her presence had a calming effect on me. But not even Aahotep knew the source of my night-time terrors; like the others, she assumed it was to do with my trial, which was public knowledge. To no-one, not even my Aunt Hasina, had I spoken of what had happened before the trial. The horror and grief were still too raw.

Apart from my nightly bouts of insomnia, I had settled quickly into the routine of life at the palace. Along with Queen Merris's other attendants, I would help her to dress, arrange her jewellery and hairpiece, and wait on her as she ate and drank. Much of the rest of the time was my own, and I would wander through the palace grounds, maybe play a game of senet, or sit and study with Aahotep, who, like me, was the daughter of a scribe, though unlike me she was a keen student and could read and write almost as well as my father. As a child I had paid scant attention to such learning, considering it of little use in life; now, however, I found myself desperate to keep my mind occupied, so I'd begged Aahotep to teach me all she knew.

Part of me – quite a large part – missed my old life. Midwifery was my calling; it had given me a sense of purpose, and without it I felt stranded, like a ship becalmed at sea without any wind to drive it. However, even had it been possible to return to my old profession, I knew that every birth would be marred by fear, and in every child I delivered I would see the face of the one who had been killed. I understood now how Thiti felt, and instead of privately condemning her for her perceived cowardice, I rather admired her for being willing to continue in her work, albeit with Egyptian women. I also empathised with her fears for Nailah and her sister. I was worried about Nailah myself – carefully guarded hints from my aunt during her recent visit had told me that she was determined to continue the work I had previously been doing – but at the same time it was reassuring to know that the Hebrew women, and especially Keshet, would not be left without a midwife.

A sudden trill of birdsong pealed through the quietness of the room, followed by another. Looking around, I could see the sleeping figures of the other girls, silhouetted in the grey light of early dawn. I exhaled softly; I needn't return to my dreams this night. Rising from my bed as noiselessly as possible so as not to wake the others, I crossed the chamber to the separate room used for the morning ablutions. The palace slaves had not yet risen and I didn't like to wake them so early, but a large pitcher of water stood ready in the corner, so I showered myself down, shivering slightly in the cool morning air.

By the time I had finished, the rest of the girls had likewise risen and summoned their slaves to help them wash. My own slave-girl, Adah, had also come through from her own quarters to help me with my clothes, hair, and make-up. My father had sent her to join me here on my very first morning, much to my surprise and delight. Whether or not he knew about my trial I did not know, but while he and I would never see eye to eye, it seemed he was proud that his daughter had been selected as handmaid to the Queen.

Once Adah had made sure that my hairpiece was fashionably styled and that the dark shadows under my eyes were concealed with a thick layer of face powder, contrasting with my black kohl eyeliner, I was ready in turn to wait on the Queen. As the most junior of her attendants, I was not yet entrusted with the more involved tasks of her hair and make-up, but rather with helping her to dress in her garments of highest-quality linen, so sheer and fine that several layers were needed to protect her modesty.

"Good morning, Ani," the Queen smiled as I entered her chamber. "As it's such a lovely day, I think I'll go down to the river for a bath. Showers are all very well, but somehow I feel cleaner after bathing properly."

It was indeed a beautiful morning. By now the sun had fully risen, drenching the rooms in a golden light. A slight breeze also wafted through the palace windows, keeping the temperature pleasant and hinting at the promise of water, the beginning of the season of Akhet when the river that now flowed low and sluggish would rise in a silver torrent and flood the land with its blessing, bringing life and prosperity to the realm.

I bowed my head in acknowledgement of the Queen's words and, after helping her into her going-out attire, began to gather together the lotions and unguents with which she would anoint her body after bathing. As I packed them into a papyrus basket, it reminded me forcibly of how I used to pack my potions and medicines ready for a birth. Without warning, I felt the hot prickle of tears in the corners of my eyes. I blinked them away quickly, glancing at the Queen, who was having her hairpiece arranged by two of the other girls. I wouldn't want her to think me ungrateful for the way she had saved my life, or for the great honour she had shown me. Luckily her face was turned away from me, talking to Aahotep, and by the time she turned back to me I had regained my composure.

"My favourite bathing spot is a bit of a walk away," the Queen told me. "Will you need any help carrying the basket?"

"I'll be OK, thank you, my lady," I replied, thinking of the many miles I'd walked with my Aunt Hasina carrying a laden basket.

"Excellent! Then let us go."

Half an hour later, we had left the city of Rowaty behind us and were following the well-used dirt track that sloped gently downward toward the banks of the Nile. The sky above us was pale blue, and the air felt crisp and clean.

Just as we reached the riverbank, the Queen turned sharply to the right down a small path partly obscured by the feathery papyrus reeds that grew all around. A short distance along the trail, a streamlet branched out from the main river, trickling downward to fill a small hollow before exiting through a bank of reeds and meandering back toward the main watercourse. Although it was the dry season and the banks were hard-baked in the sun, a small pool still lay in the centre of the hollow, its calm waters shimmering blue and gold in the morning sunlight. All around the outside grew tall papyrus reeds, a verdant border rooted deep beside the water's edge, providing shade and seclusion. It was the perfect spot for a bath.

Setting my basket down, I helped the Queen to slip off her outer clothing and held it for her as she stepped out of her sandals and down to the pool's edge, testing the water with her toes. Suddenly she stopped, shading her eyes against the reflected sunlight.

"What's that? Over there, in the reeds?"

Aahotep and one of the other girls came forward to join her, treading gingerly, reluctant to soil their leather sandals with the wet clayey earth of the riverbank.

"It looks like a basket, my lady. Yes, it's a large basket."

Curious, I stepped closer, parting the reeds with my free hand. On the other side of the pool, a small grassy outcrop jutted into the main river, barely above the waterline. Papyrus reeds grew there in abundance, and amidst the thicket of greenery I could make out a black shape a couple of cubits long – a basket daubed in pitch to seal it against the lapping waters.

"I wonder what's in it," the Queen mused. "Would someone fetch it for me?"

The other maids hesitated; I saw them fingering their fine linen dresses, clearly reluctant to get them wet. Gazing across once more to the other side of the water, an odd feeling crept over me. I couldn't say how, but I knew that basket was important.

"I'll get it," I volunteered.

The Queen smiled at me as I passed the garment I was holding to Aahotep and then gathered up my own skirts and tucked them into my belt. The water felt pleasantly cool as it lapped around my ankles, then my calves. I waded in further; at the centre of the pool I found myself submerged almost to my waist, and the wavelets splashed over my undergarments, spreading dampness up to my chest; but the water rose no higher, and soon I stood in the shallows by the island, parting the reeds that grew all around where the basket had been placed.

As I reached for the handles, I felt a prickling sensation on the back of my neck. Turning my head, I made out a pair of dark eyes watching me intently from behind the screening reeds. As I watched, the reeds were parted slightly to reveal a child's face framed by long dark hair; a finger was raised to the lips, then the face withdrew behind the reeds once more.

There was something familiar about the solemn intensity of those big dark eyes. I stared at the basket, and a suspicion started to rise inside me.

What was I to do? If I was right, how could I give over the precious contents of the basket to the wife of the King himself? Yet I had been ordered to do so, by one to whom I owed not only my allegiance but my life itself. And strangely enough, a feeling of peace was creeping over my mind – a sense that this was meant to be, that everything would turn out fine.

Those eyes were still watching me from behind the reeds, waiting to see what I would do. Looking directly at them, I smiled what I hoped was a reassuring smile. Then I took a firm hold of the basket's handles and waded back into the pool.

The top of the basket was sealed so that I couldn't see inside, but its weight seemed to confirm my suspicions, as did the muffled sound that started to rise from it when I was halfway across. Again I hesitated, but again that sense of peace washed over me, giving me the confidence to continue.

Thankfully, being made of papyrus reeds and sealed with pitch, the basket was both waterproof and buoyant; had it not been so, I'm not sure I'd have managed to carry it back across the deepest part. Finally I emerged, dripping wet and out of breath, and presented the basket to the Queen.

Queen Merris thanked me graciously and took the basket from my hands, raising her eyebrows a little at the weight of it. She placed it down on the ground in front of her, and all the girls gathered round curiously as she began to untie the knotted fibres that sealed it closed. As her fingers worked, the same muffled noise I had heard earlier began to drift upward from the basket's depths. The Queen raised her eyebrows once more but continued to work on the knots until all had been released. Then she lifted the lid from the basket and peered inside, with all of us girls leaning in for a glimpse.

There lay an infant boy, between three and four months of age. He was plump and healthy, with well-rounded cheeks and a good strong cry, which he was currently demonstrating to good effect. While a baby of that age rarely bears much resemblance to the newborns I had used to deliver, the solemn little face I had seen among the reeds earlier helped me to place him. There could be little doubt: this was Yokheved's boy. His parents must have kept his birth a secret this long, but a noisy three-month-old isn't easy to hide. I wasn't sure what they were hoping for when they put him in the basket and hid it by the river – in fact, I suspected that they didn't know themselves – but they were placing his fate in the hands of their God rather than those of the King's guards. Twice already he had survived against the odds; surely their God would protect him once again?

"This must be a Hebrew child," said the Queen, indecision playing over her features as she stared at the little boy. I remembered how confidently she had stepped in at my trial, overruling the vizier and taking me under her wing; but while her husband the King might pay little attention to who she took into her retinue, the same could not be said of a baby. I felt certain that she would not give him over to the guards; what she would do with him, however, was far from certain. I prayed silently as I studied the Queen's face.

The baby's cries subsided into a series of hiccoughing sobs. Sticking his fists in his mouth, he sucked them vigorously for a moment, then broke into sobs again. Watching him, the Queen's face softened; then a steely determination crept into her eyes.

"I'm going to keep him," she announced.

Several of the girls gasped.

"But – my lady – the child is a Hebrew – what will the King say?" stuttered one of the maids.

"It has been over a year since our wedding day," the Queen replied, "and as yet there is no sign that I will produce an heir for him."

"A year is not so long, my lady," murmured Aahotep.

"I know there is yet time," Queen Merris returned, "yet I feel in myself that my desire will not be granted – that I will not be able to conceive and bear a child of my own." She cast her eyes down to the ground for a moment before continuing. "Just last night, a dream came to me, which I believe was sent by the gods. In my dream, I was down by the Nile, and I saw one of the sacred hippopotami of Taweret. She lay by the riverbank among the papyrus reeds and suckled a little orphaned lamb." She paused to let this sink in. "After such a message, and finding this child today, it seems clear that the gods have sent him to me, to bring solace to my heart and to perpetuate my line. I will tell this to my husband; he cannot deny the will of the gods. Besides, he himself is desperate for an heir."

I felt a great sense of lightness as the Queen spoke; however, the relation of her dream raised another issue, one that I wasn't sure how to resolve. Aahotep echoed my thoughts as she spoke: "The child will need feeding, my lady, and soon. We don't know how long he's been here already."

"Your highness," a youthful voice suddenly piped.

Turning with the others, I saw a child of around seven years stepping out of the water, her head bowed so that her long dark hair hung all around her face. She must have known a better route across from the island than the way I had come, because her patched knee-length tunic was barely wet.

"Sorry to bother you, your majesty, but I might be able to help you," she said timidly.

"Speak, child," the Queen said gently.

"Perhaps you could employ one of the Hebrew women who has lost a child to nurse this baby for you."

"Of course!" exclaimed the Queen. "Since my husband issued that decree," her brow darkened, "there must be many such mothers able to nurse. But how can I find one? It would hardly befit me to go knocking on every door of the Hebrews; and besides, we don't have that much time." She turned to the girl. "Perhaps you know of a suitable woman?"

"I do, your majesty. Shall I fetch her for you?"

"Yes, as quickly as you can."

As I watched the girl run off – Miryam, as I recalled her name to be – I marvelled inwardly at the wisdom possessed by one so young. She would surely fetch her own mother, who not only would have her own baby restored to her arms, but who also, in nursing him, would come under the Queen's employ, freeing her from the heavier toils of slavery.

Aahotep's voice broke into my thoughts. "What will you name the baby, my lady?"

Queen Merris thought for a moment. "He is a child of destiny," she mused, "sent to me by the gods themselves. He needs a name that reflects that."

I recalled Yokheved's words: *Just as your hands drew him out from my womb, the hand of our God is on him and will draw him onward.* "We drew him from the river, my lady," I started hesitantly, "and the Hebrew for 'drawn out' is *mosheh* – like the Egyptian name *Moses*, 'son'."

"Perfect," smiled the Queen. "Then I name him Taweret-Moses, 'son of Taweret', as in my dream. He'll be Moses for short. From now on, he is not Hebrew but Egyptian, for Taweret watches over him and has claimed him as her own."

I gazed at the little boy as he lay in the Queen's arms. Someone was indeed watching over him, but I didn't think it was Taweret, with her pendulous breasts signifying fertility and her broad, dangerous smile promising death to any who crossed her. Three times now the child's life had been saved – from death in the womb, death by the spears of the guards, and now death in the river. I thought again of Yokheved's calm conviction that the God of the Hebrews had His hand on him. I couldn't have known then, any more than the Queen could have known, that he would be the one chosen by his God to 'draw out' His people from the land of their oppression.

-PART III-

13

Puah

One week. Seven days. Such a short span of time, especially when you have seen as many years as I have; yet so much can happen in such a brief period. Long enough, so they say, for our God to create everything from nothing. Long enough for empty darkness to blossom into vibrant life, blazing with sunlight, rich with bounties of fruit and crop, teeming with vivacity in ocean, land, and sky.

Long enough, too, for the light of hope to burst over generations of gloomy resignation, only to be extinguished so completely that it has taken with it whatever faint grey light existed before, plunging us into a darkness deeper than that of the King's mines when the candles are snuffed out. Darkness so black, it seems no light can ever burn here again.

Seven days ago, the greyness of our existence was merely taken for granted. It has been six days since that first spark, the rumour of Mosheh's arrival and the signs he had been given. How brightly, yet how briefly, it blazed!

The last two evenings, Tobit and Asher have again returned late from the brickfields, exhausted and with fresh weals on their backs. I have taken over some of the good wine Hana brought to dress their wounds. The honey and frankincense I am saving; they are hard to come by, and it seems the demand for them will only increase.

Echud's back is improving ever so slightly, but he is still bedridden. Even when he is able to rise, he, Chenya, and I have decided that he will not go back to work. Another beating will surely finish him off, and if it comes to it, he would prefer a swift death at the hands of the guards when his continued absence is reported. Such are the choices we are forced to make.

I try to stop my mind wandering down that path as I prepare the midday meal for myself, Echud, and little Amana. To focus on the present, which has enough worries of its own. Without the food allowance Echud earns through his work, we are now totally reliant on the generosity of Alim and Sekhet, and, while they are good people and frequently give Chenya and Reena food to take home, I am loth to tell them of our predicament unless it's a choice between that or starvation. I know Chenya and Reena will feel the same. We have too much pride to beg. So I try to eke out our supplies as best I can, watering the wine down more than usual and dividing one small loaf between the three of us, keeping the smallest portion for myself.

Just as we start eating, the front door bangs. I rise with a start, my mind still full of taskmasters and guards, but it is only Baruch, who dashes up the stairs shouting at the top of his voice, "Grandfather, Savta, Amana!"

"What's the matter?" I ask in consternation. He wouldn't normally be back for several hours yet, and what's more, there's no sign of the little flock he drove out to pasture this morning. Scenarios run through my head, each more drastic than the last: armed guards confiscating our livestock; detachments of soldiers hammering on doors, searching for absent slaves; fields strewn with Hebrew bodies, their backs as raw and bloody as Echud's... Baruch's voice breaks into my vision, seemingly confirming my worst fears.

"Blood – it's all turned to blood!"

"What has – what do you mean?" I ask, trying to keep my voice level.

"I was grazing the flock down by the Nile, when I saw him," Baruch begins, his words tumbling over one another in his eagerness to get them out. "Mosheh, I mean. He stood on the riverbank and stretched his staff out over the water. Then – I don't really know how to describe it – it was like a red stain spread from under his staff, all along the river. When it reached the part near where I was, I ran to see, and the water had turned to blood! Look!"

He pulls out the small waterskin that his mother had filled that morning with diluted wine for him to drink as he worked. The red liquid that he pours out into a basin, however, is clearly not wine. It is far too thick, and it stinks – a sharp, metallic tang that recalls a dozen unpleasant memories all at once. While the sight and smell repulse me, it also fills me with awe, mingled with just a hint of something else.

"Signs and wonders," I murmur, more to myself than to Baruch or Echud or Amana. "Miryam was right. Egypt will know that the Lord is God!"

And there it is, that feeling that I didn't quite dare to name. There in Baruch's flushed face, glimmering in Echud's pain-dulled eyes, even lighting up Amana's youthful features. Reflected too, no doubt, in my own expression.

That little word again.

Hope.

Ani

Sunset, and the river runs red. The smouldering sky stains the turgid waters a deep crimson.

On the near bank of the Nile, a little she-goat stands, eyeing the water nervously. She is all alone, separated from her flock and her herdsman. Across the river, on the opposite shore, is a large flock, but it's plain to see that the little goat doesn't belong with them. This flock is made up entirely of sheep, each one's fleece whiter than bleached linen.

The goat lifts up her head. She gazes at the sheep, so close yet so far away. Then she looks around her at the vacant pastureland – rich and verdant, yet empty, so empty. She bleats once, long and low, and her cry is the very embodiment of loneliness.

I opened my eyes, then closed them again and lay back on my headrest. The dream had been so vivid, so real, that I half expected to feel the waters of the Nile lapping about my feet, and to hear the plaintive cry of the little lost goat echoing through the palace. At least it was an improvement on my old nightmares. As a matter of fact, since the day I had found baby Moses on the banks of the river, that other baby – the one whose face had haunted my dreams – had been visiting me less and less. It was almost as if the rescue of Moses had made atonement in my conscience for the one I had failed to save.

The presence of Yokheved and her children in the royal palace was another positive change. As the royal wetnurse, Yokheved now had a status far above that of the average slave, and it was quite proper and acceptable for one of the Queen's handmaids to spend time associating with her – after all, the Queen would expect regular reports on the health and progress of the infant prince. Despite my friendship with Aahotep, I had been sorely missing my regular chats with Keshet, and Yokheved went some way to fill that hole in my life. She was delighted to discover my interest in the old Hebrew lore, and I spent many an hour listening with rapt attention as she told me of the creation of the world, the fall of mankind, the great flood; of Noah, Avraham and Sarah, Yitzhak and Rivqah; of Yaqob and his sons, and all their deeds; of Yosef and how he came to Egypt as a slave, yet rose to become vizier over all the land and save the people from starvation through the knowledge and wisdom bestowed upon him by his God.

Little Miryam, too, proved to be good company. Despite her youth and her lack of education, she was keen-witted and possessed a wisdom beyond her years. If I had something on my mind and didn't want to bother Yokheved, I would seek out the little girl with the big solemn eyes, who would listen intently and then, with childish simplicity, quietly suggest a solution.

Maybe Miryam would know the meaning of my dream, I pondered. It wouldn't be the first time her childlike way of looking at things had come up with an answer I had missed completely.

Within the next hour, however, thoughts of my dream had been driven out of my mind in the face of a greater dilemma.

"When you have finished, Ani," the Queen said to me as I arranged her garments, "would you pack up my wardrobe ready for travelling? Have your own made ready, too. My husband has sent word that I am to join him in Itjtawy as soon as I am able. We will leave after sunrise tomorrow."

"Y-yes, my lady," I stuttered, not knowing what else to say. Leave Rowaty? Travel all those miles south, to Itjtawy? Now, when my Aunt Hasina would be giving birth any day, and Keshet too?

Later, under the shade of a fig tree in the palace grounds, I explained my problem to Miryam.

"But how can I refuse?" I asked. "I am in the Queen's service, and besides, I am under obligation to her. Where she goes, I have to go too."

"What about Mosheh?" Miryam asked. "He's still too young for such a long journey. Even if Mother took him, she'd have to stop to feed him every few hours, and it would slow everyone down."

"I don't think he'll be expected to come," I said thoughtfully. "The King may have accepted him, but he's not exactly fond of him."

I recalled the King's last visit to Rowaty four months ago, just weeks after Moses' arrival. Along with Yokheved and Miryam, I had been desperately praying that all would go smoothly, that the King would accept his wife's explanation and allow her to keep her adopted son. He had indeed done so, but he had made no effort to visit Yokheved and the child, and he had stalked around the palace with a deep scowl on his face for many days after the interview. Aahotep, who knew something about such matters, theorised that there was a political reason behind it all.

"The Queen's dream and the need for an heir wouldn't be enough on their own to convince him," she had whispered to me one evening. "But here in Rowaty, the Queen has a lot of influence – after all, it was her family who ruled here for many generations. The King fears that, if he were to deny her the child, it would create a public rift between them that would destabilise his hold on Rowaty, and on Lower Egypt itself."

Moses, then, had been saved yet again; but there was little doubt in my mind that the King would not be keen to see him in Itjtawy. Miryam was right – her family would be staying here. But how would that help me?

"Perhaps the Queen will want one of her own people to watch over her son while she's away?" Miryam suggested ingenuously.

A smile started to spread over my face, but it quickly turned to a frown. Why should I be chosen for this job? Aside from my interest in the family, what was there to recommend me? I was the newest and most junior handmaid, without the years of service and trust that many of the others had built up. Thanks to Aahotep's tutelage, I could now read and write tolerably well, but undoubtedly there were many who would be better qualified to send written reports to the Queen in Itjtawy.

Miryam seemed to read my mind.

"Why not just tell the Queen the truth?" she suggested quietly. "She is a kind lady, and she likes your aunt."

I hesitated. It had seemed to me that my selfish reasons for remaining would hold little weight with the Queen, that my duty to her would be seen as more important than a simple family occasion. But maybe that was not doing her justice.

Miryam was right, as usual. The Queen not only gave me permission to stay in Rowaty, but she told me to take as much time off as I wanted when the baby came. It wasn't long before I had cause to take advantage of her generosity.

For someone with twenty-five years' experience of handling newborns, Aunt Hasina seemed strangely mesmerized by the sight of the tiny human being that lay in her arms.

"I can barely believe it," she repeated over and over, shaking her head as if in a daze. "I never thought I'd see the day."

"Was it a straightforward birth?" I asked. Considering my aunt's age, this had been no small concern for me.

"I couldn't have asked for a better," she replied, "though no amount of midwifery experience prepares you for the reality of labour pains! Thiti was a great help, though, and I would bear them all again in a heartbeat for the joy they have brought to me." She gazed at her little son, his eyes closed in blissful repletion after his feed; with one finger she reverently stroked the downy fuzz that crowned his tiny head.

"He's a handsome little lad," I commented. "What have you called him?"

"Your uncle has named him Mesu," said my aunt, "but I want to give him a Hebrew name as well – something to honour the Hebrew God, who gave him to me. Your friend Keshet seems to have a knack for names. Maybe you could call on her and ask."

I put a lot of careful thought into my preparations for visiting Achyan and Keshet's house. Even though this was a social call rather than a midwifery visit, I knew that Keshet would be due any day now, and I didn't want to run even the slightest risk of endangering her or her child. My slave-girl disguise would no longer provide any protection – in fact, it would only excite suspicion – so I dressed myself in the finest Egyptian clothes given to me by the Queen and took the letter she had written granting me the license to purchase anything necessary for the benefit of baby Moses. If anyone asked, I could justify my visit by buying some of Keshet's yarn. As an extra precaution, Nailah followed me at a distance, and we arranged a signal by which she could warn me of any pursuit.

As it turned out, I needn't have worried. Whether my aunt's house was no longer being watched or whether it was my royal handmaiden's attire that deterred any questioning, my journey was uneventful, and when Nailah arrived a few minutes later, she had seen neither guard nor anyone acting suspiciously.

Keshet greeted us warmly. As she enfolded me in a hug, I could feel the child kicking strongly from within her swollen belly.

"Puah, my friend," she beamed. "It has been too long. There's rather more of me to hug than there was on your last visit!"

Apart from the obvious, though, it was amazing how little had changed in six months. Keshet sat with her spindle in her hands as always, and conversation flowed as easily and naturally as if I had been there only yesterday. Nailah had been a regular visitor during my absence, so Keshet had been kept up to date with all the gossip Aunt Hasina could supply, including that of me and my doings. She was overjoyed to hear my aunt's happy news, and, as always, she came up with the perfect name for the baby.

"He should be called Anath – 'answer to prayer'," she said. Nailah nodded, and I felt an instant glow in my heart. It was just right, and I knew my aunt would agree.

As I was updating Keshet on baby Moses, I noticed her squirm in her seat, as if uncomfortable. The moment passed, but a few minutes later it happened again, and I felt my midwifery instincts rising to the fore.

"Are you OK?" I asked her.

"I think so," she replied with a slight frown. "I had a bit of stomach pain, but it's gone now."

Nailah jumped in. "It looks to me like you're in early labour."

"Really?" Keshet's eyes widened with comprehension. "I mean... it wasn't like this last time; it was much more intense."

"Last time wasn't a normal labour," I told her. "You'd had a fall, and it all started very suddenly. In normal circumstances it's more of a gradual build-up."

"I suppose so." Keshet shifted uncomfortably as another contraction mounted. "How long will it be?"

"There's no real way of telling, but it's likely to be a good few hours at least."

"Oh." She was silent for a moment, her face shadowed. Then she spoke again, in a small voice: "Will you stay with me, Puah?"

"Of course, if you want me to."

"I just... I don't know why, but I'm suddenly scared. What if something goes wrong again?"

She paused once more, and when she next spoke, her voice was barely audible. "I couldn't bear to lose this one, too."

I felt a pang in my heart; it was as if her face reflected my own fears. I spoke as reassuringly as I could: "There's no reason why anything should go wrong this time. You've had a healthy pregnancy, and your child is kicking strongly inside you. Everything should be fine."

Keshet gave me a brave attempt at a smile, but I don't think either of us was that reassured.

14

Puah

This country stinks. I stand with one hand covering my nose and mouth, trying to block out some of the smell, but here, by the very banks of the blood-red river, it is all-pervasive. The Nile itself gives off an acrid, metallic reek, but even this is overpowered by the stench of the fish carcasses, bloated and rotten, that lie piled on the banks. Here and there, a larger corpse – a crane, a crocodile, sometimes even a hippopotamus – adds its own contribution to the pestilent miasma.

Even the people stink, though here it would be impossible to distinguish the aroma of stale sweat above the general effluvium. One Egyptian custom that I have never abandoned is the daily washing of the whole body; a love of cleanliness has been instilled in me from my youth, and even now I have a horror of greasy hair or sweaty armpits. Today, though, I haven't bathed for a whole week, and neither has anyone else – there just isn't enough water.

"Are you sure you don't need any help?" I call to Reena, who has stopped digging to wipe the sweat from her brow. A white vulture, startled by my voice, glares balefully at me with its beady eye before returning to its feast.

"I'll be fine, Grandmother. You rest a while."

All along the banks of the Nile, our little scenario is replicated over and over again as people stand in small clusters, wielding spades and hefting tubs and buckets. Hebrew and Egyptian, slave and free –

distinctions of race and class have dissipated along with the life-giving water of the great river. Today is the seventh since the Lord, through Mosheh, struck the Nile, and since it is now clearly undrinkable, every family in Egypt is reduced to digging along its banks for water to drink. Yet the King, so it is said, remains unimpressed.

"Apparently his magicians could also turn water to blood," Miryam had said, "though it would benefit them more if they could change it back!" She chuckled a little at her own humour.

The miracle of the Nile's transformation has brought about an equally dramatic change in the mood of the Hebrew community. A God who can do this, it is generally felt, will not stop there. If the King persists in his stubbornness, the Lord will send more trouble upon him until he is forced to let us go. In the meantime, the inconvenience of having to dig for our water is a small price to pay.

"Mosheh is going to the Palace again tomorrow," I announce at the supper-table later that day. "Miryam told me this morning. And if the King still won't relent, he's promising even more trouble for Egypt."

"Let's just hope it doesn't result in us having to dig even deeper for our water," says Chenya, but her tone is light. Work at the brickfields has now ceased completely as everyone's main concern is finding water. No longer are we living in fear of repercussions from Echud's non-attendance, and his back improves daily. Today he has even managed to rise from his bed and join us at the table.

"The King won't relent," he grunts now, in between mouthfuls of stew. "He won't believe Mosheh until he sees the signs with his own eyes. Even then, unless it touches his own comfort, he won't let us go. After all, you won't see *him* with a spade at the riverbank!"

I nod in agreement. "Then let's hope the next sign is something to really make him squirm!"

By noon the next day, we know exactly what form that sign will take. I am sitting outside with my spindle, resting in the shade thrown by the mudbrick wall and enjoying a slight westerly breeze that freshens the air somewhat from the ever-present stench. Amana is somewhere nearby, playing with sticks and pebbles; I am ostensibly keeping an eye on her, but my mind keeps wandering into thoughts of Mosheh: whether he has met with the King yet, and what he will say.

Amana's voice drifts into my consciousness; it sounds like she is talking to someone. Glancing over, I see her crouched on the ground, stroking and crooning to a small brownish something that seems to be trying to escape her attentions. As I stare, it leaps from her hands and lands right in front of me. I see that it is a frog, quite a big one. They're common enough in the Nile, of course – or at least they used to be – but it's rare to find one this far inland.

"Look what I found, Savta! Can I keep him?"

"No, child," I tell her gently. "He needs water to live, and flies and other bugs to eat. He will soon die so far from his home."

Amana's lips start to form a pout; then suddenly her eyes light up and her grievance is forgotten as she points over my shoulder.

"Look, Savta, another one! And there's another!"

I turn. Sure enough, two more fat frogs sit gulping wetly in the dusty street. As we watch, another hops out from behind a building; then another, and another.

A moment later, before my astonished eyes, a writhing, leaping wave of frogs rises and cascades toward us – a solid mass of wriggling brown bodies, hopping on top of one another, as if the ground itself had come to life to surge through the town. Retreating before them, I pull Amana into the house, slam the door shut and flee up the stairs to the living quarters. Even there, though, there is no escape. A brown head emerges from the mouth of a small jar that stands upon the table; then the frog leaps out, kicking with its strong back legs and sending the jar crashing to the floor. Meanwhile, Echud sits up in bed, shooing weakly at a pair of large amphibians that sit blinking up at him from among his blankets.

Amana laughs aloud, and I can't keep from grinning myself at the thought that has just crossed my mind.

"They're everywhere, Echud – everywhere! Just think – all the government officials in their spotless houses – what will they make of them? And in the Palace! Hopping on the King's throne, making themselves at home in his royal bed, even popping up from inside his gold dishes when his dinner is served!"

Echud stops scowling at the frogs on his bed and laughs instead. "That should make him take notice, all right!" Then he suddenly becomes serious again. "Do you think it will be enough? Will he let us go this time?"

"I can find out," I say. "Miryam will have the news."

"Then what are we waiting for?" He makes an effort to rise but sinks back with a groan. "It will take me all day to walk there with this back of mine. You go." Seeing my concern, he adds, "Don't worry about me – Amana can look after me. Can't you, my girl?" He winks at his granddaughter. "You can start by getting these frogs off me!"

I set out promptly, but my euphoria has somewhat lessened as I pick my way carefully along the streets, stepping over a frog here, pushing one aside with my stick there. A thought has struck me, one that should have been obvious, but that has only come to my attention now that freedom is a definite prospect again. What if the King does relent? What if we have only a matter of days left in Egypt? What then? The Hebrews speak of the Promised Land, their ancestral homeland, full of green pastures and fertile soil, where corn and barley, figs and grapes grew in abundance – "a land flowing with milk and honey", as they often call it. But, as I gather, the journey to this land is a long one – a matter of weeks rather than days, even without taking into account the logistics of travelling in such a vast group of people. We will need to take our flocks and herds, which will slow down travel considerably, to say nothing of the very old and the very young. And what of the sick and wounded, such as Echud? At present, he can barely walk across the room. If we are to leave soon, how can he possibly survive such a journey?

I have come now to the banks of the Nile. Although I have grown used to the reek that pervades the whole town, here at its source the putridity still makes me choke. Nobody is digging here now; the piles of dead fish are interspersed instead with live frogs, still flopping their way toward the city.

Despite the stench, I pause for a moment to gaze out at the crimson river. It has been a sign of hope for my adopted people, but now its bloody flow reminds me forcibly of the wounds on my son's back.

What is the price of freedom? I wonder. In theory, the blood of the older generation would seem a fair price to pay for the new life of the young. But it's hard to be philosophical when the sacrifice involves those you love the most.

Given the choice, would I pay that price?

I don't know.

ANI

The blood just kept on flowing. There was nothing I could do to stop it. Even Aunt Hasina, had she been there, would have been helpless in the face of that relentless tide. Pressure, herbs, fluids – I'd tried them all, but nothing had made a difference.

She lay surrounded by the crimson rags and cloths that I had used in my attempts to staunch the flow. By contrast, her face stood out stark and white. As white as death. Her skin was cold to the touch, yet still she breathed, fast and shallow.

There was nothing I could do. Keshet, my best friend Keshet, was dying.

Achyan's little sister was scrunched up in a corner of the room, hugging her knees and sobbing audibly. Achyan himself sat beside Keshet, holding her hand. He talked to her in Hebrew, soft and low, keeping up a steady, comforting stream of words even as the tears flowed unchecked from his eyes. I wanted to weep too. Actually, I wanted to curl up into a ball like little Leah, shut out the whole scene and pretend it was nothing more than a bad dream. But I couldn't. Not yet.

"Here you go." Nailah's voice was soft, with a hint of a tremor, as she passed me a warm little bundle wrapped in clean cloths. The baby.

"Keshet," I said gently, trying but failing to keep my voice level. "Your son. He lives."

The pale lips formed themselves into a smile.

"Yechiel," she whispered. "He whom the Lord preserves alive."

With a huge effort, she lifted a ghostly-white hand and caressed the tiny cheek. Her eyelids fluttered open; a pair of brown eyes, startlingly bright in that bloodless face, locked onto mine.

"Take care of him," she breathed. Her gaze flickered from me to her son, and then to Achyan.

"We will," I promised, as my eyes prickled hot. Keshet's own eyes were now closed again, but I knew she had heard as she smiled faintly once again. Then she gave a sudden gasp; her chest rose and fell once, then was still.

The light was fading, but no-one had thought to light the lamps. It must have been an hour since Keshet's passing. Little Leah had fallen asleep in her corner, worn out by grief; even in sleep her breathing was disturbed from time to time by a sob. Achyan hadn't moved at all; through my tear-blurred vision I could see his crumpled figure, dark in the dim light, still hunched over Keshet's cold hand, washed clean by his silent tears.

Nailah had taken the baby from me and was pacing to and fro with him over her shoulder. Every now and then I heard a whimpering cry, followed by Nailah's soothing whisper of "Shhh, shhh". Now she crouched down beside me and gently touched my shoulder.

"I'm sorry to disturb you," she murmured, "but we need to decide what to do with the baby. He will need feeding very soon."

With an effort, I tore my swollen eyes away from Keshet's still figure and looked at Nailah. She was right. With her last breath Keshet had asked me to look after her son, and I couldn't let her down. But what were we to do with him? Not only did he need sustenance, but he also faced the same danger as every other Hebrew baby boy.

As I was thinking this, an image of little Mosheh came into my mind. He was the one Hebrew child who didn't have to fear the guards, because the Queen had taken him under her protection. But what if another high-born Egyptian woman should follow her example?

"My Aunt Hasina," I whispered. "He'll be safe with her. Her own son is only three days old, and if she tells people they're twins, who's going to contradict her?"

Nailah nodded. "We should take him now," she said softly.

Reluctant as I was to intrude on Achyan's grief, I had to agree. Gently, I placed a hand on his arm; he didn't seem to notice, so I said his name, quietly at first, then louder.

"Achyan, it's about your son. Keshet's son."

He started at the sound of her name and turned pain-dulled eyes toward me. I explained what had to be done, and he shook his head.

"You can't take him from me," he muttered, his voice cracked with grief. "He's all I have left of her. My Keshet... my Rainbow..." His voice broke into a great sob.

"Achyan," I said again, as firmly as I could. "You have to let him go. It's the only way he'll be safe." I hesitated. "You heard what Keshet said, just before…" I tailed off, unable to bring myself to say the word, but then pulled myself together. "It's what she wanted."

Achyan said nothing, but he made a little gesture of hopelessness and defeat. Then he buried his face in Keshet's long brown hair, his shoulders heaving.

Borrowing another idea from Mosheh's family, we hid baby Yechiel in Nailah's basket to carry him home, praying all the while that no-one would hear him crying. To our relief, he fell asleep within minutes of leaving Achyan's house, soothed by the rocking motion of the basket.

In a few words, we told Aunt Hasina what had happened. When she saw little Yechiel, her eyes softened.

"Poor little mite," she murmured. "I don't know what your uncle will say, but…"

She lifted Keshet's son from the basket and took him to her breast. As she did so, her own baby stirred and began to turn his head this way and that, his eyes still closed, searching for his share of the milk. I handed him to my aunt and helped her to find a comfortable position for feeding two babies at once. As I did so, I suddenly remembered the original reason for my visit to Keshet.

"Anath," I said. "That's what Keshet said you should call him. It means 'answer to prayer'."

"It's perfect," said my aunt softly. She gazed down at the two babies, both now feeding contentedly. "Anath and Yechiel. They will be brothers in all but blood. I will see to it."

"What about Achyan?" I asked. "He's all alone now, apart from his young sister. He needs to be able to see his son, but we can hardly take Yechiel to his house every day, and it will look suspicious if he keeps on coming here."

Aunt Hasina thought for a moment.

"Do you think he would resent it if your uncle and I were to purchase him and his sister as household slaves?"

"Would Uncle Khufu agree to that?" I asked.

"Oh, I'll talk him round," said my aunt with a twinkle. "I always do!"

Despite my grief for Keshet, I couldn't help but smile. My Uncle Khufu was a smallish, balding man in his late forties, with grey hair and a permanently worried expression. He was kind, and competent enough in his own way, but there was never any question as to who really ran the household.

Looking again at my aunt with a baby in each arm, I felt a strange mixture of emotions. My sense of mourning and loss hadn't grown any less, but though Yechiel would never know his birth mother, he was surrounded by the almost tangible presence of her love – channelled to him through his new foster-mother, through Achyan and Leah, even through me. Here was a child who would grow up surrounded by love; and that thought tempered my sadness with hope, like new green shoots pushing upward through the ashes of a fire-scorched land.

15

Puah

"Wake up, Grandmother, and get ready! Today's the day!"

I wake with a jerk to see Tobit and Asher leaning over me, laughing. Young and muscular, they are almost identical in height, in colouring, and in the matching grins that split their strong-jawed, sun-bronzed faces.

"Sorry, my dears. I must have dozed off waiting for everyone else to wake up!"

The house is a bustle of activity. Chenya has been baking bread; the dough she had left to rise overnight is now cooking, filling the room with a delicious smell, while she pounds away at a fresh batch in the kneading-trough, her arms covered in flour up to the elbows. Reena is helping her mother while simultaneously trying to keep an eye on Baruch and Amana, who are in the highest of spirits and dance around, chasing the frogs that still hop out from the most unlikely of places, and generally getting in everyone's way.

"The frogs have served their purpose, but I won't be sorry to see the back of them," Chenya states, evicting one from the kneading-trough. "They were all over my dough when I got up this morning. I won't be surprised if the bread tastes of frog!"

"They've upset the King more than they've upset you," I comment. "Miryam told me that he actually summoned Mosheh and Aharon to the palace and begged them to get rid of them!"

"What was the time given, again?" Reena asks.

"Noon today. Then the frogs will be gone – and so will we!" It is Echud who speaks. He has risen from bed with the aid of a stout wooden staff, and he leans on it heavily; the creases in his brow show his pain, but he speaks with assertion and his eyes are full of fire.

I am more cautious. "We must wait to hear from Mosheh first. It will take some time to gather all the people together. There are Hebrews all across the Goshen region, and some even as far south as Atef-Pehu. They won't even have heard yet that the King has relented."

"Then surely the best plan would be to send messengers south and west, right across Goshen, and rally the people either here at Rowaty or at Awnu in the south. Both have plenty of water and good roads used by traders from the east. Then we can march north-east along the Way of the Sea – and onward to the Promised Land!"

I look doubtfully at Echud. There is no denying his spirit, but his poor broken body is in no state for such a journey. And neither is mine, I am forced to admit to myself. The chances of a ninety-five-year-old woman surviving a journey across the desert are slim to none.

"We'll stick with you, Uncle Echud," Tobit supports him. "We'll carry you if need be!" He throws a reassuring smile in my direction; my doubt must be written on my face.

"We'll carry you too, Grandmother!" Asher adds with a twinkle in his eye.

"You'll do no such thing!" I snort. But their banter has made me feel better. Whatever obstacles there may be, we'll find a way to overcome them together. And if some of us die in the wilderness, at least we'll die free.

Time trickles past. We pass it in gathering together all that can be carried: transferring wine and oil into more portable jars; pressing raisins and figs into cakes and wrapping them in fig-leaves; tying blankets and clothes into bundles. The flocks still need feeding, of course, so Baruch has taken them out to pasture, but with instructions to return early, an hour or so after noon. We can't expect to hear from Mosheh before then.

As we work, we are constantly hampered by the frogs. They trip us on the stairs, hop out at us from behind the things we're moving, and try to jump into the wine jars. One particularly large one drops out of nowhere right onto Chenya's head as she rummages in the store-room. According to Tobit and Asher, her scream is heard several houses away.

As the sun toils toward its zenith, I start to wonder just what will happen to the frogs at noon. They can't go into the Nile; I've been with Reena to fetch water and it's still as blood-red and malodorous as ever, not conducive to any life. Surely they won't disappear into thin air?

Just as I am pondering this, Amana, who has been playing up on the roof, gives a wail and comes running down the stairs. As she approaches me, I see that she has a frog in her hands. It is obviously dead.

"I was just playing with him – I didn't squash him or anything. Honest!" She is close to tears.

"Hmmm," says Chenya. She seizes the blankets from the nearest bed and shakes them out; several more dead frogs fall out onto the floor.

"Noon," says Echud, who is standing by the window, peering out at the sun. "It's the appointed time, and the frogs are dying!"

Reena takes a broom and sweeps around the house, reaching it into every crevice, while the rest of us help by moving jars and furniture out of the way. From the rooftop to the downstairs storeroom and stable, the pile of dead frogs is swept out onto the street, where we see our neighbours doing the same thing. Together with those that have died in the dust outside, the street is now filled with heaps of frogs, already starting to shrivel in the noontide heat.

"It's a good job we are going to be leaving soon," I remark. "The dead fish were bad enough, but at least they're down by the river and not right outside our houses. This lot are going to really stink!"

There is nothing left to do now but to wait for news from Mosheh. We sit down to share a loaf of Chenya's bread, but none of us feel like eating much. Quite apart from the reek that drifts in through the windows, turning our stomachs, we are all on tenterhooks, anxious to hear what instructions Mosheh will send.

When Baruch returns with the flock, he has another revelation for us.

"The Nile – it's back to normal!" he says excitedly. "I mean, it still stinks from all those dead fish, but the water's running clear again!"

"It must have happened around the same time as the frogs died," I realise. "It was still blood when Reena and I were there, an hour before noon."

"The Lord keeps his promises," says Echud solemnly. "The King has let His people go, so the plagues have been lifted."

It is nearly evening by the time we finally hear from Mosheh. We have accepted by now that we won't be starting on any journeys today, and so we are just unrolling the bundle containing our bedclothes when there is a knock on the door. It is Yared, Aharon's granddaughter's husband, and one look at his face tells me the news isn't good.

"The King has changed his mind," he informs us shortly. "He won't let us go."

Echud is incensed. "He can't do that! He made a bargain with Mosheh! Mosheh has kept his side of the deal; he prayed that the plagues would be lifted, and they have. So how can the King go back on his promise?"

"Mosheh and Aharon have been reasoning with him all afternoon," says Yared. He sounds weary, as if he has told this story many times already. "They told him that he has broken a covenant, not with men, but with our God. They have warned him of the consequences, but he wouldn't listen. He said it would take more than a cheap conjuring-trick to convince him to release his entire labour force."

"He dared say that?" Echud's fury is incandescent. "He dared to tempt Yahweh, the Lord Almighty?"

"He will regret it." Chenya's voice is quiet, but certain. "Our God isn't to be trifled with. The King will have to let us go in the end. The only question is how much Egypt will suffer first."

ANI

"Do you mind if I ask you something?"

Today, like every day this month, I had spent the morning at the palace helping Yokheved. Returning to Aunt Hasina's house at mid-afternoon, I was enjoying a break, sitting in the courtyard under a shady sycamore. Aunt Hasina was indoors feeding the babies, who were now nearly two months old, and Achyan was outside with me, pruning the trees and bushes. He had proven himself to be quite green-fingered, to the delight of Uncle Khufu, whose garden was his pride and joy. Achyan had told me he was pleased to justify my uncle's purchase of him, as he didn't like to feel under obligation to anybody. Besides, he said, he enjoyed the work, and it helped to alleviate his grief.

Talking about Keshet was another way to come to terms with her loss, and for this reason I ended up spending a lot of time sitting under that particular tree, listening to Achyan's stories about his wife as he busied himself around the garden. His voice was tender, and the tears flowed often as he spoke about her kindness, the little things she would do for him, the shawl she wove for an elderly neighbour, the gentleness with which she would gather little Leah into her lap when she had fallen and grazed her knee. His tears were healing tears, cathartic both for himself and for me.

One thing I noticed, listening to Achyan, is how he would often call Keshet his "Rainbow". I remembered that he had used the word before, in the first throes of his grief, but I had wanted to wait until the wounds were a little less raw before asking him about it.

When I put the question to him, he was silent for several minutes, and I feared that my timing was wrong and I had upset him. But then he turned toward me, a wistful half-smile on his face.

"Because that's who she was. My Rainbow. It's what her name means, and it's exactly what she was to me."

He paused again, trimming off a few more twigs before continuing.

"When I first met her, it was during a very dark time. A wasting sickness had swept through my family. First my grandparents were taken ill and died, within two days of each other. Then my mother fell sick. She had never been strong, and her frail body didn't stand a chance.

"Even while we mourned our loss, the sickness tightened its deadly grasp upon our home. My father, my brothers and sisters, my uncle, aunt and cousins were all taken ill, one after the other. I alone was spared – why, I will never know.

"Keshet was an orphan herself; her mother had died when she was a little child. Her father followed some years after, and she had been raised by her elderly aunt, who had no children of her own. This aunt was a sister to my own aunt and, seeing the trouble we were in, came to help nurse my family. Keshet, who was thirteen at the time, came with her.

"I'll never forget the black despair of those days. Morning by morning I was forced to go to work, never knowing if I might be saying goodbye to a loved one for the last time. Night by night I nursed them, each cough echoing around my head until it felt like the life was being leeched from my own body. And through it all, Keshet was there beside me. She mourned with me when my two younger brothers, my three cousins, my aunt and uncle, my father, and finally my elder sister all succumbed to the disease, one by one. She rejoiced with me when little Leah, who wasn't much more than a baby, grew miraculously stronger. The day her fever broke. The first time she accepted some morsels of food. The night she slept without being woken by that terrible racking cough."

Achyan's voice quavered, and he turned away from me, attacking the branches with his pruning-hook with unaccustomed force. I wondered if I should leave; I hadn't intended to make him relive still more painful memories. But even as I turned, his voice, now steady again, called me back.

"Do you know the story of Noah and the great flood?"

I nodded, wondering at this sudden change of subject. Of course I knew the story. Even before Keshet had told me of Noah, I had known the Egyptian legend of a flood that had swept over the whole world, and of one family who escaped through the intervention of the gods. The version that Keshet had told me, though, had immediately seemed more real; as she spoke, I had pictured myself aboard the ark, looking out over a world of nothing but water. I had felt the fear of being tossed to and fro by the waves, wondering if we would ever walk on dry land again. Above all, I had sensed the isolation of that little group, knowing that the frail timbers of their vessel contained all the life left on the earth, and understanding that, come what may, nothing would ever be the same again.

Achyan seemed to read my thoughts.

"You've pictured what life was like onboard the ark; but have you ever thought about afterwards? Noah and his family had never seen rain before the flood. Can you imagine their fear the next time the clouds started to gather and water began to pour from the sky? They must have thought that the Lord was angry with them, that he had decided to finish the job and wipe life from the earth completely. After all, Noah was a good man, but he was only human. Every sin he'd ever committed, in thought, word and deed, must have flashed across his mind when those first drops began to fall.

"And then he looked up, and there above him was a rainbow – shimmering and beautiful, like a bridge between the earth and the heavens. And he remembered the promise: no matter what happened, however he messed up, there would never be another flood like the one before. The Lord had sworn it, and His promise would stand. However dark the clouds, however fierce the storm, hope would survive, a promise as unshakeable as the One who made it."

Achyan said no more, and I could see from his face that his thoughts were no longer with Noah and his family, but back with his beloved wife. Keshet, who had never lost her hope, even when the clouds were darkest. Like the rainbow, beautiful but transient – too close to heaven to stay on this earth for long.

16

Puah

At nightfall, I join Reena, Amana, and Baruch up on the roof to watch the orange sun slowly set over our once-proud city. The heaps of dead frogs form dark shapes in the street below, like grotesque anthills. I try not to think about how much they will stink in the morning.

The events of the day and the anticipation of what may happen tomorrow have left the children buzzing, so I promise to tell them a story to help them settle down. As I recount the familiar tale of Noah and his ark, I find my mind wandering back to my youth, to the places and people who in my mind are inextricably linked to the story. Keshet, Achyan, Yokheved – so many good and faithful people have died without ever seeing the freedom they so longed for. Is the promised deliverance really as close as we have dared to hope, or must we, after all, see another generation suffer and die as slaves?

"Since that day, no storm has darkened the sky without the rainbow shining above us, a reminder from the Lord of his faithfulness and love for his people." As I finish the story, I see that Amana and Baruch are already asleep. Reena smiles at me, her eyes telling me that she, too, has taken comfort and encouragement from the age-old story.

"He is faithful indeed," she says softly. "Who knows what new wonders tomorrow will bring?"

The next wonder, it turns out, is to begin in a very public way. As a matter of fact, I myself am there to witness it, along with a mixed crowd of several hundred Hebrews and Egyptians.

The sun has risen less than an hour ago, yet already its remorseless rays have drawn out from the piles of decaying frogs a putrid stench that makes me gag. As I walk toward the centre of town, the stink increases, and I pull the cloth of my headscarf over my nose and mouth in an attempt to block some of it out. Many of the other Hebrew women I pass on the street have done the same thing, and I can see no more of them than their eyes as they hurry past, anxious to get back to their homes on the outskirts where, maybe, the air is a little clearer. I, however, need to visit my daughter, so I press on through the malodorous streets toward the temple district.

The temples of Hathor, Ra and Amun are all busier than usual today. As I pass each one, I find myself jostling against a steady stream of worshippers, most carrying gifts of jewellery or votives. It seems the Hebrews aren't the only people who are anticipating further trouble for Egypt, and many Egyptians have decided to invoke divine favour upon themselves.

The crowd outside the temple of Amun is particularly large, and I soon see why. As I pause in frustration, unable to progress any further toward my destination due to the dense mob that blocks the street, a cry goes up: "Way for the King!" As bodies press backward, scrambling and shoving to make way, I spy a flash of royal regalia. The King has been praying in the sanctuary and, having availed himself of the protection of his gods, is on his way back to the palace.

Suddenly a change of mood seems to come over the throng. Those who had been craning forward, trying to catch a glimpse of their glorious ruler, now scatter backward, fear written in their faces. The crowd dissipates, and at the centre of a widening circle I see two figures standing tall with arms upraised, one holding aloft a stout wooden staff. Mosheh and Aharon.

Mosheh's voice, loud and clear now, rises above the hubbub and brings the crowd to silence.

"O King! You have defied Yahweh El-Sabaoth, the Lord of the hosts of heaven's armies. You seek protection from your gods, but today you and all your people will witness the power of Yahweh, God of gods and Lord of lords."

With that, Aharon raises his staff high into the air and brings it down forcefully upon the dusty ground. Where its end strikes the earth, a cloud of reddish dust is kicked up into the air. But instead of settling and fading away, the dust-cloud continues to expand, swirling thicker and thicker around Mosheh and Aharon until I can no longer see them; and still it spreads outward, enveloping the whole crowd in a dense blanket of dust.

Except that it is no longer dust. With rising horror, I see that each individual mote has tiny legs and wings. The next moment they are upon me, settling on my hands and face, swarming over my clothing and raising itchy bumps all up my legs. Reaching up to brush several dozen of the creeping, crawling pests away from my eyes, I see scenes of chaos all around me as people desperately flap and brush at their bodies in vain attempts to dislodge the tiny invaders. Once again I am glad of the protection my headscarf offers – with it wound tightly around my nose and mouth, I at least avoid the danger of being suffocated by insects swarming over my lips and nostrils. The bare-headed Egyptian women are not so lucky. I hear choking and gagging as those around me splutter and spit, trying to keep their airways clear. Women tear their elaborate wigs and hairpieces from their heads, trampling them underfoot as the hair seems to move and writhe of its own accord. The Egyptian men, with their bare chests and short shendyts, are in an even worse way as the vermin swarm over every inch of exposed skin. The modest dress style of the Hebrews shields much of my body from the creatures' ravages, so even as I shift from foot to foot in discomfort, scratching at a multiplicity of itches, I know that the Egyptians are feeling it all a hundred times over.

Still worse for the Egyptians, though, is the psychological torment. Even I, who have lived as a Hebrew for nigh-on eighty years, still retain an element of the Egyptian aversion, almost a phobia, toward anything that creeps or crawls over the human body. While I no longer shave my head and body for fear of lice, or smear myself and my clothing with concoctions of herbs and fats to deter vermin, I know that this puts me in a minority in this crowd, which is composed mainly of Egyptians. Whatever remedies those around me have partaken of today, however, their effect seems to be the exact opposite of what they intended. While the small number of Hebrews in the crowd are by no means exempt from this plague, we have certainly got off lightly compared to many of my neighbours, whose very skin seems to be crawling and writhing.

"Grandmother!"

A female figure is pushing her way through the crowd toward me. Most of her face, like mine, is obscured by a tightly-wound headscarf, but her eyes and her muffled voice identify her as Hana.

"Are you all right, my dear?" I ask, my own voice thick and indistinct through the layers of fabric.

"Better than them." She inclines her head toward the two Egyptian women next to us. One of them seems to be having a panic attack; she is hyperventilating, her eyes wide with horror as she swipes desperately at her face. Her friend tries to help her but is barely in a better state herself. Both are bare-headed, their hairpieces abandoned, their naked scalps adorned with nothing but a living, moving mantle of insects.

"I was on my way to visit Mother and Father," Hana adds, concern evident in her voice.

"Me, too," I say, glancing again at the two hysterical Egyptian women. Hana's father is an Egyptian; he and my eldest daughter live in the wealthy part of town, near where I grew up. They serve our God and treat their Hebrew staff as friends rather than slaves, but in appearance and dress they are no different to the Egyptians in the crowd around us. How will they have been affected by this judgement?

"Let's go the other way round," Hana suggests. I nod. To attempt to press on through the massed crowd, many thrashing and hitting out indiscriminately at each other in their panic, would be foolishness. I take Hana's arm and we retreat the way I had come, back toward the temple of Hathor.

As we approach the temple, an extraordinary sight meets our eyes. The sacred cow of Hathor is being driven from the temple by a group of priests. Men and beast alike are swarming with insects, and between the cries of the priests, the lowing of the cow, and the wailing and pleading of the assembled worshippers, the confusion and din are quite overwhelming. The dilemma, of course, is that while the instinct of every Egyptian is to seek divine deliverance from this plague, the religious code stipulates that no-one afflicted by vermin may enter the temple – and this applies not only to the general populace, but also to the priests and even the bovine representation of Hathor herself.

Hana and I don't pause to wonder at this pitiful sight but hurry on past, our concern for Hana's parents mounting with every stricken Egyptian we pass. By a roundabout route, we come eventually to Mesu and Aliza's home, and I knock tentatively on the wooden door.

It opens, but only a crack. "Who's there?" Mesu's muffled voice sounds through the narrow opening.

Hana and I glance at each other. Hana's anxiety is etched in her face, no doubt reflected by my own.

"It's me, Father," she answers uncertainly.

"Hana? Hana, my darling, you mustn't come in. We – there's some kind of bugs, they've invaded the house – they're all over us, the staff, even the cats and the cattle... You'd better leave, darling. I don't want you to catch it, too."

This doesn't sound good. I take a deep breath, the air stale and fuzzy-tasting through my headscarf.

"Anath." I call him by his Hebrew name, the one he prefers to use with his Hebrew friends and family. "Anath, this is a nation-wide plague. It's not just you. This is God's judgement on Egypt – I saw with my own eyes as Mosheh called it down on King and country. The insects are on everyone, us too."

The door opens further, and I find myself grinning with relief under my scarf. It's not nearly as bad as I had feared. Mesu, a slimly built man who works as a government surveyor, is dressed in the Egyptian style, bare chested with a white shendyt skirt. However, in contrast to the other Egyptian men we had passed on the way, relatively few of the swarming, biting insects are crawling over his bare skin. Like us, he has tied a cloth around his face to keep the bugs out of his nose and mouth; but, having feared to see him quite literally blanketed by the crawling pests, I realise now that our God has reserved His full hand of judgement not for those who are Egyptian in race or appearance, but for those who fail to acknowledge His name.

"Mother! Hana!" My daughter Aliza appears from one of the doorways leading off the long hall. As tall as her husband, with hazel eyes and olive skin creased with laughter lines, she is dressed, as is her custom, in a curious mixture of the Hebrew and Egyptian styles. Her fine linen kalasiris is ornamented with beads, her neck and wrists hung with jewellery, as befits the wife of a wealthy government official, but the neckline of her dress is worn higher than the current Egyptian trend, and her unshaven head is modestly covered with an undyed linen scarf, the tail of which she has used to protect her nose and mouth from the insects. She clucks with consternation at the sight of the creatures crawling over Hana and me, makes a vain attempt to brush them off, then gives up and enfolds each of us in a hug.

"So this is the new plague the Lord has sent?" she comments, holding her own arm out in front of her and watching in revolted fascination as the insects creep up and down it. "I thought it was something we'd caught from the cats, maybe. We didn't know everyone else was affected too."

"Yes – in fact, we have all got off quite lightly," I say, and in a few short words I describe the scene outside, Hana occasionally jumping in to elaborate.

I have just started to recount Mosheh's words to the King when there is a knock at the door. Mesu and Aliza glance at one another, then Mesu goes to answer it. As the door swings open, however, he recoils as if he had been struck.

The figure outside is a grotesque caricature of a man, swaddled from head to foot in broad strips of linen, almost like a mummified corpse – except that the sheets are moving, teeming with bugs. Judging by the overpowering odour that assails our nostrils, the linen has been soaked or smeared with a concoction of garlic, oils, spices, and I don't know what else, presumably in a fruitless attempt to deter the creatures. The only visible feature is a pair of brown eyes that stare wildly out from a gap in the swathing bands. In another context the figure might have been either funny or macabre, but today the word that comes to mind is "tragic".

The man seems to me to be unrecognisable, but Hana's younger eyes have identified what my rheumy old ones cannot, and she gives a little cry.

"Alim!"

"Help me, Mesu – I didn't know who else to turn to."

His voice is cracked with distress and muffled by the layers of linen, yet it is indeed Alim's voice – my cousin Nanu's son. But what a difference! He is normally so neat and dapper, so particular about his hygiene and appearance. But why should he have been stricken so severely? He is a good man, honest in his dealings, and a kind master to

Chenya and Reena and his other Hebrew house-staff. There must be many who are less afflicted yet deserve it more.

I am still pondering this question an hour later, as I make my way home through the unusually quiet streets with Hana by my side. When I voice my thoughts to Hana, she, too, grows pensive.

"There's something else I've been wondering," she says after a while. "If the Lord has placed a distinction between those who acknowledge Him and those who don't, then why not distinguish fully? I mean, why couldn't He have kept us completely free from these bugs?" She brushes irritably at her forearm.

"I'm sure He could have," I reply thoughtfully. "So maybe He's trying to teach us something? Could it be that we're not totally free from this plague because we're not totally free from the sin that causes it?"

Neither of us speaks for a moment. Then Hana breaks the silence.

"I have this old amulet; it belonged to my father's grandmother and has been passed down through the family. It has the image of Bast on it. I often wear it to bring me luck."

I say nothing, but I finger the blue-and-gold pin that fastens my dress. How many Hebrews might have some token – bought, found or given – with an image or symbol of Egypt's gods? But all these things are just a scratch on the surface, I realise suddenly. We can shun the graven images and throw away the tokens, but harder to cleanse ourselves from are the ingrained thoughts and habits of the culture that surrounds us. Even if we should soon be taken out of Egypt, how many generations will it be before Egypt is taken out of us?

ANI

The blood-red river. Sunset on the water. The flock grazing on the far bank. And the little lost she-goat.

The herdsman. Across the water, she can see him with the flock. The sheep mill around him, looking to him for pasture and safety.

The she-goat has no shortage of pasture, but she doesn't feel safe. Sniffing the air, she looks this way and that, scenting danger, vague and undefined, but undeniably present. She stands, shivering, poised to run but not knowing which way to turn.

I lay with my eyes open wide in the dark, my heart thumping, covered in a cold sweat. The little goat's fear had seemed so real. More than that, though: even on waking I sensed her loneliness, a deep-down ache that drained the strength from my limbs and brought the water to my eyes.

I supposed I could get up, or else try to go back to sleep, but I felt no real inclination to do either. I don't know how long I lay there, staring up into the blackness, listening to Aahotep's deep, regular breathing, Tali's gentle snores, and an occasional cough from Iseret.

I had been back at the palace two weeks now, since the Queen's return to Rowaty. On the surface, things were carrying on just the same as ever. I waited on the Queen, studied reading and writing with Aahotep, and helped Yokheved and Miryam with Moses, who was just beginning to walk now and kept us all busy hauling him away from potential hazards. Yet beneath all this busyness, there was a sense of unfulfilment. Even in the hours I spent playing with Miryam and listening to Yokheved's stories, it nagged at me, like an empty place inside that nothing could fill. I had never in my life experienced homesickness, even in the months I had spent as a child studying at the temple of Neith in Zau, several days' journey away from home and family. Yet now I found myself looking forward with longing to my few days' leave, when I could abandon the decadent splendour of the palace and return to the familiarity and comfort of Aunt Hasina's home.

Beside me, Aahotep stirred in her sleep. The first grey fingers of dawn were reaching in through the narrow windows of our chamber. I decided I might as well get up.

A couple of hours later, I sat with Aahotep in our usual spot in the garden arbour. The air was fragranced with the heady scent of rare lilies and orchids and filled with birdsong from the nearby aviary. Yet in my heart I kept picturing myself back under my shady sycamore tree in Aunt Hasina's courtyard, sipping a drink and listening to the drone of insects and the rasp of a pruning-hook.

If my mind wasn't on my studies that day, I wasn't the only one. Aahotep, who had returned only yesterday from a week's leave, also seemed preoccupied. After half an hour of staring at my own blank writing-tablet, I glanced over at Aahotep's tablet, expecting to see her usual neat rows of hieroglyphs, and was astonished to see instead a series of meaningless doodles. Suddenly aware of my gaze, she blushed and covered her tablet with her arm.

"Are you OK?" I asked, with some concern. It wasn't like Aahotep to shirk her studies.

"Fine, thanks," she replied, but her blush continued to deepen as she spoke.

Tali, one of the other girls, happened to be passing at that moment; hearing our conversation, she changed direction and plonked herself down next to me.

"I know what the problem is," she said confidentially. "Aahotep is in looooooove!" She drew out the last word and followed it up with a high-pitched giggle.

"Tali!" Aahotep reprimanded her, her face now a deep scarlet.

"Really?" I asked, trying to hide my own confusion. Of course I was happy for my friend, so why did my insides feel all twisted up?

"Apparently he's young, intelligent and very handsome!" Tali continued, ignoring the warning glances Aahotep was shooting her. "Not short of money either, from what I've heard. Her father has approved the match, and they just have to set a date for the wedding! I thought she'd have told you by now." A slight frown creased Tali's face as she finally noticed Aahotep's expression.

"Oh Ani, please don't hate me!"

"Why would I hate you? I'm happy for you." Yet even as I spoke, there it was again: that feeling that my guts were writhing like snakes in my belly.

"He was there, in Itjtawy. I couldn't believe it when I saw him there, but it seems the King has appointed him as one of his personal scribes. Oh Ani, I wanted to hate him for what he did to you, really I did, but I just couldn't."

She didn't need to say his name. For almost a year now, ever since I had first come here, I had said it over and over to myself, sometimes with a note of longing, but more often in pure bitterness and anger, picturing elaborate revenges that I knew I could never carry out. Yet today, strangely enough, I felt nothing. If I'd been told this news a month or two ago, I'm not sure what I would have done. I probably would have shouted a lot. I'd have wept. I'd have pleaded with Aahotep to see Tothi for who he really was, to leave him now before he betrayed her like he had betrayed me. Maybe I should do this still. I couldn't explain the strange indifference I now felt at the thought of him, but Aahotep was my friend and I didn't want her to get hurt.

Before I could open my mouth, Aahotep had pre-empted me.

"He's changed, Ani. If you saw him now, you'd realise it for yourself. What he did to you was despicable, but he never truly wanted to see you hurt. When he thought his actions had condemned you to death... it broke him. It made him realise there's more important things in life than ambition. Every day he tries to atone for what he did – by praying to the gods, by giving alms to the poor, by treating everyone with kindness and gentleness, even his slaves. That's what I saw in him, and that's... that's why I love him."

She looked at me pleadingly, tears standing in her eyes, willing me to understand, to forgive her, yet expecting an outburst of tears and fury.

"It's fine," I said, surprised by my own sincerity. "Maybe he *has* changed. Either way, it's not up to me to tell you who to love."

Aahotep's face registered bewilderment and disbelief.

"No, really," I said. "You can't choose who you fall in love with. Even if no-one else agrees, if everyone thinks he's unsuitable... even if you were to fall in love with a man with no wealth and no status... a commoner, or even a slave..."

My voice faltered and I broke off, realising that both Aahotep and Tali were staring at me.

17

Puah

"Early this morning, before the sun had risen, the bug-ridden King and his bug-ridden retinue left Rowaty as swiftly as their bug-ridden beasts could carry them."

Ironic cheers and titters ripple through the crowd at Miryam's irreverent remark, showing just how far the tide has turned over the last couple of weeks. Not so long ago, few would have dared to speak so lightly of the King even within the safety of our own walls, let alone in public. I look around at the people: young men, sunburnt and muscular from their labour in the fields; careworn mothers with babies in their arms; older faces, deeply lined from decades of toil; laughing children, darting in and out among the crowd – and not a bug in sight. I woke up this morning to find them vanished, so I set off to Miryam's in search of an explanation, to find that half of Israel had had the same idea. I think we were all wondering whether the lifting of the plague meant that the King had relented, and, while Miryam has disabused us of that notion, spirits are nonetheless high.

"Does he think he can escape from the Lord's hand in Itjtawy?" someone calls out.

"Maybe so," Miryam returns. "At the least, he hopes to put some distance between himself and my brothers."

"Will Mosheh and Aharon go after him?" another voice enquires.

"They are on the way already."

A genuine cheer follows this announcement. It is hard to believe that this is the same crowd that harangued Mosheh and Aharon only two weeks ago, when things were at their blackest.

Yes, they are far from perfect, this nation among whom I cast my lot so many years ago – even as I myself am far from perfect. Yet they are the Lord's chosen people, and His hand is with them. I am truly blessed to class myself among them.

Ani

At last the day had come. One last time, I checked my appearance in my polished bronze hand-mirror. I looked good – my favourite white kalasiris, soft against my skin, was complemented by the lapis lazuli beading and the exquisite blue-and-gold scarab pin that had been gifted to me by the Queen. I touched this now for luck, humming a little ditty to myself as I packed my things together, regardless of the giggles and nudges of the other girls.

"Someone's looking forward to her week's leave!" Tali commented, with a wink at Iseret and Pipui.

"Well, yes," I answered. "I've missed my aunt and the babies. It'll be great to see them again."

"Just your aunt?" asked Tali slyly. "Are you sure there's not someone else you're looking forward to seeing?"

I couldn't help it – I felt the blood rising to my cheeks, confirming Tali's suspicions.

"Oooh, come on, Ani. Who is he? We won't tell anyone – promise!"

"Oh, leave her alone." Aahotep came to my rescue as my blush spread deeper and wider. "Ani knows better than to trust you with any secrets, Tali!"

As Tali stalked off in a huff, followed by her friends, Aahotep put her arms around me. "I'm going to miss you, Ani."

"Me too," I said, returning her hug. The day I returned from my leave would be Aahotep's marriage day, when she and Tothi would begin their new life together. As Tothi was the King's personal scribe, the couple would be moving to Itjtawy shortly afterwards.

Part of me longed to open my heart to Aahotep, but prudence counselled otherwise. For one thing, she was marrying Tothi, and however much he had changed on the surface, I doubted that he had completely reformed his attitude toward slaves. After all, I thought wryly, a man can be kind to animals without considering them to be human.

But more than that – it had taken me long enough to untangle the thoughts of my own heart and come to the resolve that I had now formed. If I told Aahotep, she would undoubtedly try to talk me out of it, and that wasn't a conversation I wanted to have.

The sun's golden barque was sailing above the eastern horizon as I left the palace, bathing the earth with its rosy light and warmth – not yet the fierce, dry heat that saps the energy and makes you want to stay indoors, but a gentle warmth like a lover's caress. I sang to myself as I strode along the street with big, swinging steps, my bundle on my shoulder and a lightness in my heart. I was going home!

As I neared Aunt Hasina's house, though, my steps slowed as doubt came flooding in. What would I say? I had run through words in my head a thousand times, but now that the moment had nearly come, they felt poor and feeble, insufficient for what my mind and heart wanted to express. What if I lost my nerve? What if I tripped over my own tongue and made a fool of myself? Most importantly of all, even if I could get the words out, how would he react? Well, there was only one way to find out. Taking a deep breath, my pulse quickening, I pushed open the front door, selected the corridor that led toward the garden, and set off along it, my legs weak beneath me.

Achyan was on his hands and knees digging weeds out of the flowerbed, but he turned his head at the sound of my footsteps and straightened up, smiling as he wiped his hands clean on his tunic.

"Miss Ani! It's good to see you back again."

"Please don't call me 'Miss', Achyan. We've known each other too long for that."

"As you wish... Ani." His eyes met mine for the briefest of moments, then his own face coloured and he looked away, staring intently at the sycamore tree. Somehow, this unspoken sign was all I needed.

"Achyan, I... I really missed you when I was away."

"I missed you, too." The words were barely perceptible and seemed to be directed toward the roots of the sycamore tree.

"Then why miss each other any longer?" It came out in a rush, louder than I had intended; I then compensated by dropping my voice to little more than a whisper. "When my leave is over, I don't want to return to the palace. I just want to stay here... with you."

Achyan froze. He stood stock-still, his face still toward the sycamore tree, his expression hidden. Then, slowly, deliberately, he turned his back to me and took up his gardening tools. It looked like his hands were shaking.

"Achyan?" I ventured.

"Miss Ani."

His voice was stiff and formal, so unlike his usual warm tone that I had to look around to see if it wasn't someone else that had spoken.

"Miss Ani, I have work to do. Master Khufu is very particular about his orchids. I am very sorry, but I need to concentrate."

His words went through me as though he had taken his pruning-hook and driven it into my heart. All the soul-searching and agonizing of the past months, all the depth of meaning I had read into each word, each glance, as I had replayed it in my mind while lying in bed at the palace – no more than a foolish girl's dream, shattered like a clay drinking-vessel that is cast over the shoulder and then trampled underfoot.

Time seemed to slow, the garden around me blurring out of focus. I was stupid, so stupid. The words kept repeating in my head like a mantra: *stupid, stupid, stupid...*

I didn't know what else to do. Clenching my fingernails into my palms so tightly they drew blood, and biting down hard on my own tongue – anything to stop the tears that threatened to brim over – I stood for a moment as if turned to stone; then, my senses returning, I spun around and ran from the garden.

"Ani."

I lay motionless. If Aunt Hasina thought I was asleep, maybe she'd leave me alone.

"Ani, I know you're awake."

No, she didn't. She was bluffing. I'd pulled the blanket right over my head; all she could see of me was a shapeless lump. How could she possibly know?

The bed creaked as my aunt sat down.

"Achyan told me what happened, Ani. He asked for leave to return to his home for the night. I told him to take the rest of the week off."

Good. That meant I wouldn't have to see him before I returned to the palace.

"He was in a bit of a state, emotionally."

This irked me so much that I sat up and pushed off the blanket. "*He* was in a state?"

If my aunt noticed my red, blotchy face, my ruined make-up, the puffiness of my eyes, she made no comment.

"Yes," she said evenly, ignoring my indignation. "It wasn't easy for him to do what he did."

"Not easy for *him*?"

Aunt Hasina sighed. "You are young, Ani, and impulsive. You have yet to learn that there's more to love than mere feelings. Did you think of the consequences at all before you opened your mouth and put your foot in it?"

This was too much. "I've thought of nothing else for months!" I blurted, glaring at her through a new mist of tears.

She sighed again. "I'm sure that's true. And in the fantasy world you created in your head, what exactly happened once you and Achyan had declared your undying love for one another?"

The tears were falling again now, but I brushed them away furiously. How dare my aunt make light of my feelings like this?

"What would you know about love?" I spat at her. "Whatever you have with Uncle Khufu, it's not love. You only married him because he won't stand up to you and lets you do whatever you like!"

I saw a momentary flash of pain in her eyes, showing that one of my darts had hit home, and it felt good. It was as if the shards of my broken dreams that cut into me so painfully could be dug out and hurled at my aunt instead. I wanted her to shout back at me, to give me more ammunition to fuel the fire of my anger, because when I was angry I could forget about the pain.

She didn't rise to the bait, however. "Your uncle is a good man. I married him for his good heart, and yes, I love him. Love isn't always a raging fire, you know. That's not to say that emotions don't come into it, but feelings are very transient things. They rise and fall like the river, but true love is more like a rock – not always new or exciting, but always there. It's in the choices we make every day to put the other person before ourselves. That's why Achyan's love for you is far more real than your love for him."

"But he doesn't love me at all," I whispered. My anger had burnt itself out, and the tears now fell unchecked.

"Are you so blind?" said Aunt Hasina softly. She edged closer and put an arm around me; my first instinct was to shove her off, but I ended up burying my face in her shoulder instead.

"Achyan loves you enough to put your future before his own feelings. You might not have thought about the future, but he did. A high-born Egyptian girl can't marry a slave."

"Of course I've thought about the future!" Some of the indignation had crept back into my tone. "I don't care about wealth or status. And under the law, a free-born Egyptian can marry whoever they like."

"That law was written by men and for men. Sometimes an Egyptian man may fall in love with his slave-girl and choose to marry her. It's rare, but it does happen. But remember it's the husband's status that determines the status of both. If an Egyptian man marries a Hebrew girl, she becomes an Egyptian in the eyes of the law. But if a Hebrew slave marries an Egyptian girl, she would lose all her rights as an Egyptian and be classed as a slave."

"I don't care! I'd rather be a slave with Achyan than an Egyptian without him."

"You may not care now, but you've never experienced life as a slave. Achyan has, and he's not willing for you to throw away what you have for his sake. Besides, remember that your uncle and I won't be around forever, and when we die, the two of you – and all your children – would revert back to being slaves of the state. Do you really want your daughters to go through what Keshet went through? Could you bear to see your sons sent to work in the brickfields, beaten if they didn't work fast enough? And that's if any of them even survive infancy. Don't think that your children would be safe from the King's decree just because you were born an Egyptian." She paused to let this sink in.

When she spoke again, her tone was gentler. "I know it's hard now, Ani, but in time you'll realise that Achyan did the right thing."

I had no answer. My tears soaked Aunt Hasina's kalasiris through to her skin, while she just stroked my hair and let me weep.

Eventually I must have fallen asleep, because I woke, sweating and shaking, from my old nightmare – the one I hadn't had now for nearly a year. Except this time, I was the young mother, and the baby I tried desperately to shield from the guards had Achyan's hazel eyes.

18

Puah

The human heart is a great mystery. Sometimes I feel that the older I become, the less I understand it. The physicians tell us that it is the organ from which our blood, tears, and every other fluid of the body proceeds. Yet also proceeding from this same organ are many less tangible things: love and hatred, joy and sorrow, courage and fear. Again, the physicians describe it as soft and vulnerable; yet I believe that this is not always the case. There are those whose hearts are harder than stone, harder even than iron. Maybe they were not always so. Maybe it was the pain of a past wound that caused them to fortify their heart against future attack, to raise the bulwarks high and build an impregnable fortress within their chest. Whatever may have caused it, it's easier to harden a heart than to soften it again.

In my long life, I have seen quite a few hard hearts, but none so hard as the King's. When people talk of the heart ruling the head, they are generally talking in terms of love, but the King's case shows how hardheartedness and stubbornness can also overrule common sense in an otherwise intelligent man. The sicker his country becomes, the more obstinately he rejects the cure. Rumour has it that even his own magicians and counsellors are now begging him to let our people go, to open his eyes to what the hand of our God has wreaked upon the land, but still he refuses to listen.

Every trading vessel that travels north from Itjtawy to Rowaty brings new and stranger tidings. First it was flies. They say that Mosheh confronted the King early in the morning as he went to the river to bathe. I would have loved to have seen the King's face when he saw that leaving Rowaty had failed to rid him of his nemesis. Still, maybe he hoped that our God's power would be lessened out there, away from the land of Goshen where His people dwelled. If so, he was sorely disappointed.

The traders we spoke to were badly shaken and vowed that they would not be returning to Upper Egypt any time soon.

"By Set's forked tail, speak not to me of flies!" swore the leader, a swarthy and grizzled man in his fifties. "Agents of Apep! Faugh! Never have I seen the like, and I pray Hathor I will never see it again. We lost half our livestock to flystrike, and the grain and figs were completely ruined. The flies were so dense, it was like walking through a sandstorm, but one that buzzed and bit. And yet" – he lowered his voice – "these were no natural pests but the malice of the Chaos-Serpent given form and wing. For, should you believe it or nay, as soon as we crossed the border into Lower Egypt, they were gone. I looked behind the ship and there they were – a black cloud so thick I couldn't see the water's surface – but for some reason they weren't coming any further. Not that we stood gazing for long, I can tell you. We took up oars and rowed on as if Apep himself pursued us, in case they changed their minds."

We didn't need the traders to tell us about the next two plagues. The very day after we had received word about the flies, Chenya and Reena were at Alim and Sekhet's house. Many of the wealthy Egyptians thought that, now Mosheh and Aharon had left Rowaty, the plagues would go with them. Whatever was happening in the southern kingdom, at least life could return to normal here in the north. The bugs had gone, meaning that the priests and the sacred animals could return to the temples, and teams of slaves had been diverted from the brickfields to remove the stinking piles of frog carcasses from the streets and throw them into the Nile. The temporary respite we had received from our slavery was over, and, while I doubted that Alim and Sekhet would punish Chenya and Reena for their absence, we nonetheless thought it best that they report for duty once again.

"I do feel sorry for Alim and Sekhet and their family," I say pensively, interrupting my own train of recollection to voice a thought that has been simmering for a while.

Chenya, Reena and Amana all nod and make noises of assent. We are sitting by the riverbank near the entrance to a small, sheltered cove – the very place where Queen Merris had found baby Mosheh eighty years before, though the river is high now and the reed-covered outcrop lies submerged beneath several feet of water. The channel, no more than a stream in the dry season, is now wide and deep enough to be navigable by all but the largest of vessels, and the Queen's favourite bathing hollow has become a calm anchorage. Over the last few decades, Hebrew residents have installed stout wooden mooring-posts to encourage trading ships to dock here rather than downstream at the temple of Amun, which we are forbidden to enter.

It is for such a trading vessel that we watch as we sit under a rough palm-leaf shelter, sipping thin beer from our waterskins. Miryam's network of relatives have sent word that a ship is due this afternoon, and no doubt the news will quickly spread; soon the serenity of the riverbank will be broken with the cries of the traders and the eager gossip of the townsfolk, but for now all that disturbs the quiet of the afternoon siesta is our own voices, the drone of dragonflies and the ever-present buzz of insects. On a rock by my feet, a solitary fly sucks with its long proboscis at a few drops of spilt beer. It was the sight of this fly that started the conversation about the events of the last couple of weeks.

"Alim is a good man," observes Chenya, "but he is almost as stubborn as the King. Considering how badly the third plague affected him, I thought maybe he'd have realised how powerless his own gods are to help him. But the household staff all told me he's been spending more time than ever in his private chapel, prostrate in front of the statue of Amun. In fact, that's where he was when the first of his herdsmen came back with the bad news."

"Who was it first?" Echud asks. "The boy who looks after the sheep and goats?"

"No, it was the donkey herdsman – an Egyptian fellow called Aau. He's worked for Alim for years. He came bursting in, white as a sheet, demanding to speak to the master. Alim came out of the chapel, and poor Aau more or less collapsed at his feet, begging his forgiveness. He said he didn't know if it was something the donkeys had eaten, but one minute they were fine, the next they started staggering around in circles, foaming at the mouth. One fell to the ground, then another and another. It was so sudden, there was nothing at all he could do.

"Before Alim had had the chance to get his head around this tragedy, the herdsboy had arrived, and his story was the same. Every goat, every ewe and ram, every lamb and kid – not one had survived. He had passed other flocks on the way back, and they had suffered the same fate. The kites and the vultures had carrion aplenty that day.

"Alim's face had been getting greyer and greyer, but he didn't know what to do. It was Sekhet who gave the order to send Aau to the cattle herd to see how they fared."

"Sekhet fears our God," puts in Reena. "She recognised the news as yet another judgement. By the time Aau returned with the cattle herdsman, she had resigned herself to what had happened. It was still a huge blow to her, but she wasn't shocked. Alim, though – I thought he was going to pass out when they told him that not one beast had survived. He was a broken man."

"Sekhet even warned him," Chenya continues. "'This is the hand of the Hebrew God,' she said. But he wouldn't listen. He just stood there, dazed, then went straight back into his chapel and wouldn't admit anyone for the rest of the day."

"Well, I just hope his stubbornness doesn't cost the lives of those sheep we sold him," grumbles Echud. "I still say we could have got a better price for them."

"I'm sure we could," I say. "All of Egypt is looking to buy livestock right now, and many Hebrews have grown rich through it. But Alim and Sekhet are family, and they have been good to us. Besides, I'm not sure it's right to become rich through the misery of others."

"But it's the judgement of the Lord – He is blessing His people and cursing our enemies."

"If He were only interested in judgement, He could have just wiped out every Egyptian and set us free that way," I retort. "Look at the most recent plague – those terrible boils that have broken out among the Egyptians. Could He not have made that affliction deadly? But I don't know of one Egyptian who has died from it. It seems to me that He's giving them the chance to turn to Him."

"Do you think the Lord would spare them if they did?" asks Chenya doubtfully.

"Look at Mesu," I reply. "Look at me! Are we not both Egyptians by birth?"

"Then why is Sekhet still afflicted? You heard what Reena said – she acknowledges the Lord's hand in all this, and she fears Him as much as any Hebrew does."

"I think it's not enough just to fear Him," I say thoughtfully. "Did not Cain fear the Lord's judgement after he had killed his brother? Yet still he went his own way, setting up a city in defiance of the Lord's word that he should be a wanderer on the face of the earth. There has to be a turning – a deliberate breaking away from the old ways. And that's not an easy thing to do. I know that better than anyone." I pause for a while, remembering, and the others respect my silence.

Around us, a hum of chatter rises above the drone of insects and the lapping of the water. While we have been talking, a small crowd has congregated on the riverbank, concentrated around the narrow entrance to the cove. Groups of neighbours and relatives talk amongst themselves, but frequently a hand is lifted to shade the eyes as expectant faces are turned upriver.

"What made it possible for me," I say after a moment or two, continuing my train of thought, "was the attraction I saw in the Lord's people. Not just your father, Echud," I add with a smile, "though that was obviously a big part of it! But the Hebrew people as a whole. To many it might have seemed that I had everything and they had nothing, but I came to realise it was the other way around."

"Listen, Mama!" pipes up Amana suddenly. "The ship is coming!"

She's right. We hear it before we see it: the shouts of the coxswain, the grunts of the rowers, the splash of oars. Then timbers creak as the pitch-blackened prow rounds the river's bend, sending wavelets rippling outward to the shore to lap at the bare feet of children who throng the waterline, jostling for position as they wave and gesture emphatically to the helmsman.

Reena, Amana and Chenya have already pushed their way in among the growing crowd. Echud and I follow more slowly on account of our limited mobility. Several of the younger people shift aside to make way for us out of respect for my age and Echud's status as an elder, and soon we find a place just upstream from the mooring posts, where a dozen beckoning hands invite the helmsman to cast out his rope toward the shore. The merchant, his small, dark eyes gleaming at the sight of the crowd, gives a signal to his helmsman, and soon the vessel is made fast to the post and the gangplank is lowered.

"I see you're eager to buy today!" calls the portly merchant as he steps ashore, followed by two young men stooped beneath the weight of their wares. "What will it be? I have pottery, oil, and wine. Come and see – made from the best grapes out of Atef-Pehu, fit for the table of the King! Come, sir, see for yourself. Have a smell of it – you don't get wine like that in Rowaty. No? Then how about some clothing? For the right price, I can even let you have some finest Itjtawy linen, dyed in blue or scarlet. Get it while you can – there won't be any more linen out of Itjtawy this year, I can tell you that!"

"Why not?" several eager voices ask. "What's happened in Itjtawy?"

"Come, now," says the merchant, the glint of his eyes belying the hurt expression he assumes. "It's been a long day, and the sun will be setting soon. I can't stop just to share stories."

"Very well," I say, stepping forward. "I'll take two *heqats* of wine. What's your price?"

"Well, considering the short supply and the trouble we've been through to get it..."

"Your sales patter will be more believable if you tell us the whole story," puts in Echud tersely. He has never had much time for the traders and their profiteering.

The merchant stops talking, but his lips curve upward and his eyes flash shrewdly as he takes in the crowd. He is a regular visitor, known to many of us here by sight, if not by name, and while doubtless at least some Egyptian blood runs in his veins – as evidenced by his close-shaven face and the scrupulous cleanliness of his scarlet shendyt – he has never had any scruples pulling his vessel in here to scrape a few *debens*' worth of trade from us unwashed infidels before proceeding downriver to the more hallowed moorage of the temple of Amun. Now, his gaze sweeps over us, lingering on the lapis lazuli pin that fastens Echud's cloak, the gold bangles worn by Chenya and Reena – all part of Alim's purchase price for our livestock; the nose-rings, earrings and necklaces scattered liberally among this once impoverished crowd. Truly, every Egyptian in

Rowaty has been desperate to purchase sheep, goats, and cattle from their Hebrew neighbours this last week, and many of the latter have been less accommodating than we have with the prices they've asked.

"Very well," I concede, slipping a gold ring from my finger and weighing it in my palm, unwilling to hand it over until I have what I'm after. "This should be at least double the price of the wine. If you have reason to think otherwise, now's your chance to persuade me."

"You'll be begging me to take four times that amount once you've heard my tale," scoffs the merchant, his eyes following the gleam of the gold. "It began when I heard a rumour that the King was anxious to buy horses. More than anxious; he was willing to pay well over the odds for them. Now I'm never one to pass on the opportunity to do good to my fellow man, especially when he's the King. So I acquired – at great expense, mark you – a dozen of Kush's finest horses, then made my way overland to Itjtawy, telling Kashta to follow with the ship." He nods toward his dark-skinned helmsman, who acknowledges the gesture with a slight dip of his bald head.

"I found the keeper of the King's stables in a real state," the merchant continued. "I'd made some enquiries on the way up, and it seems that some mysterious malady had wiped out every one of his warhorses. All those gleaming chariots, the very latest in military technology, and not a single beast to draw them. I could have named whatever price I liked, but, being a compassionate sort of guy, I let him have them for a very reasonable cost."

"I'll bet you did," mutters Echud under his breath, eyeing the rolls of rich fabric, the jars of fine wine, and the unopened cargo that has been left aboard the ship under Kashta's watchful eye – no doubt stuffed to the brim with gold and jewels.

"Anyway, just as we'd finished haggling over the price, a lad came running up to the fellow and they had a long, whispered conversation. Quite rude, I thought it; but it seems the long and the short of it was that some prophet chap had said that a huge hailstorm was coming. Now, I don't generally set much store by prophesyings, but there was something about the fellow's eyes when he told me – he looked genuinely terrified. I guess when you've just lost one stable-full of horses, you don't take any chances with the new ones. So he rushes off to get the horses under cover, and the lad tells me I'd better round up the crew and come and take shelter with him. I was in two minds about it, as it would put me behind schedule, but by all the gods, I'm glad I did!"

"The hailstorm came, then?" someone asks.

"Didn't it just! Hailstones the size of melons! I thought the whole house was going to come down with the force of them! And not just hail, but almighty thunderclaps and lightning fit to rend the skies in two. My ship was spared, thank the gods, though it was badly pitted by the hail, but when it was all over and I went to check the damage, the royal anchorage upriver was blazing away like the fiery lakes of Duat – one of those fancy barges of the King's had been struck by lightning and drifted into the rest of the fleet, setting them all alight. I don't know which god the people of Egypt have angered, but Set's rage at Osiris has nothing on this. They say Set hacked Osiris into fourteen pieces, but Egypt has been shattered so badly that I doubt even Isis could put it back together again."

"Our God has done this," Chenya informs him. "This is His vengeance for the years of misery we have suffered under the Egyptians."

"Hmm. No doubt the Canaanites and the Kushites would give the credit to their gods, too. Egypt has many enemies!" He scratches his head thoughtfully. "Mind you, maybe there is something in what you say. Did you see anything at all of the hail down here?"

As we shake our heads, he says, "I thought not. In the whole delta region as we passed through, the fields are still green and blue with ripening grains and flowering flax, but all around Itjtawy it's a different story. The devastation it's caused – craters all over the fields, some black and charred where the lightning struck, and anyone who was foolish enough to remain outside was killed outright, together with the livestock. Although actually, surprisingly few animals were lost – the master of the stables told me that whatever it was that killed the last lot of horses had also wiped out the flocks and herds, and whatever beasts the people had scraped together since then were mainly indoors and under cover, thanks to the warning of this prophet fellow. Of course, there were some who just thought he was a nutcase and laughed at those who listened to him – but the joke was on them, that's for sure! Either way, the wheat and the emmer might bounce back, but the barley and flax will be dead losses. No linen from Itjtawy this year, and no beer, which makes this wine all the more valuable!" He grins and measures out one *heqat* of wine, pushing it toward me. "This is all I can give you for that little trinket. It'd fetch five times as much in Itjtawy, but I'll let you have it since you remind me of my own grandmother, may the gods prosper her soul. Does anyone else want to buy? Or maybe trade? I'll pay gold for grain or livestock, premium prices. I think I'll head back south in a few days, once I've got myself together – after all, we wouldn't want those poor folks in Itjtawy to starve, now, would we?" He grins again, and I can't help but picture a Nile crocodile basking open-mouthed on the mud flats as it waits for its prey to float by.

I think of Itjtawy as I remember it – an affluent city of beautiful buildings, set within the green and fertile valley of Atef-Pehu, irrigated by the Mer-Wer canal and the great shimmering waters of Osiris' Lake. I picture those fruitful fields storm-blighted and pitted by hail, dotted here and there by the broken and bloodied bodies of beasts and men. A shudder runs through my body. That could have been me. My family, my grandchildren and great-grandchildren.

ANI

"I'll be leaving for Itjtawy again in three days' time. Would you like to stay here and help care for Moses again for me?"

The Queen's question seemed like the very opportunity I'd been praying for.

"No," I said, a little too quickly and too loudly. "That is – it would be an honour to accompany you to Itjtawy, my lady. If it's OK with you. Please."

Queen Merris' face registered surprise for a moment, then a smile of understanding dawned across her features. "Of course. You're missing Aahotep, aren't you? I've noticed how lonely you've seemed, these last two months since her marriage."

Lonely, yes. So lonely I'd found myself wishing that the Queen hadn't stepped in to rescue me from the sentence pronounced by Neferkare Iymeru. Not only had I been avoiding Tali and the other girls as best I could, unable to face their inevitable questions about my love life, I had even stopped spending time with Yokheved and Miryam. Yokheved reminded me too much of Keshet, and that was a train of association I didn't want to set in motion. I just wanted to put as much distance as possible between myself and *him*, and Itjtawy seemed to fit the bill perfectly. Given time, maybe I would even be able to confide in Aahotep, if I could catch her away from her husband. *Husband...* at the mere thought of the word, my eyes began to prickle as I felt myself engulfed by a fresh wave of loneliness.

Suddenly, an idea struck me. I swallowed once, then spoke up quickly before I changed my mind.

"May I... may I ask a favour, my lady?"

"Certainly." She smiled encouragingly at me, and I ploughed on:

"When we're in Itjtawy, if you know or hear of a suitable man who's looking for a wife..."

There, I'd said it. The mixture of feelings that surged through me once the words were out was so overpowering and so confusing that I almost missed the cloud that passed over the Queen's face.

"Why so anxious to marry, Ani? Are you not happy in my service?"

Realising my breach of etiquette, I hastily tried to cover it up. "It's not that, my lady – it's just, well, I'm seventeen years old now, and I don't want to leave it too late and miss my chance."

The Queen laughed gently. "You think no men will be interested if you leave it another year? I think you place too little value on yourself, but very well, if you're sure it's what you want, I will see what I can do."

Was I sure? Of course I wasn't, but I needed to put *him* behind me, and I desperately needed an answer to this suffocating loneliness. Maybe it would even help to heal my relationship with my father. Yes, I would badly miss my Aunt Hasina and the babies – I swallowed again – but I was sure they'd come to visit me in Itjtawy when they could. I couldn't go to see them now, anyway – there was too great a risk of bumping into *him*.

Three days. I should send messages to Aunt Hasina and my father, saying goodbye. Should I ask my aunt to come and visit me before I left? I wouldn't tell her of my plan to get married, just that I would be going to Itjtawy for a few months. Who could I ask to take the message? Maybe little Miryam could do it?

After searching high and low, I finally found Miryam in the flower garden – another place I rarely visited these days because the associations were too painful. When I told her what I wanted, her face fell.

"You won't leave without saying goodbye to Mama and Mosheh, will you?"

"Well, I..."

"Don't you like us any more? You never come to see us like you used to."

"Of course I like you, Miryam. I like you all very much. It's just that I've been, um, busy."

"You don't look busy when I've seen you. You do look sad, though. My mama can cheer you up. She's the best at cheering people up when they're feeling sad."

"Very well." I forced a smile. "I'll come and say goodbye to your mama."

I found Yokheved in the slave quarters, sewing clothes for Moses, who, as a royal prince and potential heir to the throne, couldn't just run around naked like other children his age. He looked quaint in a miniature dark-blue shendyt, his single short, dark braid flicked over his left ear as he crouched on the floor with his brother Aharon, playing with a set of beautifully crafted toy animals made from brightly-painted wood. Yokheved looked up and smiled as I edged sheepishly into the room, Miryam at my heels.

"It's very good to see you, Ani. It's been a while."

"I know. Sorry." I shifted uncomfortably.

"Mama, Ani is going away to Itjtawy. Maybe she'll stay there forever, like Aahotep, and we'll never see her again." I was dismayed and touched to see tears in Miryam's eyes.

Yokheved paused in her work to give Miryam a hug. "Darling, the reason Aahotep stayed was because she got married. I'm sure Ani will be back in a couple of months."

Embarrassed, I chewed on my lower lip, my gaze toward the floor. Yokheved looked up, a frown creasing her brow.

"You are coming back, aren't you, Ani?"

"I, um. I don't know. Maybe," I muttered, not meeting her eyes.

If I felt awkward right now, things were about to get a whole lot worse.

"But Ani can't marry someone in Itjtawy," Miryam piped up. "Ani's going to marry Achyan!"

I didn't even hear what Yokheved said in reply; at the sound of his name, the blood rushed to my head and my ears were filled with the furious thumping of my own pulse. My first instinct was to get away, to run out of the room, but I felt sure that Yokheved would come after me, even as my Aunt Hasina had done. So I stood my ground, clenching my hands and staring at the floor, wishing I could sink into it and disappear.

"Ani?" Yokheved's voice probed gently; my reaction must have given me away.

"No, he doesn't... I mean..." I glared at Miryam. "How did you...?"

"You used to talk about him lots, before you stopped coming to see me. And I heard you tell Aahotep that you can't help who you fall in love with, even if he's a slave."

Even through the tempest of emotion, in a part of my mind I still found room to marvel at the acuity of this child. Yes, admittedly I had chattered away to her, sharing more perhaps than I would have done with one of the older girls, but at that time I hadn't even fully realised my own feelings; never in a million years would I have expected an eight-year-old to connect the dots with such perspicacity.

"It is no easy thing, for an Egyptian to marry into the children of Israel."

Yokheved's tone was gentle and sympathetic, yet I did not look up. I didn't want to hear it again. It was bad enough to have my Aunt Hasina tell me that Achyan had only acted out of love, to spare me all the hardships of slavery. I couldn't stand to be told the same things by someone who barely even knew him.

"Puah."

The use of my Hebrew name, unused and forgotten for so many months, startled me into raising my head. As I met Yokheved's deep brown eyes, the warmth and understanding in them caused fresh tears to well up in my own.

"You have always loved hearing the history of our people; let me tell you some now. When our forefather Avraham wanted to find a wife for his son Yitzhak, he instructed his servant not to go to the Canaanites, but to journey back to the land of his father's kin. Yitzhak was the son of the promise, from whose seed would come a people set apart for the Lord, and this couldn't be compromised by intermarrying with the people of Canaan with their false gods.

"Years later, Yitzhak's eldest son, Esaw, did indeed marry two women of Canaan, and this was a source of great grief to Yitzhak and his wife Rivqah. But it was the younger son, Yaqob, through whom the promise would be fulfilled. Knowing this, his parents sent him to Paddan-Aram, to his mother's brother Laban, again to find a wife who was not subject to the idolatry of the Canaanites.

"Yaqob's sons eventually came here to Egypt with their families, as you know, but the principle established by Avraham, Yitzhak, and Yaqob still stands today. Children of Israel may not marry a worshipper of false gods, whether the gods of Canaan or those of Egypt."

I glanced around nervously, willing Yokheved to stop talking. If she were overheard decrying the gods of Egypt as false – especially in front of the young prince for whose care she was responsible – the consequences for her would be harsh.

To my relief, there was an interruption at that point in the form of little Aharon, who came running to his mother with an injured look on his face.

"Mama, Mama! Mosheh took my lion, and I had it first!"

Moses, toddling on podgy legs, came tripping across the room in pursuit of his brother, hampered somewhat by the blue shendyt that seemed in danger of unravelling and sending him headlong.

"Mama, Mama!"

"Hush, Mosheh, don't call me Mama. The Queen is your mama. Aharon, remember that all the toys belong to Mosheh really. He's just letting you share them. But Mosheh, remember that it's nice to share. Come now, let me tell you the story of Noah and all the animals, and you and Aharon can play that you're on the ark with him, feeding the animals together."

Seemingly forgotten for the time being, I stood and watched as Yokheved gathered both boys onto her knee, complete with armfuls of wooden animals, and began to tell them the story. How it must have broken her heart each time she had to tell Moses not to call her 'Mama'! Maybe Aunt Hasina was right; maybe sometimes the best way to love someone was to do what you had to do to keep them safe, even if that meant pushing them away and causing pain to both of you. Yet that wasn't what Yokheved had said. All along, I had been thinking that the insurmountable barrier to a life with Achyan was what I stood to lose by it. It hadn't crossed my mind that Achyan had barriers of his own.

But was it a barrier? I had embraced the God of the Hebrews; I had even taken a Hebrew name. Admittedly I never used it around Egyptians for fear of what they would think; but when I prayed in private, it was to the Hebrew God. Yes, I still went regularly to the temple of Hathor and prayed in front of the sacred cow, but that was just so that the Queen and the other maids wouldn't think ill of me. And the offering I brought to the temple of Amun each week, that was to try to build bridges with my father...

Great. So now I had two insurmountable barriers instead of one. At that thought, the pain returned, throbbing away at my insides with a deep physical ache.

Yes, to go to Itjtawy and stay there was the only plan, even if that meant marriage to a faceless stranger. Pain was sure to fade along with memory.

My interview with Yokheved had left me emotionally drained, so I slipped into my chamber, undressed, and climbed into bed before any of the other girls could turn up and ask questions. When the others did start coming to bed, I feigned sleep. But sleep itself was elusive this night, and when it finally came, my dreams fluctuated between the old nightmare and that of the little she-goat, whose lonely bleat went straight to my heart.

19

Puah

"A message from Mosheh!"

It's the hour after noon and the sun is relentless and scorching, but the streets are full of people, dashing around, calling out to one another and knocking on doors. From the rooftop, craning to see what all the excitement is about, I can make out one phrase only: "A message from Mosheh!"

My pulse quickens and my aching joints are forgotten as I head for the stairs. In all the time Mosheh and Aharon have been in Itjtawy, this is the first time they have sent word to the people. Miryam, of course, has received news occasionally via her network of grandsons, nephews and great-nephews who have travelled backward and forward for that very purpose; one of her grandsons owns a skiff, a light fishing vessel made of woven papyrus reeds, and in this they can navigate the Nile faster than any trading vessel, shooting downstream with the current to convey word of all the latest events to their family in the delta. Through this grapevine we have learnt that the King has twice more promised to let the people go, but Mosheh, grown wise through experience, has delayed sending word until he has had a confirmation from the Lord. The wisdom of this policy has become apparent, since the King again changed his mind each time, and the people's hopes would only have been raised to be dashed again.

I feel a surge of excitement as I navigate the final steps. Could this be it? Even as I raise a hand to the door, it shakes with a frantic knocking from outside. I push it open to reveal Shimeon, my great-grandson, husband to Aharon's granddaughter.

"Mosheh has sent a message from Itjtawy," he says, before I have the chance to ask the questions that burn on my tongue. "Upper Egypt has been completely devastated by a vast swarm of locusts. Everything that was growing has been destroyed."

"And the King?" I ask quickly, but Shimeon gives a little shake of his head.

"No, he remains stubborn. He initially relented, but as soon as the locusts were gone he changed his mind – yet again."

As my anticipation fizzles and dies, Shimeon continues: "He's sent his soldiers throughout all of Goshen to see if the Hebrews have grain, and to seize whatever they find. My father-in-law and his brothers came just ahead of them. This is the word they brought from Mosheh: 'Stand firm. Do not give them so much as a grain of barley. Yahweh your God will deliver you out of their hands.'

"I must go; they will be upon us soon. Spread the word throughout Rowaty: stand firm!"

And he is gone, hurrying to the next door, the home of my younger son Elchanan, and of Tobit and Asher and their families. I meet eyes with Echud, who stands at my shoulder, and we are silent for a moment, digesting this news. Then Echud claps a hand to his forehead.

"The flocks! If they can't get grain, they may target the livestock. Baruch and the other young lads can't stand alone against them. I will go to them."

"But Echud, your back!" I protest. "And they'll be armed."

"You heard what Shimeon said. If it comes to a fight, the Lord will fight for us."

"At least take Tobit and Asher with you," I plead.

"I intend to. Their sons are also out with the flocks."

I watch helplessly as he grasps his staff and strides out of the door. Before he has taken more than three or four steps, however, a thought seizes me, and I call after him:

"Echud, wait!"

He stops.

"What of Mesu and Aliza? Their house is far from the Hebrew side of town. Who will tell them?"

"Mesu is an Egyptian," snorts Echud. "He has no need to worry."

"They ought to be told, just in case." Echud is probably right, and I don't know why it is, but I can't shake the feeling that this is important.

Echud sighs and drums his fingers on the head of his staff. "Very well. Send Amana, if you must. But I don't know why you're worrying. The guards have been sent to Hebrews, and Mesu is no Hebrew."

"He's as Hebrew as I am," I retort.

"No, he's not. You gave up your wealth and privileges to live as a Hebrew. Mesu is wealthy, and he serves the King."

This is an old argument, and I answer as I always do: "Avraham was wealthy. Yosef served the King."

"Yes, and look where that got us!" Echud returns. "I'm sorry, Mother, but I have to go. From what Shimeon said, the soldiers could be upon us any minute, and Baruch is out there alone with the flocks."

"Very well. God be with you."

"And with you."

I watch until he is admitted to the house next door, then I go back inside with a small sigh. Echud has never had much time for Mesu; he was sullenly silent all through the celebration of Aliza's marriage so many years ago, and he has rejected all Mesu's attempts to build bridges since then. When we do leave Egypt – I am no longer saying "if" – I hope and believe that Mesu, Aliza and their family will all come with us. But if Echud's attitude is reflected by the majority of Hebrews, then I fear that they may never fully "fit in".

A short while later, Amana, full of self-importance, has been despatched to the other side of town with the message for Mesu and Aliza, and I am left alone. Of late, Chenya and Reena have been returning early from Alim and Sekhet's house. I hope they are home soon. I don't want to face the King's revenue-collectors alone.

No sooner have I thought this than there is a pounding on the door. My heart is in my mouth as I descend the stairs to open it. What will I say? What will I do? There is no time to hide the stores of grain, nor could I lift the sacks by myself. Still, I have the promise of divine aid. Stand firm.

The pounding intensifies, accompanied by shouts in Egyptian: "Open up! Come on, we don't have all day!"

An unpleasant sense of déjà vu washes over me, coupled with the recollection of an old nightmare. All of a sudden, I'm not so sure I can do this. *Help me,* I pray silently, as I reach out a trembling hand toward the door and push it open.

The guards are more or less what I expected – well-muscled, well-armed, and young. Even the senior officer can't be more than twenty-five, while his colleague is barely out of boyhood. Behind them, an even younger lad holds the donkeys, each of which bears a pair of empty panniers. This sight gives my waning confidence a boost. Surely they would have called at other houses before mine, yet, for whatever reason, they have come away empty-handed.

"Out of the way, old woman," says the senior officer brusquely. "We have orders to requisition whatever stores of grain you might have, in the name of the King."

I run my gaze over the two men, sizing them up. The younger one appears nervous, his glance shifting between me, his boss, and the sky. I remember the traders' description of the hail mixed with lightning that had devastated Upper Egypt, and I wonder whether he's half expecting to be struck down by a bolt from heaven. If the other man shares his misgivings, though, he hides it well. As I hesitate, he lifts his spear, tilting it slightly toward me, his eyes hard.

I swallow. This would be easier if I didn't keep having flashbacks from eighty years ago.

"No," I croak, my throat dry.

"What?" The spear-tip is now levelled straight at my head. I tear my eyes away from it and try to focus. Think of Mosheh's message. Think of Echud's conviction. I may seem alone, but I'm not.

"No," I repeat, somewhat louder. "You will take no grain from here, nor from any house of the Israelites."

"And who's going to stop us?" he sneers.

"The same One who destroyed your grain. The One who afflicted you with flies and boils, hail and locusts. Take care that He doesn't do anything worse to you."

I'm not sure where the words came from, but they seem to have an effect on the younger man. He rocks nervously from one foot to the other, edging back from the open door as he shoots anxious glances at his superior. The officer, however, seems unimpressed.

"So you have one god. What is he to the many of Egypt? Now stop your bluster, old lady, and stand aside, or do I have to make you?"

"Sir..." the younger soldier tries, but his colleague isn't listening. Shoving me roughly aside with his spear-shaft, he strides through the doorway into the store-room. I stagger and clutch at the doorframe to keep myself from falling.

Even as I struggle to regain my balance, a sharp cry pierces my senses. I manage to retain my footing, but when I look round, the senior soldier is on the ground clutching at his ankle, his face deathly white. Both spears clatter to the ground as the younger guardsman runs to crouch beside him.

"Snake... cobra..." the officer manages through gritted teeth. His lips are already tinged with blue.

I hesitate, but only for a second.

"Give me your knife," I order the younger man. As he stares distrustfully at me, I stretch out my hand impatiently. "Every second you wait, the poison spreads further. I need to draw it out."

The young man glances at his commander, but he is in no fit state to comprehend what has been said, let alone give an order. With doubt still evident in his eyes, the youth draws his knife from his belt and passes it to me.

"Now see if you can find the snake," I say brusquely, my hands already busy around the wound site. Locating the two tiny punctures that cause so much harm, I swiftly draw the knife's tip over and around them, again and again, letting the venom-infused blood spill over my hands and soak into the packed earth of the floor. Delirious with pain and only semi-conscious, the officer seems barely even to feel the knife.

Sensing a presence over my shoulder, I look up to see the lad who had been holding the donkeys. Presumably they have been left to wander where they will. His face is pale, and he looks like he could be about to vomit.

"You, make yourself useful and cut up an onion," I snap. "In the sack beside those jars."

Without looking to see if he has obeyed me, I take up the knife again and use it to tear a wide strip from the hem of the officer's shendyt. With a few swift strides around the store-room, I gather a small pot of salt and a jar of wine. Soaking the linen in the wine, I sprinkle it liberally with the salt, trying not to think about the expense of this treatment for my enemy.

The boy comes over with the chopped onion; I don't know whether the tears in his eyes are from emotion or onion juice. I add the onion to the poultice and bind it tightly around the wound. As I adjust the knot, the other soldier returns, shaking his head.

"No sign of the snake," he reports. "It's disappeared."

I'm neither surprised by this news, nor concerned that there may be a cobra hiding in my store-room. Somehow I know that this snake will cause no harm to me or to my family.

"There," I say, straightening up. "That's all I can do. Now he needs to rest the foot. It might be best if he stays here..."

"No!"

There's as much venom in the commander's voice as there is in his wounded ankle. He forces himself into a sitting position, his face livid. Each word forced through his blue-grey lips clearly costs more strength than he has to spare, yet they are none the less forceful for it; fear, pain and malice contend in his bloodshot eyes.

"Get me out... accursed house... find... physician... proper spells..."

"Those spells can't help you," I tell him bluntly. "None of the gods of Egypt can save you now. Your only hope is to pray to the God of the Hebrews. He holds the keys to death and life. If you repent, maybe He will have mercy on you."

The stricken man turns his eyes to mine. He draws a deep, laboured breath – then spits right in my face.

"That's... for your... God!" he snarls, his pain not masking his contempt.

As I search for a rag and some water to wash my face clean, the lad hastens to round up the donkeys and redistribute their loads, then he and his colleague lift the wounded man onto the back of one of the beasts. I notice that the young soldier keeps shooting doubtful glances between me and his commander as he does so.

I watch them out of sight, torn between thankfulness for my own deliverance, natural concern for the plight of a fellow man, and wonder at the stubbornness of the human heart.

Ani

Safely inside the women's quarters of the palace at Itjtawy, I let out a sigh and fell back on the comfortable bed. Glamorous as it might seem to travel aboard the Queen's barge, with its gold-painted prow and blue-and-crimson hangings, I was glad to be back on solid land.

The royal residence at Itjtawy was impressive, even more so than the palace at Rowaty, but after such a long journey I was interested in little more than finding my bedchamber. I'd slept little the nights we'd been compelled to spend afloat, finding the gentle rocking motion of the barge a disturbance rather than a sleep-inducer, and my legs were stiff from the enforced inactivity. All I wanted now was a good stretch followed by a long sleep.

I'd lost track of the number of nights we'd been travelling. Of course, we hadn't been confined to the barge the entire journey. Some nights we'd moored at one of the cities that clung to the banks of the Nile, such as Per-Bast or Ankh-Tawy, and we'd been able to sleep in actual beds within the small administrative palaces. From Hetep-Senusret, the last town we'd visited, we'd set sail in the early morning past the militarily laid-out buildings of the Hebrew ghetto, men and women eyeing us with undisguised hostility as our flotilla went by in all its pomp and splendour. These were the workers who had been settled here against their will, away from friends and family, to work on the construction of the pyramid and then of the Mer-Wer irrigation canal, into which we turned southward from the Nile toward Osiris' Lake and the city of Itjtawy.

"Ooooh, my poor stiff legs," moaned Tali, sinking down on the bed next to me. "I'll swear that journey gets more uncomfortable every time we make it."

"Mm-hm," I agreed noncommittally. I had nothing in particular against Tali, but I didn't think I had the energy right now to cope with her constant stream of gossip. Sure enough, stiff legs or not, it was soon apparent that her tongue wasn't too tired to wag in its usual fashion.

"Did you see Aahotep? Less than three months married, and I'd wager all my jewels that her waist's looking thicker already."

That got my attention. Much as I missed Aahotep, I couldn't face seeing her just yet, especially if, as Tali implied, she was carrying Tothi's child.

"Where did you see her?" I asked.

"I passed her in the corridor, just now as I came in. Hey, let's go and look for her – she can't have gone far. I want to see if you agree with me about her belly!"

"No thanks. I need a rest first."

"You're not kidding! I didn't sleep a wink at that last place we stayed – I'll swear there were bedbugs!"

I lay back on the bed and let Tali's chatter wash over me. Step One of my plan had been accomplished: I had made it to Itjtawy. The next step would be the hardest – to find a man with whom I wouldn't mind spending the rest of my life, and to persuade him to marry me.

The Queen was to dine with the King that evening. We girls bustled around her like bees around a cornflower, arranging the sky-blue folds of her fine linen gown and fastening gold and jewels around her neck, wrists, earlobes, and ankles. As the last brooch was pinned into place, the last golden bead threaded into the elaborate hairpiece, we fell back to admire our handiwork, and I thought to myself, not for the first time, that she was the most beautiful woman I had ever known.

With a smile and a murmur of thanks, the Queen dismissed us to go and attend to our own dress. Tali and the others trooped through to our adjoining room, chattering excitedly about the feast and which young men of the King's entourage were yet unmarried. With little appetite for such prattle, I fell to the back of the line, but as I reached the doorway, I felt a hand on my shoulder.

"Hold a moment, Ani, if you will."

"My lady?" I stepped back and turned to face the Queen. Her tone had been light, but there was something unreadable in her expression.

"I have not forgotten the promise I made to you. Among my husband's officials is a young man called Suten-Ka, assistant to the Chief Treasurer. I will arrange for you to be seated with him at dinner."

I felt my pulse speed up; I hadn't expected this so soon.

The Queen had been studying my face. "Is this what you want? If you've changed your mind..."

"No," I said quickly. "I mean yes, I do still want it. Thank you, my lady."

"Then you had better go and get yourself ready." The Queen smiled at me once again, but it didn't quite reach her eyes.

"The pale green. Yes, I'll wear this one."

Rarely had my choice of dress seemed so important. I'd potentially be meeting my future husband tonight, and it was vital that I made a good first impression. In a court filled with pretty young girls, a maiden of seventeen was at a serious disadvantage. What if this Suten-Ka started asking himself exactly why I hadn't married yet? What if he preferred a girl of thirteen or fourteen, a girl with three or four extra years in which to bear him a healthy heir? So it would have to be green, the colour of fertility, cut in a simple yet suggestive close-fitting style that would make me look young while simultaneously emphasising my womanly curves. I needed him to be smitten at first sight, otherwise my plan would fail, and I didn't know whether I'd get a second chance.

Adah, my maid, raised an eyebrow at my choice. She lifted the kalasiris obediently and began to dress me, but I saw how her brow creased and her lips pursed as she straightened out the folds of linen beneath the low-cut neckline. Adah herself was always modest in her dress, covering head and shoulders in the Hebrew style, and while I hadn't worn a headdress myself since the day that guardsman had ripped it from my head, it was rare for me to reveal as much as I was today. Still, times change. Whatever games I had played in the past, I wasn't Puah the slave-girl but Ani the Egyptian, and I'd have to be a bit more Egyptian in my fashion sense if I was to compete with the likes of Tali.

This thought was still uppermost in my mind when half an hour later, bedecked with jewels, my hairpiece arranged in the latest style and my dark eyes and high cheekbones emphasised with careful makeup, I followed in the Queen's train through to the great banqueting-hall of the palace. Noting with displeasure that Tali was also wearing green, I had taken care to position myself ahead of her; it didn't take a genius to know that she would be on the lookout for eligible young men tonight, and I wanted to ensure it was me that Suten-Ka saw first.

So preoccupied was I with my thoughts that it took me a moment or two to realise we had reached the great hall. As my senses awoke to the scene around me, my eyes widened in awe.

The hall was truly palatial in size, the high vaulted roof supported by endless rows of pillars, intricately carved and gilded so that they shone like the sun. Together with the polished stone floor and brightly painted walls, inlaid in many places with precious stones of every colour, the effect was truly dazzling.

Most of the court were already present, seated at wooden tables throughout the hall. Gorgeous outfits, gold, and jewels featured in abundance. The order of precedence could be told by proximity to the top table, and also by the seating; carved chairs were provided for the higher officials, while the less prestigious made do with low wooden stools.

At the far end of the hall, at a table higher than all the others, the King was seated on a grand cedarwood chair, richly cushioned and beautifully carved in the likeness of a lion. At his right hand, a second cushioned chair, slightly lower and without arms, stood ready for the Queen. On his other side – my heart missed a beat – it was my old enemy, the vizier Neferkare Iymeru. Only now did I see the flaw in my grand plan. A life in Itjtawy would mean a life under his baleful gaze. As my eyes rested on him, he lifted his head suddenly and looked directly at me, causing me to flinch. *I haven't forgotten,* he seemed to say. *I haven't forgotten, and I'll make you pay.*

I shook my head slightly at the childishness of my thoughts. I had nothing to fear this time. I was an Egyptian lady, serving the Queen, doing nothing to warrant his ire. What could he do to me now?

"Suten-Ka." The Queen's voice called me back to the present. "May I introduce Ani, a young lady of my retinue."

Suten-Ka rose gravely, took my hand, and lifted it to his lips. He was young, well-dressed, and relatively good-looking, seated halfway across the hall – not too far from the King's table, but not too close either. He studied me for a moment, taking in my face, my dress, the way I stood. Then he smiled.

"Welcome, Lady Ani. I would be honoured if you would join me."

So far, so good, I thought to myself as I returned his smile. Glancing sideways at Tali, I wasn't surprised to see her with eyes wide and a hand to her lips as if to hold in all the gossip that longed to spill from them. No doubt her tongue would wag freely once released from the constraints of the formal dinner setting. Well, let her gossip. Everything was going according to plan.

The meal, of course, was a sumptuous and drawn-out affair, featuring course after course of dainties from every corner of the country: whole roasted oxen, salted and herbed cuts of pork, spiced goat and mutton, quail and waterfowl of every kind, game such as ostrich and gazelle, and other exotic meats that I couldn't even name, nestled alongside dishes of onions, squashes and cucumbers, twenty varieties of sweet and savoury bread, confections of raisins, figs and pomegranates, and delicate little honey cakes flavoured with lotus flower. The wine flowed freely, and this, too, was mixed with lotus to make it stronger. I took care to watch how much I drank; I needed to keep my wits about me if I was to pull this off, and the last thing I wanted was to embarrass myself in front of Suten-Ka. He, on the other hand, drank freely, and by the end of the feast he was ready to announce our engagement then and there.

"Slow down just a little bit," I told him, laughing. "We need permission from my father in Rowaty first."

"I'll travel back there with you," he said earnestly. "Whenever you like. Then we can marry straight away." His brow creased a moment. "You won't mind moving to Itjtawy after the wedding, though, will you? I know your family are all in Rowaty, but my life and my livelihood are here..."

"That's fine," I said quickly. "I'll start a new life here. With you."

He beamed, and I smiled back. It had been easy – much easier than I had expected. Suten-Ka was everything I had hoped for – thoughtful and attentive, financially well able to support me, and even courteous to the slaves who had served the food. My great escape plan was going without a hitch, and my future seemed assured. So why did every mention of our marriage make me feel as though a deep pit had opened up inside me?

20

Puah

"You did WHAT?"

Echud's voice is heavy with disbelief. He stares at me as though I were some strange being rather than his mother whom he has seen every day since birth.

"I treated him," I repeat, somewhat abashed. Faced with Echud's incredulity, I find it hard to explain why I did what I did. "With an onion poultice. You know, wine, salt, onion..."

"Let me get this straight." Echud speaks slowly and deliberately, as if talking to a young child or someone hard of understanding. "The King's guardsmen tried to take our grain. The leader pushed you over and forced his way into our house, blaspheming against our God as he did so. The Lord graciously rescued you by sending a snake to judge him for his actions, and what do you do? You patch him up – using our best wine, no less, and the last of the salt store – and send him on his way, still breathing out curses against us and our God, so that he's free to rob and assault still more of our people!"

It's useless to object that it felt like the right thing at the time. The way Echud puts it, I'm beginning to feel as though my actions were indeed the height of stupidity.

I'm grateful that a knock on the door saves me from attempting to reply. Rising from my stool, I follow Reena down the stairs, only to come face to face with the young soldier from yesterday.

Seeing the expressions on our faces, he holds his hands up, palm outward as a gesture of peace. "No need to fear – I'm not here in the King's name this time. I've come on my own behalf." His eyes find mine. "I wanted to thank you. For what you did for my commander." A moment's hesitation, eyes lowered to the floor. "He died about an hour ago."

"I'm sorry," I say with as much sincerity as I can muster. Behind me, Echud shifts impatiently from one foot to the other.

"So why exactly are you here?" he asks brusquely. "Is one death not enough to persuade you to leave us alone?"

The young man bridles. "I wouldn't expect an uncouth, unwashed slave to understand courtesy and good manners."

Echud's face purples with rage, a vein bulging in his temple. I open my mouth to intervene before he says something he regrets; after all, this youth still has the authority to arrest him and have him flogged. Chenya is obviously thinking along the same lines as me; she rests a restraining hand on each of Echud's shoulders as I try to placate our visitor.

"It was good of you to take the trouble to come. But I sense there may be another reason for your visit?"

The soldier masters himself with a visible effort as he returns his attention to me. "You are astute, Mother." I smile inwardly at the term; I am old enough to be his great-grandmother, let alone his mother. "There was indeed something I wanted to ask you." He hesitates, glancing over his shoulder before continuing in a lowered voice. "It's not just my commander, you see. This whole mission has been a catastrophe from start to finish. With the King's fleet badly damaged by that freak hail and lightning storm a couple of weeks ago, we commandeered every fishing and merchant vessel we could for the journey, but we've had ships run aground, beasts go inexplicably lame, and outbreaks of sickness among the men. Between that and all these 'accidents'… well, we'll be returning to Itjtawy with half the number of men that set out – and without even a single grain of barley to show for it."

Out of the corner of my eye, I see Chenya's eyes widen slightly at this echo of Mosheh's own words to us. Echud's anger is forgotten; the spark has returned to his eyes, and a smile of triumph curves at the corners of his mouth.

"There's not one of our brigade now who will dare try to take grain from the Hebrews," the young man continues. "We have faced barbarian raiders and Kushite armies without faltering, but a God who controls the beasts of the earth and summons the storm-clouds at his bidding, who can strike a man down without warning by sickness or by serpent – how can we stand against such a power?"

"So what will you do?" I ask, suddenly feeling pity for this young lad, barely out of boyhood, caught between a merciless King and a vengeful God.

He sighs. "The only thing we can do. We can't return empty-handed – our families in Itjtawy will starve to death if we do, to say nothing of the King's wrath. So we'll have to requisition grain from the Egyptians in Rowaty. They won't like it, but it's our only option." He hesitates. "What I came to ask – could you, would you, pray to your God for us? If I bring a lamb, would you sacrifice it on our behalf? We need our journey back to Itjtawy to be more fortuitous than our journey here; if your God doesn't turn aside his wrath from us, none of us will make it back alive!"

"Only our priests can offer sacrifices," I tell him gently. "But I can speak for you to them. Oh, and in return," I add, a thought striking me, "you can tell your brigade not to seize any grain from the house of Mesu the surveyor, near the temple of Amun. His wife is Hebrew, and he worships our God."

"They will be left in peace," he promises immediately. "None of our men dare risk angering your God any further!"

Ani

"But why? Why would you risk it?"

I turned to glare at Adah. Clearly the liberties I'd allowed her, the confidences I'd shared, had gone to her head. I had treated her as a friend rather than a slave, but that didn't give her the right to speak to me in such a way.

"There's no risk. And it's none of your business." I knew I was snapping, but I'd been nursing a headache all afternoon, and Adah's questioning was making it worse.

She didn't back down. "I'm sorry if I speak out of turn, my lady – "

"You do."

She ignored my interjection. "I just don't want you to make any decisions you'll regret. Suten-Ka seems nice enough, but you barely know him."

Adah's fingers worked deftly as she spoke, smoothing the fabric of my gowns and folding them carefully to minimise creasing. As each one was completed, she placed it carefully into my travel chest, ready for our journey to Rowaty tomorrow.

"I've known him two months," I retorted.

"Yes, and how many times have you seen him during those two months?"

"He's been busy," I muttered. "He's had to work overtime to earn the time off this month."

"So he says," replied Adah darkly. "But why marry someone you know so little about? You've been hurt once before."

The reference to Tothi irked me still further. The flaw in my escape plan was that, living in Itjtawy, it would be hard to avoid seeing him. I'd run into him twice in the last two months, and each time was profoundly awkward. On the second occasion, Aahotep had been there, too, and though she was my friend and I'd been missing her gentle smile and easy conversation, I couldn't get over the awkwardness I felt at the unmistakeable rounding of her belly. Nonetheless, I couldn't avoid everyone from my past, and despite what Tothi had done, the man who had hurt me the deepest didn't live in Itjtawy.

"Phew!" Tali flounced into the room carrying a wooden chest similar to mine, which she dropped onto her bed before collapsing melodramatically next to it. Behind her, her slave girl, Hadassah, staggered under the weight of a second, much larger chest.

"Is that all you're taking?" Tali questioned, craning over to peer at my luggage. "I'm sure you had more than that when we came."

"Well, I'm not staying in Rowaty long, am I?" I returned. "As soon as we're married, Suten-Ka and I will be returning to Itjtawy with the next merchant ship."

"Why the rush?"

"Suten-Ka has to get back to work. He says the Chief Treasurer is a miserly old eunuch who knows nothing of affairs of the heart and needed a lot of persuading to spare him at all. Besides," I added, "it suits me. I like it in Itjtawy."

"Which kalasiris will you wear for your marriage day?" Tali asked, reaching into my chest and fingering the different fabrics. "Or are you having a new one made?"

"Stop it," I said, annoyed, "you're creasing them all up. There's no time to have anything made; we're getting married just as soon as we have my father's permission." I couldn't see there being any issues there; my father would be delighted that I had found such a suitable husband, and happier still to get rid of me for good.

"But you ought to have something special to wear," Tali insisted. "You should ask the Queen. She likes you. Maybe she'll have one of her old dresses altered for you. Oh, that reminds me." She clapped a palm to her forehead in mock chagrin. "She sent for you. I was supposed to tell you to go to her in her quarters."

I scowled in frustration. "Why didn't you tell me sooner, Tali? I'll have to run. Adah, could you re-fold those dresses while I'm gone?"

Without waiting for a response, I hastened out of the bedchamber and through the complex of rooms and corridors that made up the women's quarters before arriving, slightly breathless, at the entrance to the Queen's private parlour. As I pushed open the elegantly carved door with its tracery of gold leaf, Queen Merris turned to face me.

"Ah, Ani. You got my message, then? I was in some doubt as to whether Tali would remember to tell you; she seemed quite preoccupied with her packing."

"Yes, she remembered." I resisted the temptation to add *eventually*; no-one likes a tattle-tale.

"I gather that your marriage will be taking place soon after we arrive in Rowaty." She waited until I had signalled to the affirmative before continuing. "If I can help you with anything – if there's anything you need – just let me know."

"You are very gracious, my lady."

"I wanted to be sure that you are… happy. With your decision." She hesitated, studying my face, then added quickly, "If not, it's not too late to change your mind. You needn't worry about the future; you have a place in my retinue for as long as you want it."

Moved as I was by the earnestness in her tone, I kept my face impassive as I met her eyes. "Thank you, my lady, but you needn't be concerned. I am certain this is what I want."

She held my gaze a moment longer, then sighed almost imperceptibly. "In that case I won't keep you any longer from your packing."

I bobbed my head and turned to go. But as the gilded door began slowly to swing back into place behind me, I heard her voice again, low and wistful: "To be able to choose whom to marry is a great gift. Don't throw it away."

By the time I got back to the ladies' chamber, my headache had reached a crescendo. Mercifully, Tali had gone and the room was empty save for Adah. Casting myself down on my bed, I closed my eyes, covering them with both palms in an effort to block out the glare of the sunlight.

Adah had finished repacking my clothes and was now sorting through my collection of jewellery and hairpieces. Stopping what she was doing, she crossed to me and placed a soothing hand on my brow. "Is everything all right, my lady?"

"Fine," I mumbled, pushing her hand away. The last thing I needed was Adah fussing over me as if I were a child.

"What did Her Majesty want?"

I scowled in irritation. "None of your business," I snapped, for the second time that afternoon.

Adah backed off and went back to the jewellery, polishing each piece before wrapping it in linen and placing it carefully on top of the clothes in my travelling chest. Watching the care with which she attended to my possessions, I began to regret my harsh manner. After all, my headache was hardly Adah's fault, and she was only trying to help.

"She just wanted to wish me well," I volunteered in a gentler tone. "For the wedding." I kept the rest of the conversation to myself.

"She thinks highly of you," Adah observed. "And of your Aunt Hasina. Why, Achyan once told me…"

"What?!" The word was out of my lips before I could stop it; at the very sound of his name the blood had risen to my face and I had jerked upright, my eyes blazing.

"My lady?" Adah looked at me in confusion. "Did I say something wrong? I was just thinking of the time, before we left Rowaty, when I met Achyan at your aunt's house…"

The blood was pounding in my ears now. "You… you what?"

She took half a step back from me, her brow furrowed. "I've been there many times – how else was I to bring all your possessions to the palace? And your aunt likes to hear news of you… and Achyan, he always stops for a chat – poor man, he's been so lonely since his wife died. And him so young, too, and handsome…"

I barely knew I was doing it. My hand seemed to move of its own accord, and suddenly Adah was staggering back, a look of shock in her eyes, the imprint of my heavy gold rings clearly visible on her cheek.

"You're not to go there again, do you understand?" I was shouting, my eyes wild. "How dare you talk to… him! If you speak to him again, if you even mention his name, I'll, I'll – I'll *sell* you!"

And with that I turned and fled from the room, the little audience of watching slaves recoiling from me as I passed, heedless of my throbbing head, my stinging hand, the tears of shock and pain in Adah's eyes. Heedless of anything but the need to get away.

21

Puah

The stars are beautiful tonight. Finding the main room unbearably stuffy, I have dragged my heavy goatskin bed up to join Reena and the children on the roof, and now I lie wide awake, gazing at the night sky draped above my head like an ink-black garment studded with precious gems. The moon is on the wane and has yet to rise, so there is nothing to dim the splendour of the celestial pageant of lights. Many years ago, the breathtaking wonder of the sight would have led me to whisper a hymn of praise to Nut, star-sprinkled goddess of the sky; now, of course, I know that it was woven by another, the Creator of the heavens and the earth, who formed and placed each star with the skill of a master silversmith crafting a work of utmost beauty. Whether Nut herself is forced to prostrate her mighty arching form before the power and majesty of such a Creator, or whether she yet strives against His mastery over the domain that the Egyptians see as her own, I cannot yet see.

    I think of the King, said to be himself divine, a manifestation of Horus and son of Osiris. He continues to wage war on the God of the Hebrews, yet even Horus – even Osiris himself – cannot stay His hand when it is lifted against them. The casualties of this conflict continue to mount: those soldiers sent to collect grain who will never return to Itjtawy; the population of Upper Egypt who teeter on the brink of starvation; the many struck down by lightning, hail, and plague. Yet this is a struggle that has been raging for generations, and the Hebrew side has also suffered great loss, starting eighty years ago with the innocent children killed without mercy at the King's command. With such a beginning, who can say where this warfare will end?

I shake my head slightly, trying to banish such gloomy thoughts. Above me in the glimmering darkness, my eyes are drawn to a band of three bright stars, glinting coldly in a row: the crown of Sah, father of the gods. Whenever a king dies, they say that he is taken up to join his divine progenitor as one of the points of light visible within his form in the night sky. The very beauty of these stars is then a malevolent one, a set of baleful eyes blinking vindictively down on us. I shiver and turn over, burying my face in the reassuring coarseness of the goatskin.

When next I open my eyes, it is still dark, though I feel refreshed as after a good night's sleep. Rolling onto my back, I blink up at the sky for a few seconds before I figure out what's wrong.

The stars have disappeared.

"Reena?" My voice sounds thin and tremulous to my own ears.

I can just make out a moving figure, a patch of darker blackness against the tarry sky. "Grandmother, it's me," Reena whispers, her own breath catching as she does so. I grope toward her, my right hand finding hers and seizing it tightly.

"What's happened?" I ask stupidly. "What time is it?"

"It's morning, or at least it should be," she murmurs back, her voice soft and tremulous. "When I got up, the dawn was lightning the horizon and the stars had started to fade. But the sun never rose. The stars disappeared, but the horizon got darker, not lighter. It's as if someone pulled a blanket over the sky."

Even as Reena speaks, the darkness seems to intensify, to thicken and congeal. My eyes can no longer make out Reena's form, though her hand in mine is reassuringly solid and warm; I can't tell if the clamminess of her palm comes from her or from me.

I turn my face automatically toward the east, but there is no sun, and no horizon. The darkness is stifling me; it's behind my eyeballs, in my throat, and in my nostrils. I can't breathe. Something brushes against my left leg and I scream, except no sound comes out; I can only gasp like a landed fish. The Something screams, too, and my heart starts beating again as I recognise the voice.

"Amana, it's me, it's Savta. It's OK, little one. It's only me."

I find her arm and squeeze it; she is sobbing now, breathy, terrified sobs, and I try for her sake to keep my own breath steady and my hand from trembling.

"What's happening, Savta? Is it the end of the world?" Baruch has joined us, and in his boyish treble I hear his determination not to show fear, to be a man; but he is belied in the last word by the quaver he can't quite keep out.

"Mother? Reena? Are you all right?"

Wonderfully, miraculously, the darkness seems to roll back. Chenya's face appears at the top of the stairwell, illuminated by a warm halo of light from the oil lamp that she holds high in front of her. Right now, she appears to my eyes like an angel straight from the heavenly realms.

"Mother, thank goodness! And Father," Reena adds, as Echud appears behind his wife. Soon we all stand huddled together in our little circle of lamplight as Reena recounts again what she has seen. Yet our small oasis of light is no more than a speck in the bleak desert of blackness. The luminescence of our little flame reaches no more than an arm's length from the wick of the lamp, as if afraid to venture any further into the suffocating darkness. I step for a moment outside the bubble of light and strain my eyes, gazing outward in all directions, but if any other lamp is ablaze anywhere in this unnatural night, no trace of its glow can be seen. The sense of total isolation sends cold fingers down into my very soul, and I shudder and shrink back inside the friendly yellow orb, pressing close to my family, yet careful all the while not to upset that frail clay vessel that is all that stands between us and the enveloping dark.

We stand in silence now that Reena has finished her tale. It seems pointless to discuss what is happening; none of us can do any more than speculate, and talking about the darkness seems to make it more real – solid, even, like a thick blanket pressing in on us to steal the breath from our lungs, held back only by our flickering wall of lamplight. Yet the silence, too, seems suffocating.

"If anyone knows what's happening, Miryam will," I say eventually. Yet as soon as the words have left my mouth, I regret them. Miryam's house is over half an hour's walk away by daylight; the thought of making that journey in this choking darkness causes my chest to tighten and my breath to come fast and shallow.

"I'll go," says Baruch immediately. His eyes glisten in the lamplight, his fear forgotten in the anticipation of adventure. When I was a girl, I'd have felt the same way. Suddenly I'm ashamed of my cowardice.

"No," I say as firmly as I can, "it ought to be me. I know the way better than anyone else; I've even walked it in darkness before, the night that Miryam's eldest was born. I'll take the torch."

"You can't go alone, Mother," Echud rules. "Baruch will go with you."

"Don't worry, Savta." Baruch puffs out his chest as far as his bony frame will allow. "I'll take care of you."

Chenya carries the lamp with care, shielding its fragile flame with her hand as she leads the way down the steep staircase to the room below. The chamber that was unbearably humid yesterday evening now feels dank and chilly, the darkness spreading its clammy arms throughout it like a thick fog. Even when Chenya places the lamp on its high stand, its glow seems stifled, leaving the deep black shadows to loom menacingly all around the edges and corners of the room.

"I'll light the fire," Echud decides, "and we'll keep it lit until this accursed darkness has lifted. We have plenty of fuel in the store-room, but we're low on kindling."

Taking the bow-drill from beside the fireplace, he twists the string around the shaft, positions the drill end on the fireboard, and draws the bow briskly backward and forward until the dark-red glow of the ember appears, a second point of light to challenge the darkness. Soon the kindling is ablaze, and under Echud's skilful hand the fire grows and blossoms like an acacia shrub planted by the Nile, gladdening our hearts with its merry crackling.

"I'll get the torch," Chenya volunteers. "I know just where it is." Leaving the lamp on its stand, she gropes her way through the door and down the dark stairway toward the storeroom.

Despite her optimism, it takes Chenya some time to locate the torch. In my younger days I would have kept it handy beside my bed, ready to grab at a moment's notice if I was called out urgently in the night to assist a labouring mother. But those days are gone, and while the torch is still kept for emergencies, it is tucked away at the back of the storeroom amongst the cracked jars and empty sacks. I fret at the delay, and Echud drums his fingers nervously on the table; without a light, Chenya runs the risk of disturbing a snake or a scorpion down there in the pitch blackness.

But all is well; we hear the tramp of her feet on the mudbrick steps, and moments later she emerges back into the light, torch in hand.

The torch is a heavy wooden stave, wrapped around at one end with strips of tallowed linen. Grateful now for my foresight in making sure the linen windings were refreshed after each use, I grasp the smooth wood of the handle and thrust the end into the middle of the fire, hoping it's neither too dried-out nor too damp to burn properly after its years in storage. It takes a little while to light, and I feel the pressure of five pairs of eyes watching me anxiously, but finally it catches and I breathe out a silent prayer of thanks.

From past experience I know that I have less than an hour before the torch is burnt out; if this happens before we reach Miryam's house, Baruch and I will be left completely stranded, alone in the smothering darkness. I allow myself one last moment to take in the faces of those I love the most, pale and solemn in the flickering lamplight, and to clasp each hand in turn; then, drawing Baruch close to my side, we descend the stairs together and feel our way step by step, eastward along the dirt path toward the edge of town.

I've been out after dark many times, but never in such eerie blackness as this. From time to time as we pass a house we can dimly make out the hazy glow that tells of a lamp burning within, but no more than a few steps further and even this is swallowed up into the all-consuming maw of the night. The darkness seems to steal sound as well as light and warmth from the surroundings; our footsteps are muffled and even the crackling of the torch seems distant and remote, though we hold it close in front of us in an attempt to bring our footsteps within the limited reach of its glow. Despite our caution, each of us stumbles more than once, and there is a heartstopping moment when Baruch, taking his turn with the torch, catches his foot on a stone and falls flat on his face, our precious light flung from his grip as he instinctively splays his hands out to break his fall. Miraculously, though the flame gutters, it does not go out, and I stoop to take it up again with trembling hand before helping my much-abashed great-grandson back to his feet.

It is a nerve-shredding journey, and one I earnestly hope I need never repeat, but to my infinite relief the torch holds out all the way to the little riverside settlement. As we approach Miryam's home, Baruch gasps and I feel my spirit lift. The house materialises out of the darkness in a warm shimmer of light. Every niche, every cranny, is hung about with lamps and torches, some burning smokily like our own tallow lights, others shining with the clear steady flame of flax oil mixed with salt. I daren't even try to estimate the cost of such excess; it seems that Miryam is intent on burning several months' supply of oil in one day.

Miryam herself opens the door, lamp in hand and a beaming smile on her face. She sends one of her granddaughters up to the roof to tie our torch to the side of the house, promising to replenish it when it burns out. Then she ushers us into her living quarters. I have never seen a more welcoming sight. A roaring fire blazes cheerily in the grate, while on stands all around the room are placed yet more lamps, enough to banish the darkness even from the corners. We are not Miryam's only guests: most of her neighbours are here, standing engrossed in conversation or warming themselves by the fire, and they are joined by several others who, like us, have travelled further to be here; theirs, no doubt, are the torches that hang with ours from the roof, turning the house into a beacon of light.

"Welcome, welcome; make yourselves at home," says Miryam affably. "Stay as long as you like. I can have some more blankets and fleeces brought up if you want to stay the night – though since no-one knows when night actually is, just sleep whenever you feel tired!"

"How long do you think the darkness will last, then?" I enquire.

"Well, that depends on the King's stubbornness," answers Miryam with a twinkle in her eye, "so it could be a while yet! On the other hand, most of his advisors are terrified of Mosheh by now, so he'll be under pressure from them. A few days, maybe."

"A few days?" exclaims a neighbour who has overheard. "What are we to do for that time? We can't take the flocks out to pasture, nor can we gather crops or thresh corn."

"Do you have any grain stored away?" Miryam asks the man.

"Yes, but that's to last until next year's harvest."

"Use your stores," says Miryam, now talking to the room at large. "Eat and drink, feed barley to your animals, and fill your lamps with oil. Those who have plenty should share with those who have little. Neighbours and relatives should come together under one roof to eat and drink, and to share their lamps and their firewood. Don't worry about laying up stores – before many days have passed, we'll be gone from this country!

Whatever you can't carry with you will be left behind, so you may just as well use it as lose it!"

To show that she is taking her own advice, Miryam and her family set about preparing a hearty meal for us all. She has had a goat slaughtered, and soon the meat is simmering in a huge pot over the fire, together with onions, lentils, celery, garlic, herbs, and spices. A delicious smell fills our nostrils, reminding me that Baruch and I have not breakfasted this morning – if indeed it is still morning; who can tell?

Whether it's the aroma of goat stew, the welcoming light that surrounds the house, or – most likely – just a general feeling that Miryam will have the answers to whatever is happening, the crowd of people inside Miryam's home gets bigger and bigger as time goes by. Although Miryam's house is a large one by Hebrew standards, it was not built to contain so many people, so the houses on either side – one belonging to Aharon and the other to one of Miryam's sons – are also opened up to guests, hung about, like Miryam's, with the torches of the travellers. Just as Miryam's daughter begins to dish up the stew, accompanied by flat cakes of unleavened bread, there is yet another knock on the door. Young Ghila is sent to answer it, but when I hear the new guests' voices, I rise quickly from my stool and hurry down the stairs to greet them, a huge smile upon my face.

"Aliza!" I enfold my eldest daughter in my arms. "And Hana! How on earth did you make it right the way across the city in this darkness? It must have taken you hours!"

"We carried spare torches," says Hana, showing me two staves with blackened and burnt-out linen bindings. "Mine was already half consumed from my journey to Mother and Father's house, so we borrowed another from Alim. Do you know" – she turns to Miryam, who has joined us – "while we were under his roof, it just wouldn't light. He couldn't get a single one of his lamps to burn, and even my own torch went out as I passed through the door. Yet in Father's house, it lit just fine."

"What of your other Egyptian neighbours?" asks Miryam keenly. "Did you see any lights from their homes?"

"Not one." Hana shakes her head. "I thought it was strange, as they have lamps and oil enough. But it's possible they just weren't visible from outside; this darkness seems to hide every light until you're right up close to it."

"No." Miryam's tone is definite, her eyes ablaze in the torchlight. "I suspect that what you experienced at Alim's house is the same in every Egyptian dwelling. Just as the Lord spared His people from the flies, the hail, and the boils, He has spared us the worst of this plague too. We have light, while the Egyptians languish in total darkness."

We follow Miryam back up the stairs. As we climb, a thought strikes me, and I turn to my daughter.

"Where is Mesu, Aliza? It's not like him to leave you and Hana to undertake such a dangerous journey by yourselves."

"He stayed to take care of Alim and Sekhet – well, of Sekhet and their household. Alim wouldn't leave his house, dark as it is, though he was happy to see Sekhet and the rest go with us." Aliza glances at Miryam and lowers her voice. "There's another reason, too. Mesu wasn't at all sure of his welcome here, in a houseful of Israelites."

"But that's…" I start to say *ridiculous*, but realise it doesn't ring true. My Echud's not the only one to think that if you're born an Egyptian and live in a fine house, you have no place among the Lord's people.

We've reached the living quarters now, and I suddenly become aware that our conversation is no longer private. While most of the guests are sitting or squatting, preoccupied with their bowls of stew, Mosheh's wife Zipporah remains standing, empty-handed, by the doorway. Her eyes make contact with mine, and a sad sort of half-smile touches the corners of her lips for a moment; then Miryam bustles forward, pressing plates of food into our hands, and when I look around again, Zipporah is gone.

All through the meal, which is excellent, I can't get Zipporah's expression out of my head. With the dishes cleared away, many of the guests think of departing; Miryam delegates various family members to prepare torches for them, and the fat from the goat, far-sightedly held back from the cooking pot and rendered into tallow, is pressed into service as torch fuel, along with much of Miryam's dwindling oil supply. One by one, people head back out into the darkness, with instructions from Miryam to call on others along the way, spreading the word to gather together and pool lamps and fuel. Knowing from this that Echud and the rest of the family will be OK, I am happy to accept Miryam's repeated offer to stay until this unnatural night is over. Besides, it will give me the opportunity to talk to her in private.

My chance comes an hour or so later, when I go up to the roof with her to retrieve the last couple of guttering torches before they burn out. It's only my torch and Miryam's left now, and compared to the cheery fire- and lamp-lit parlour below, the rooftop feels cold and isolated, our torch flames a futile defiance to the all-encompassing blackness.

As Miryam brushes past me to head back down the stairs, I lay a hand on her arm. "Just a moment. I wanted to ask you something. It's about Zipporah."

Miryam's face is unreadable in the flickering torchlight, but her tone is guarded. "The Midianite. Yes?"

"Your sister-in-law," I add, and it may be the light, but it seems to me that Miryam winces.

"She is a guest in your house," I press on, "yet she always seems to be alone. Her husband is in Itjtawy, and her two sons have gone with him to carry messages back and forth. Her father and sisters remain in Midian, and you are the only family she has here. But in all the time she has lived under your roof, I have never once seen you speak to her – you, nor any of your children or grandchildren."

I have phrased the rebuke as gently as I can, yet Miryam is no fool, and she has all the pride of a matriarch used to ordering her household as she likes without question. She bridles at my comment, taking half a step back and shaking free from my touch on her arm. Then she meets my gaze and droops, sagging her shoulders.

"It is no easy thing," she says quietly, "for a foreigner to marry into the Children of Israel."

Though I had suspected some such reason, her choice of words hits me with a jolt of emotion, and it's my turn to take a step back. Though eighty years have passed and the setting couldn't be more different, looking at Miryam now I see not her but her mother, Yokheved's eyes surveying me with grave sympathy, her lips forming the same words, virtually unchanged with the intervening years, that still have the power to send waves of pain and rejection crashing through my body.

But wait a minute; surely there's a difference. Zipporah is no foolish young girl, desperately in love with a man she can't have. She's Mosheh's wife and the mother of his two sons – not infants but grown men. Miryam, with her usual intuition, seems to sense my argument before I voice it.

"I know it's a bit late now to object to their marriage," she says with a sigh. "But Mosheh is God's chosen leader and will set the standard for the whole Israelite community. He should have followed the example of Avraham, Yitzhak, and Yaqob, and taken a wife from among his own people. If he's married a foreigner, what's to stop others from doing the same?" Seeing the look on my face, she stops. "Sorry," she concedes and sighs again. "Sometimes I forget that you're not an Israelite by birth."

And I? For most of the community, it's beyond living memory since I was last called an Egyptian. I live, dress, speak, and even think as an Israelite. But as for me, I will never forget.

Ani

"Tomorrow morning. At the temple of Amun."

Suten-Ka's tone was triumphant, and, as he came impetuously forward to embrace me, I tried my best to look pleased. Something in my expression must have given me away, however, because he pulled back, hands on my shoulders, and studied me anxiously.

"That is OK, isn't it? I know it's not the usual place for ratifying a marriage contract, but your father was insistent – he is serving as lector priest this month, after all, so it is his duty to remain within the temple."

"No, that's fine," I said quickly.

"Great." He smiled. "Your father and I drew up the marriage contract today, so it just needs to be witnessed. Of course, you won't officially enter my house as my wife until we're back in Itjtawy, but I've made enquiries and there should be a merchant ship leaving in three days' time with space for two passengers, so it won't be long."

I tuned out and let Suten-Ka's enthusiasm wash over me as he talked on and on about arrangements for the witnesses, the sacrifice, the feast, the dower. Of course, I had entered the temple of Amun many times since my trial, but that was just to leave an offering, and even then I'd never felt exactly comfortable inside its tall, frowning edifice. I'd got into the habit of making the offering as quickly as possible, keeping my head bowed in case anyone was watching, then retreating as soon as I could without drawing attention. But this time I wouldn't be able to do that. Standing before witnesses, all eyes fixed on me – the occasion might be a happy one this time, but the setting was all too familiar, and even now I felt my breath coming fast and shallow at the very thought. With a deliberate effort, I focused on breathing deeply, forcing my tense limbs to relax. I just had to get through this, and then I would be free – free to start a new life in Itjtawy and leave my past behind forever.

The she-goat stands on the banks of the river. But today she is not the only one. Just a short distance away, the main flock browses – sheep and goats of all shapes, sizes and colours, feasting on the abundant greenery that is the gift of the Nile. Amidst the flock, towering head and shoulders above the largest of the other beasts, is an enormous ram. He struts proudly to and fro, tossing his massive curved horns as he surveys his estate. Both sheep and goats defer to him, lowering their heads submissively and skipping this way or that as he drives them.

Spotting the little she-goat, he glares haughtily at her for a moment, then throws his head back and gives an imperious call. The she-goat looks at him uncertainly, then takes a couple of hesitant steps toward him. Then she stops.

Across the river, the herdsman is grazing his flock. Pure-white sheep feed on the pastureland all around him, but his gaze is fixed across the river. At the little she-goat.

She wavers. She looks backward and forward; first at the ram, then at the herdsman, then at the swollen crimson torrent of the river. Then she makes up her mind. Turning her back on the ram, she trots down toward the water.

Quick as a flash, the ram runs to block her way. Head down, horns lowered menacingly, his eyes flash fire as he stands between the she-goat and the river.

On the far bank, the herdsman raises his crook and extends it out across the water. Then he calls out one word: "Come!"

With a great leap, the little she-goat springs toward the river. The ram is powerless to stop her as she plunges into the rushing flow. Striking out as hard as she can, she swims for her life, fighting against the swift current that threatens to sweep her downstream, struggling to keep her head above the crimson torrent. Just as it seems she will be swept away, the herdsman stretches out the hooked end of his crook and draws her toward the bank. Her cloven feet scrabbling for purchase on the silty shore, the little goat heaves herself from the water and shakes herself dry. As the drops are scattered from her body, shining vermillion under the sunset sky, the sheep gather around her, bleating softly. She is no longer alone.

The day dawned bright and fresh, with a pleasant breeze that held the promise of rain. I rose early – sleep had eluded me for much of the night, and vivid dreams had troubled the little I'd had, but I had more than enough nervous energy stored in my body to ward off any feeling of tiredness. I showered and applied my usual lotions and fragrances, then sent for Adah. Adah made no comment as she helped me into the close-fitting light-green kalasiris in which I had first met Suten-Ka. While Tali was probably right that the queen would have lent me a finer dress, I hadn't asked; apart from the fact that I was beholden enough to her already, my last private audience with her had left me feeling distinctly uncomfortable, and I was reluctant to repeat it.

Suten-Ka was waiting for me just outside the door of the women's quarters. His eyes lit up as I stepped out to join him; his gaze travelled appreciatively over my dress, lingering on the low-cut neckline and the way the fine linen clung around my hips and waist. Then he met my eyes and, smiling, took my hand.

Together we made our way out of the palace and westwards toward the temple. The palace stood at the northernmost edge of the city, and the road along which we walked, flanked by mudbrick buildings on our left, commanded an unobstructed view to our right of the mighty waters of the Nile. A little further upstream the river would divide into two branches, one rushing and tumbling northwards in its hurry to reach the sea; the other, alongside which we now passed, meandered eastward on a broader and more leisurely course. Right at the point where they separated stood the temple, its long landing-stage jutting north across the silted banks toward the water. The road, too, bent toward the north before turning westward again to meet the temple approach.

I felt my palm sweating in Suten-Ka's grip as we walked those last few steps toward the two towering pillars of the temple gate. In a double row flanking the walkway on either side, ram-headed images of Amun glared accusingly at me as we passed. I forced myself to look straight ahead, not meeting their cold stone eyes, which nonetheless seemed to bore into the side of my head, causing sharp prickles to run up and down my neck.

As we approached the gates of the temple, my father came out to meet us, dressed in his priestly garments: the bleached-white linen shendyt, with the white sash across his chest showing that he held the office of lector priest. This was one meeting I had been dreading, but he beamed at the sight of me and came forward to clasp my hands between his own.

"My daughter," he greeted me warmly. "You look radiant."

I wasn't sure how to reply. This was the first time in a year and a half that he had referred to me as "daughter".

"Your Aunt Sera and Nanu have come to witness the signing of the agreement," he told me, "and your Aunt Hasina and Uncle Khufu are here, too."

Sure enough, as Suten-Ka led me by the hand through the gateway into the courtyard, I saw Aunt Hasina, a baby on one hip – whether it was Mesu or Yechiel I couldn't tell, as in the five months since I had seen them last they had grown beyond recognition. Behind her, Nailah in her slave-girl disguise carried the other baby, who squirmed in her grip, twisting his head around to take in the bustle of sights and sounds. I smiled despite myself at his antics, and Aunt Hasina smiled back, although I noticed the little crease in her forehead that meant she was not quite at ease.

Nanu, by contrast, seemed in her element as she pulled away from Aunt Sera's side and dashed forward to give me a hug. I'd seen little of her since her marriage the previous year, but there was a new roundness to her belly, and it suited her. I returned her embrace affectionately; though we had grown apart in recent years, as girls together we had been as close as sisters, with only six months between us in age. I realised suddenly that this could be the last time I saw her; that I would never meet the child she carried, or watch it grow. Mesu and Yechiel, too, and even little Moses – children who had been a part of my life, and would be so no longer. I didn't even dare think about how much I would miss my Aunt Hasina.

My father had appointed a scribe, a junior colleague of his, to perform the public reading of the marriage covenant and record the names of the witnesses. Despite the momentousness of the occasion, my mind and gaze wandered as the scribe's voice rose and fell, intoning the clauses with a steady solemnity.

Suten-Ka son of Ankhareoutef, assistant treasurer under Uar-Mu the Chief Keeper of the King's Treasures, says to this woman, Ani daughter of Sapthah...

A faint breeze lifted the banners that hung from tall poles atop the pylon; they danced briefly, momentarily, before falling to hang limply once more. Behind our little party, the young sun's pale yellow rays seemed powerless to heat the smooth, white stone of the obelisks, whose sharp-tipped shadows pointed across our heads to the flagstones within the entrance.

If they beckoned me in, it was a welcome devoid of warmth.

...today I have made you my wife, both being freeborn, and bringing to the marriage...

A freeborn Egyptian woman was free to marry as she chose. I had made my choice. So why didn't it feel like freedom?

...sixteen garments of fine linen; four woven headpieces; six armlets of pure gold...

The air beneath the pylon was cool, yet I was sweating. The back of my neck prickled and burned. I looked up – and wished I hadn't. Towering over my head, the malevolent stares of two colossal Amun figures bored into me, standing sentinel one on each side of the gateway. Where could I go to escape that baleful presence? Could I find sanctuary inside the Temple itself, where the daily sacrifices my father offered would appease the god's vindictiveness and purchase his favour? Or should I turn tail and flee? Could I escape, or would the god's disapproval follow me, haunting my days with anxiety and my nights with nightmares?

...and if I should abandon you as my wife, or if you should abandon me...

Suten-Ka loved me. He was a good man, and he'd been good to me. What sort of slinking dog would I be if I left him now? No, lower than a dog – even a *tjezem*-hound is loyal to a man who treats it well.

Gone now was any trace of a breeze, and I felt simultaneously chilled and stifled. Goose pimples rose along the bare skin of my arm. Seeing them, Suten-Ka enfolded my shoulders with his own arm, pale from long days spent in the treasury yet reassuringly warm and strong. Heat from his chest surrounded me and I relaxed into him, letting some of the tension slip away. The path he offered me may not have been my first choice, but it was a smooth one: life, comfort, security. What lay the other way? Nothing but precipice after precipice, littered with the dry bones of my broken dreams.

At the corner of my vision, the stone guardians that towered above my head seemed to wear identical smirks on their cold faces. It was only a split-second glimpse, but something in me snapped.

"I... I can't."

My voice was faint, little more than a whisper, but as I said the words, resolve grew in me. It was as if the pieces of my jumbled-up mind were finally slotting into place.

Suten-Ka drew his arm back and turned to face me, a furrow of concern on his brow. "What's wrong, Ani?"

I flinched but forced myself to look into his eyes. "I can't. I'm really sorry."

Confusion in his brown eyes mingled with hurt, and I had to look away. My father and Aunt Hasina appeared either side of me, my aunt handing the baby to Nailah as she spoke in a low tone.

"You can't what, Ani?"

There was compassion in her voice and eyes, but also a flicker of fear. This was a woman who'd faced down the King and put her life on the line day after day. I wavered, swallowing nervously, but I couldn't go back now.

"I can't live a lie."

"It's natural to be nervous..." my father began.

"No," I stopped him. "It's not that." I swallowed again; this wasn't going to go well. But it had to be said. The smoothest of paths is no good if you don't like the destination. It was time to jump off the precipice.

I turned back to Suten-Ka. "You have been nothing but kindness to me, and I'm deeply sorry for the pain I know this must cause you. But I can't live any longer in the court of a King who orders the deaths of infants, nor serve the gods to whom such innocent blood is offered."

A gasp went up from my Aunt Sera's direction, but it was Suten-Ka who occupied my gaze. He looked as though he'd been trampled by a herd of wild asses. I couldn't blame him. My own eyes were wet as I continued.

"I can't expect you – or anyone else – to walk this path with me. But it's the path I must walk. I serve the God of the Hebrews." *May He protect me now,* I added inwardly. I couldn't help another upward glance at the stone colossi. Trick of the light or no, there was no trace of a smirk now. Instead, the receding shadows darkened their features with black menace.

A pregnant silence hung in the air for a moment. My father was the first to break it. I had expected anger, but I wasn't prepared for the quaver in his voice, his face pale and suddenly old.

"Then I have no daughter."

While a part of me had anticipated it, his words still cut like a blade deep in my heart. I swayed slightly where I stood. Aunt Hasina's hand found mine and squeezed lightly, her touch imparting courage in the knowledge that I wasn't abandoned completely.

Courage that evaporated as a cold, commanding voice rang out from the temple gate.

"An admirable stance. I would expect no less from the lector priest of Amun."

My father was the only one who didn't jump. A fine-robed, corpulent figure had emerged from the inner sanctum, bulbous face and small, dark eyes shadowed by his richly striped headdress. Nonetheless there was no hiding the malice that gleamed in them, and they were trained fully on me.

"Y-your Grace," my father greeted the vizier, an uncharacteristic tremor in his voice. "Did the great god Amun smile upon your offering?"

"He did," Neferkare Iymeru returned. "And it is by Amun's providence that I have come forth earlier than I had planned – just in time to apprehend a traitor."

As he spoke, two guards materialised from the shadows of the gateway and came forward to flank him. Simultaneously, Aunt Hasina shifted forward on my left and Suten-Ka on my right. In unspoken accord, they stepped together in front of me to form a human shield between me and the vizier. My aunt's mouth brushed my ear as she passed and she breathed a single word: "Run."

For a second I hesitated, rooted to the spot. Then the wave of fear crested and broke over me. My feet moved of their own accord, darting back and to the left. There was a ripping sound as the restrictive fabric of my kalasiris gave way to the force of my momentum as I hurtled toward the walkway, instinctively seeking the shelter of the statues that lined its edges.

"Bring her to me!" The command rang out behind me, clear and cold.

"Your Grace—"

"Do not obstruct my guards, woman! She is a double traitor and this time I will see her punished!"

Sparing half a second to pray that my Aunt Hasina would not pay too dearly for her effort to protect me, I sprinted along the walkway. The guards were well trained and fit, but I had a decent start on them, and fear lent wings to my feet. I gained the end of the walkway and, with no time to think, hurled myself left toward the sloping banks of the Nile. Papyrus reeds grew thickly here, and I plunged among them, face down in the sticky river mud, my heart hammering so hard I felt sure it would give away my hiding place.

"Which way did she go?"

"We'll split up. You take the riverbank, I'll take the town and gather some more of the boys to help the search."

They sounded horribly close. The muddied green of my kalasiris blended with the vegetation, but all the same, I felt exposed. Any second now, a bronze spear would push the reeds aside and I'd be discovered and dragged before the vizier. I knew that if I faced him again, there would be no escaping my fate.

The slap of sandalled feet grew closer, and I squeezed my eyes closed. *This is it.* But miraculously, they went on past, swallowed by the sound of birdsong, the wind in the reeds and the rushing of the water.

I lay where I was, weak with relief. I knew I should give thought to what to do next – more guards could be along at any minute. But right now, I didn't have the emotional strength to keep running.

"Miss Ani?"

I jolted upright, blood pounding in my head. But the whisper was soft, the voice familiar.

"A-Adah?"

I looked up. Soft, long-lashed brown eyes met mine, and a small smile flitted across her face.

"I was waiting just outside the temple. I heard it all, and I saw where you hid. You were very brave."

Below her eye, the imprint of my rings could still be seen, the bruising faded to yellow. Guilt surged through me. It was too much on top of all my other emotions, and tears tracked the mud on my face.

"Adah, I…"

"Shh, Miss Ani, there isn't much time." Her hands were already working, loosening my hairpiece. "We have to swap clothes. They won't be looking for a slave girl, you can make it to safety while I lead them away." The headpiece off, she began working on my jewelled collar.

"But…" I couldn't let her put herself in danger like this.

"Don't worry. Once they bring me before the vizier, it'll be obvious I'm not you. I'll just say you left town and gave me the clothes as a parting gift." She grinned. "But they'll have to catch me first!"

My heart still protested, but I was half dazed and out of arguments. Reluctantly, I tugged off my rings, then lifted my kalasiris over my head and slipped on the tunic Adah offered me.

"Could you help me with the headpiece, Miss Ani? It feels so different, putting it on myself!"

Numbly, I obeyed, tying Adah's headscarf over my own bare head instead. Then I surveyed Adah. If it weren't for the rips and the mud, she could easily have passed for a wealthy Egyptian woman. My heart fluttered with fear for her, mingled with gratitude.

"Why would you do this for me, when I…?"

But she wasn't listening. "You can't go to your aunt's, it's the first place they'll look. Go to Achyan's house. Your uncle gave him the day off, so he should be there. He'll help you work out what to do next."

"I…"

"Shh!" She pulled me down. Toward us on the light riverside breeze, voices were carrying, faint but drawing closer:

"…don't see why Neferkare had to send out a whole unit, just for some girl."

"He has his personal reasons."

"Personal vendetta, more like. I would say he's obsessed, but…"

"Shh! He has ears everywhere. And the girl could be somewhere along here. My old wound's playing up, I don't fancy another chase."

Holding a finger to her lips, Adah nodded at me once, then went down on her belly and crawled from one clump of reeds to the next, working her way stealthily along the riverbank. When the guards were level with my hiding place, she suddenly stood up and began to run, my tattered kalasiris trailing in muddy ribbons behind her. A shout went up from the guards and they were off, bronze spearheads flashing in the sunlight as they gave chase. I watched, heart in my mouth, guilt gnawing my insides; then, when the sweeping turns of the river had hidden them from view, I cautiously rose and headed back toward the town.

My heart pounded erratically all the way to Achyan's house. I came on a pair of guards suddenly as I rounded a corner, and instinctively I shrank back against the wall, but when they paid me no more attention than if I'd been a stray dog, my fear for myself began to dissipate, leaving room for other emotions: fear for Adah, fear for my Aunt Hasina, all mingled with a terrible, overriding guilt that it was my decisions for which they risked their lives. Then there was Suten-Ka: he'd moved to protect me even though I'd broken his heart. This was now the second betrothal I'd broken off, and I wondered dully if I could ever offer a man anything but trouble and pain.

My steps faltered; was it even fair to go to Achyan's house? He was the last person I wanted to hurt. But where else could I go?

And so my steps carried me down that familiar path, and my heart pattered irregularly as I knocked on the door, but it was little Leah who answered, and when she told me Achyan was out, the greatest feeling that swept over me was relief, closely followed by exhaustion. Leah ran to fetch me a stool and a drink, but before she'd even returned with them, I had collapsed in a heap in the corner of the room, overcome by a mercifully dreamless sleep.

When I opened my eyes, the light was dim. The single lamp hadn't yet been lit, and the evening air was clear, free from the smoke and scent of tallow. I looked up into a pair of hazel eyes, their gaze intense and serious. He rose, arching his back and stretching stiff limbs.

"Achyan, I—" I began, before realising there were no words for what I wanted to say. He ignored me.

"You threw it all away," he said, his voice rough with emotion.

I said nothing, trying to analyse his tone. Was he angry? Worried? Resentful of the danger I'd placed him and Leah in by coming here?

"Nailah was here," Leah supplied. "She told us what happened." There was something like wonder in her own voice.

Achyan spoke again. "Your aunt sent a message. She suggested you stay here until the royal party returns to Itjtawy. As for your father, she fears there's no repairing that rift. You've lost your dowry, your inheritance, your status – your very freedom." He swallowed. "After you ran away, the vizier apparently decreed that, since you'd spurned the gods of Egypt for the God of the Hebrews, henceforth you should be treated like a Hebrew. Officially, you're now no more than a runaway slave, and if caught, you'll be treated as such." He looked away. "Your father agreed to this."

The strangest mix of emotions bubbled up inside me. Fear was still present, of course, and pain over my father's abandonment – but with it came an odd sense of release. I sat up.

"Achyan."

He half-turned toward me but kept his gaze lowered to my feet.

"For a long time now, I've been living a double life in one shape or another. An Egyptian pretending to be a Hebrew slave-girl. A convict posing as a courtier. A girl running from her past, carving out a new life she didn't believe in. Now all that has gone. I may have sacrificed my freedom, but it feels like shaking off my bonds."

Briefly he looked up, and his hazel eyes were wet.

"That's only because you've never experienced the bonds of slavery," he muttered. "Someone like you should never have to."

"Neither should you. Neither should Leah, or Adah – or Keshet. But you do, and now I will, too. You're right, I've never experienced it, and maybe I'm not strong enough. Maybe I will come to regret it. But I don't think so. Better to suffer injustice than to be on the side that administers it."

Achyan blinked rapidly and passed a hand over his eyes. A small frown appeared on his brow as if seeing me for the first time and trying to figure me out. Placing a hand on each of my shoulders, he studied me at arm's length for a moment. His hands felt hot as branding irons on my skin, and emotion swirled in the hazel pools of his eyes. I found that I was trembling.

"You are brave," he said thickly, "but stupid."

The next thing I knew I was in his arms, and our tears mingled like the many waters of the Nile.

22

Puah

"What happened next?" asks nine-year-old Ayla. She leans across the table toward me, her long-lashed eyes wide.

"I know!" Amana answers for me. "Savta married Achyan, of course – our Saba – and lived happily ever after."

I smile at her childish innocence. "Close enough," I reply. "You never knew your Saba, but we had more than sixty years together. There were plenty of clouds as well as sunshine, and I won't say there were never times when I regretted my decision – but yes, we were happy."

"What about Adah?" Baruch chimes in. "She was a real hero, wasn't she?"

I suppress a chuckle. Adah's great-granddaughter is Baruch's age and pretty as they come, which may have something to do with his eagerness to glean flattering details about her family history – stored away, no doubt, for future conversations.

"She was indeed," I tell him. "I have no doubt that she saved my life that day, at great risk to herself. She led the guards a merry dance, keeping them tied up long enough for me to reach Achyan's house. They caught her eventually, of course, and dragged her before the vizier, who was livid when he saw how she'd tricked them. It would have gone badly for her, but my Aunt Hasina intervened. Since my father had disowned me, she said, she was my next of kin now, and punishment of my slave was her responsibility." The corners of my mouth lift. "She treated Adah like a daughter from that day forward."

We sit on low wooden stools or on the floor, the rough wooden table having been moved out to make room for our guests: Udiel and Maakah and their four children, and Udiel's sister Peninah with her three children. They are but two of many families to have come north over the past weeks, deserting their home in Atef-Pehu and their work constructing the great stone tomb of the King. First it was a trickle of people, leaving the locust-blighted fields of the south for the promise of grain in the north, but since the most recent word sent by Mosheh and Aharon, the trickle has become a flood, an inundation, leaving every Hebrew dwelling and settlement across Upper Egypt standing silent and empty. Their masters and foremen were powerless to stop them; indeed, many of them have also come north, sensing that only starvation and death await them in the south. The families of Rowaty have opened their doors to distant relatives, never before met, and a house built for ten now sleeps twenty or more.

Chenya and Reena are busying themselves over the fire, and the delicious aroma of roasting lamb fills our little home. It is to be a strange feast: each of us is dressed in our travelling clothes, and my walking staff leans against the table within easy reach.

The door creaks as Echud stumps through, calling for water. Chenya leaves her place at the fire and hurries down to the store-room, returning with a jar of water and a small pot of paste made from a mixture of oil and ash. She pours the water over Echud's hands as he scrubs them with the paste, washing the darkening bloodstains from his fingers and palms.

"It's done, then?" I enquire.

"It's done," he affirms. "I was one of the last – our family and neighbours are already covered."

I nod my thanks for the information. Echud and Baruch are safe under this roof, but I appreciate the confirmation that Tobit and my other grandsons and great-grandsons will also be protected.

Excusing myself a moment, I climb slowly up the stairs to the roof, gripping the banister firmly to support my weight. Already the sunlight is starting to fade – that newly-restored sunlight, how we now appreciate it! – but in the gloaming I see the town spread out before me, and every doorpost, every lintel, painted red with fresh lamb's blood. The sharp, metallic tang of it is in my nostrils. It is a sight at once sinister and hopeful.

Satisfied that what is needful has been done, I descend the stairs once more and rejoin the group. Echud has finished washing and he joins us, tightening his belt around the outside of his cloak before taking a seat.

"So, what are we talking about?" he says lightly to Baruch and Amana. It's not like him to join in with the children's prattle or listen to their tales, but I sense he's seeking a distraction from the weightier matters that have occupied him today.

"Savta was telling our guests of the day she became an Israelite," Baruch informs him.

"And when Saba fell in love with her," adds Amana with a giggle.

"Your Saba loved her long before that day, I think," says Echud. His eyes take on a faraway expression. "Father used to tell me that he was blessed to have known true love twice in one lifetime. Keshet was his Rainbow, the hope amidst the storm, and you, Mother, were his Radiance, the sunlight bursting through the dark clouds."

I duck my head to hide the tears that threaten to spill over.

"It must have been hard for you," says Reena softly; I hadn't realised she was listening. "Going so suddenly from privileged Egyptian to status-less slave."

"Yes and no," I reply thoughtfully. "Achyan was still in my aunt and uncle's service, so they made sure we were provided for. And once the initial danger had passed, I was able to go back to my midwifery, which I loved. But my first pregnancy was an anxious time. That's true for any young woman, of course, but the King's decree was still in force and I kept having nightmares..." I have to stop. Even eighty years later, I'm still haunted by the vision of that young family, the savage cruelty of the guards, and the newborn I was unable to save.

The shadow passes, and I go on. "I needn't have worried. By the time you were born, Echud, the old vizier had died and it was common knowledge that the King and his queen had taken in a Hebrew boy. The decree became unenforceable – no-one could accuse another of breaking it without seeming to point a finger at the King."

There is a knock at the door and Reena goes to answer it. At the sound of the voices below, I rise in surprise and make my own way down the stairs to greet our visitors. Echud follows me, his face grim.

"Madame Sekhet, I..." Reena stands face to face with her employer, my cousin Nanu's daughter-in-law. She looks exceedingly uncomfortable.

Behind Sekhet stands a young woman, swathed in layers of cloth that obscure her face. Strapped to her back is an infant, no more than a month old. Between us, Sekhet's face is tracked with tears. Then, to my discomfiture, she falls to her knees.

"Please! I have nowhere else to turn. If I am to lose husband, son and grandson, please save my granddaughter and her innocent child."

I hear a sharp intake of breath behind me as Echud steps forward toward the young woman.

"Then you are..."

"Yes." The girl's accent is that of the highest class of Egyptians, but there is a tremor to her voice. "I am Atinmerit, daughter of King Merneferre Ay."

By now, the whole family is gathered behind me in the dim-lit storeroom. Chenya, Reena and the children gasp and draw back at the princess's words, but Echud stands his ground.

"Then begone from my house. You ask too much, Sekhet. I am grateful for your kindness to my wife and daughter, but this I cannot do."

Sekhet gives a wail and sinks forward, her forehead striking the dirt of the floor in her distress. The young woman has turned away, shoulders slumped in resignation, and I hear the catch of her breath in her throat.

"Wait," I say. Echud glares at me, but he holds his peace for now.

The princess turns back. Her veil has slipped, and I see that she is very young, no more than fifteen.

"Tell us more," I encourage her. "Why do you defy your father? What of your husband?"

Keeping her eyes lowered to the floor, she replies in a quiet voice, "My husband... is also my brother, eldest son of the King. Such is the custom with royalty, as you know."

"Hmph!" snorts Echud. "I would say such inbreeding explains a lot, but the current King has no such excuse, does he? He wasn't born to rule."

"Echud!" says Chenya, appalled. She looks nervously for the princess's reaction.

"Indeed," Atinmerit replies. "My mother Ineni is not of royal blood but is daughter to Sekhet, as you know. My father is grandson to King Khaneferre Sobekhotep, but through the female line – from his first wife, Queen Merris, who bore him no male heirs. My father took the throne from his cousin, Wahibre Ibiau – the king who sent your Moses into exile."

"We know all this," says Echud impatiently. "What of your husband? Does he know you are here? Or do you expect us to shelter him, too?" He laughs humourlessly.

"He stands by our father," says the princess quietly. "As the firstborn, I believe the curse will fall on him." Sekhet, who had lifted her face from the ground when I spoke, now buries it in her arms.

"He has made his choice," Atinmerit continues softly. "But our son – he is an innocent. I beg you – not as a princess, but as a mother – please, let him live!"

To my amazement, she falls to her knees and prostrates herself in the dust at our feet. The child, still strapped to her back, wakes and begins to whimper. Even Echud is taken aback; he rubs his eyes as if not believing what he sees.

"Get up, child," I say to the girl. Rising to her knees, she looks up at me through dark eyes framed with kohl that has smudged and run over the dusky pink of her cheeks.

"Your father has decreed that any Egyptian who paints the blood over their doorframe, or who takes shelter in such a house, will be forever cut off from family and people. Do you accept this?" I ask her.

She nods. "I have no choice. Better to live as a slave than to die as royalty. But I believe that living as a Hebrew will not mean living as a slave for much longer."

"Then, by the King's own decree, you are no longer an Egyptian. I name you Batyah, daughter of Yahweh, as you have chosen Him above your own father. When we go from Egypt, you will go with us. And just as your great-grandmother once took in a Hebrew baby and named him Moses, so I name your son Yisbah, son of Israel."

Echud can keep his peace no longer. "You can't do this, Mother!" he blusters, his face livid. "This boy is the King's own grandson – his heir!"

I face my son, my eyes and voice serious. "Eighty years ago, I defied the King's decree to protect infants and their mothers. Must I now defy my own son to do the same? Or are we no better than the King who ordered that decree?" Echud opens his mouth to reply, and I hold up a hand. "I know what you're going to say – that it is God Himself who has pronounced the curse on the firstborn. But He has not left the Egyptians without a choice. Why do you think He commanded the ritual with the lamb's blood? Why not simply smite the Egyptians and pass over the

Israelites? Do you think His angel can't tell the difference between an Egyptian house and a Hebrew one?" I pause to let this sink in. "No, the choice is for all people, and any who harden their hearts after all they've seen of our God's power are bringing the curse upon themselves."

I turn to Sekhet. "Was it only Hebrew houses that you saw painted with the blood as you made your way here?"

"No," she answers. "Most of the other slaves, both Kushites and Greeks, and not a few Egyptians have heeded Moses' words in defiance of the King."

I nod. "As I thought. When we go from here, there will be many with us who were not born Hebrews, but whose own choices have made them children of Avraham – not by blood, but in spirit. Just as I am."

Still Echud's jaw is stubbornly set. "If it were any other child, Mother, I would be ruled by your arguments. But the King's grandson, his heir… what will come of him when he is grown? Foolish is the man who takes a serpent to his bosom."

"Heir to what?" says the princess softly. "Egypt is no more. When you… when *we* go from here, we will leave behind nothing but a barren wasteland."

Echud holds her gaze a while, and when she does not look away, he shrugs and sighs. "So be it," he says grudgingly. "Reena, I suppose you'd better set two more places for dinner. It's getting dark, and we don't want the meat to burn."

Reena hurries up the stairs to tend to the meal, while Chenya helps to unbind the baby from the princess's back and fetches a jar of water for her to wash. This done, she leads her up to the living quarters, carrying the infant in the crook of her arm. I hold back to offer washing water to Sekhet in turn, and to ask some questions that are burning on my heart.

"I am sorry to talk of what is painful to you, but I have to ask. I understand that your grandson, the princess's husband, will not leave his father. The blame lies with the King for his stubborn unbelief and refusal to spare even his own son. But what of your son, Queen Ineni's brother, and his family?"

She heaves out a breath, her face and voice betraying her agony.

"I pleaded with him. I knelt in the dust at his feet and begged him to save himself. But he fears the King more than the curse – even after all that has happened. He said it's nonsense, that no plague takes only the firstborn son but spares the rest, and so he's in no more danger than anyone else. He's locked the door and drawn the shutters – as if that will help."

"I'm sorry." I draw a shaky breath. "And Alim? Surely he has seen sense by now?"

Slowly, she shakes her head. "No. He's as stubborn as my son." She sighs. "I left him prostrate in front of his altar. He still believes that Amun and Osiris can save him. I'm sorry – I know you and his mother were close."

"Yes, Nanu and I were like sisters, once upon a time." I smile sadly. "I just wish her only son had inherited some of her common sense."

There's one more burning question I must ask, but I need to find a way to do so without being insensitive to Sekhet's grief. I think for a moment.

"Maybe Alim will yet see his way before night falls. He only has to go next door – I'm sure Mesu and Aliza would take him in." My voice falters. "I take it they have…"

"Yes, I saw Mesu painting the blood on the doorposts even as I left," Sehket reassures me. I let out a deep breath. I had been certain they would, and yet… Mesu is a rich man, one of status and influence. Among the Israelites, he will be a nobody, even looked down on by many as an outsider.

Sekhet has finished her ablutions, so we follow our noses upstairs to the living quarters, where Chenya is carving the roasted lamb while Reena cooks barley flatbreads over the open flames. Soon all is ready, and the women pass around large platters of meat and flatbread, together with chicory, fennel and coriander leaf in a wooden bowl and two earthenware vessels of watered wine.

"We give thanks to the Lord," says Echud, "and feast with joy in our hearts, for tonight he delivers us from the hands of our enemies and draws us out of the land of our suffering!"

I glance at the princess – or Batyah, as I must now call her, for she will bear a royal title no longer. Is this a feast of rejoicing or mourning for her? Certainly, she and her baby are safe beyond her hope, but she joins us in expectation that many she loves will not see the light of another day. Sekhet, too. I glance at the ridges on Echud's back, visible even through his linen tunic, and feel again the agonising fear of losing a firstborn. If our positions were reversed, would my Echud be any less bull-headed than Sekhet's son?

Meal finished, Reena takes Amana and the other children to the rooftop for some sleep; Baruch proclaims that he couldn't possibly sleep and, given the momentousness of the occasion, his mother agrees that he may watch with the adults, as long as he makes himself useful. Amias, the eleven-year-old eldest son of Udiel and Maakah, is also staying up to help. There is much still to do: bundles of bedding and clothes to be tied up; dough to be made and wrapped up in the kneading trough, so that when we camp along the way we will have bread to eat; livestock to be inspected for thorns in their hooves or any other ailments that might slow us on our journey. Old and sick animals have already been sold, at premium rates, to our Egyptian neighbours, along with other non-portable and bulky items such as Chenya's loom and the largest clay amphorae of oil, beer, and wine. In return, our necks and wrists glitter with gold and silver, our fingers and earlobes weighed down by heavy rings. If an Egyptian and a Hebrew were to stand before a stranger in these latter days, he would likely mistake the slave for the master and the master for the slave.

The work is good because it occupies both hands and thoughts for a while. But when the last roll of bedding is tied up, the last of the wine decanted into goatskin bladders and sealed tight with leather thongs, we convene on the rooftop in the cool night air, silent but for the splutter of the tallow lamp and Amana's gentle snores. Gazing over the parapet to the town spread out before me, I see pinpricks of lamplight from every house in the Hebrew quarter, like reflections of stars in the ocean of rooftops. A sudden gust of wind makes them flicker one by one, like ripples on the surface of the water. My eyes wander northward, in the direction of the palace. Whether the King sleeps I cannot tell, but all Israel watches tonight.

Echud stands next to me and I draw closer to him, leaning into his chest to feel the reassuring thump of his heart. He's a head taller than me and double my weight, but I recall the night I first held him, when he weighed no more in my arms than two omers of barley. I feel again that fierce rush of protective love, spiked with fear that reason tells me is groundless, yet is no less sharp. I felt it again through every childhood illness, every rash decision made in adulthood – most recently, and keenest, when he lay in my bed with his back torn to ribbons. I held on to him then, and I must trust that I'm permitted to keep him now. On my other side, Reena draws Baruch to her and Maakah grips Amias' shoulders, while Peninah stoops over her sleeping children and Batyah cradles her tiny son. Sekhet gazes northward, her face pale in the lamplight.

The silence is portentous, and Chenya is the first to try to lift the mood with a conversation, speaking in Egyptian out of courtesy to our guests.

"Batyah," she addresses the girl, who blinks and turns belatedly at the unfamiliar name. "Were you present when Mosheh – Moses as you'd say – last came before the King?"

Batyah nods, the movement disturbing the baby, who snuffles and roots for a feed. She waits until he is suckling contentedly before answering.

"Yes, we were all together in the throne room. The darkness was absolute, and we clung together for comfort. We had been but four days in the royal residence of Rowaty, having fled thither seeking sustenance and refuge from the calamities that had befallen us in Itjtawy."

Echud, who had been huffing with impatience at the flowery language of the well-educated Egyptian, now smiles grimly. "Yes," he mutters in Hebrew. "When the King's grain-gatherers returned empty handed to their locust-riven land, I suppose he had little choice but to come north with his household and his horses, leaving his people to starve."

"We had barely settled in to our new abode when the darkness descended. I had not yet been delivered of my child, but my time was nearly upon me. I had feared that my travail would overtake me upon the journey; now my apprehension was that the pains would come upon me in the darkness, with none able to guide me or help if anything were to go amiss."

I reach out a hand to clasp hers. Princess she may have been, but her tale tells of a frightened girl facing her first childbirth in extraordinary circumstances.

"At first, my father called for lamps and torches, but they would not light. Then he sent for the magicians and sages, commanding them to lift the curse or at least create fire through their arts to pierce the gloom. My mother and I implored him to swallow his pride and send for Moses the Hebrew, but not until we had endured three days of stifling blackness, unable to move about or even to eat, did he heed our entreaties. How the messenger found Moses is beyond my knowledge. I could not see the man's face when my father gave him the order, but from the tremor of his voice when he replied it is clear he thought he had been sent to his death. Yet Moses came.

"No light illuminated his path as he entered the palace, yet he strode through the throne room with surety in his step. Though the darkness cloaked him, there was no mistaking his presence. It filled the room. As the rap of his staff rang on the flagstones, not one among us questioned who it was or called out a challenge."

Flowery language or not, she knows how to tell a tale. Every one of us listens entranced; even Echud leans forward, grey eyes intent on her, and when she pauses for breath he motions for her to continue.

"My father knew him, too, and he called out to him: 'Moses! Cursed be the day my grandmother found you, O bringer of destruction! Thankless wretch, to deal thus with the house that fed and nurtured you for forty long years! Will you now steal even the light of the sun from us?'

"'How dealt you with my father's house, O King?' he answered. 'How deal you with us now? Will you let us go, that no further disaster shall come upon you?'

"My father hesitated, but the darkness pressed around him, and dark was his voice when he replied. 'Go! Take your men, your women, your sons and daughters. Only leave your flocks and your herds.'"

"He let us go?" pipes Baruch, his face a mask of puzzlement. "Then why…?"

"Hmph!" Echud interrupts. "Even the darkness was less dark than the King's heart. Leave the flocks and herds! How did he expect us to take an entire nation across the wilderness to settle in a far-off land with no livestock? He didn't, of course. He thought we'd take the bait, go running off into the desert and then crawl back with our tails between our legs, as a dog returns to the master that beats it."

He has spoken in Hebrew, and Batyah looks at him quizzically, so Chenya translates and she nods her head. "Alas! That, I fear, was my father's intent. Moses, the eyes of whom your God has favoured with wisdom beyond the reach of mortal man, immediately discerned the ruse. 'No!' he cried, his clear voice piercing through the blackness. 'We must take our livestock to use in worship of our God. Not a hoof will we leave behind.'

"My father's voice was black as the darkness itself. 'Unnatural demon! Serpent-tongued spawn of Apep! Not a hoof! Nay, neither hoof nor foot will your people set beyond Egypt's borders, or the full force of Montu's wrath shall fall upon you! Begone, agent of Isfet! Darken not my presence with your stench of death! Begone from my sight, and let my eyes behold you no more. The day you see my face again, you will die!'"

Echud lets out a short bark of laughter. "He said that? In the dark? 'Let my eyes behold you no more…' – ha!"

"Indeed." The princess is grave. "That is when Moses, his voice imbued with power from the Almighty God like thunder within the hall, pronounced the curse – the curse upon the firstborn." With a shudder she draws silent, folding her arms protectively around the infant at her breast.

Time passes. Moments lengthen into hours. We do not speak again but stand in silence, gazing northward. The night breeze has stilled. Rowaty holds its breath.

Around midnight, the wailing begins.

Epilogue

The Nile. For Egypt, it is the source of all life. They say it carries the seed of Osiris himself, bringing blessing and fertility wherever it touches the land.

From Swenett, far in the south, the river rushes through the night like a black-and-silver serpent, flecks of reflected starlight dancing upon its surface. As it tumbles over the cataracts, its flow is broken by small rocky islets of acacia and sedge; the waters jostle and worry the rock like a tongue over a loose tooth, while heads of white foam roil and surge over underwater obstacles. On it speeds, pushing ever northward, past Wetjeset-hor on the left, Nekheb on the right; and now the first gleamings of dawn touch the sky above, imbuing the waters with a silver-grey glow.

Through valleys and fields it runs, the promise of life and abundance fulfilled through the thick black silt deposited in the *akhet*, the season of inundation. Yet as the rosy lips of dawn stoop to kiss the riverbank, the promise withers and dies. Where those early rays should caress vast fields of ripening golden grain and blue-blossoming flax, the land lies brown and desolate. Scattered bones of sheep and cattle lie in heaps in the scorched pastureland, picked clean by jackals and bleached by the sun. If not for the constant roar and burble of the river, one might think it no more than a continuation of the desert.

The river cannot halt to determine the source of this misfortune; it must run on. Past the temple of Hathor at Inerty it winds, pale wavelets lapping at the wooden landing-stage, but no answering sound can be heard, no lowing of the sacred cow or chanting of the priest. Leaving the barren temple, it presses on toward the town of Waset; and here, amidst the gleaming palaces and prosperous dwellings, the silence is broken. A loud keening fills the morning air, many notes from many sources rising in an anguished symphony of grief. From every house, rich and poor, the macabre tones drift upward like the morning mist. All but the scattering of Hebrew houses on the outskirts; they lie in silence, deserted and still.

Onward the river flees, but the sound pursues it. From the temple of Min in Gebtu it undulates sharply to the left, past Iunet and on toward Abdju, where looms the monumental mastaba tomb of King Khaneferre Sobekhotep. From every town and settlement along the way, the wail of grief carries with the flood, crying a reproach to the sleeping king as it passes.

Tjebu, Zawty, Khemenu – each city tells the same story. The sun-barque rides on in the heavens, but no royal barge adorns the waters of the Nile today, no fishing skiff or trading ship. Even the crocodiles are absent from their basking spots on the mudbank, driven underwater by the weeping and moaning from the towns. Bare-breasted women prostrate themselves in the streets, plastering their heads with mud and striking their chests again and again as they howl out their anguish. As far as the necropolis at Beni Hasan their cries are heard, and the dead sleep uneasy in their limestone tombs.

A little further on, the river divides, the Mer-Wer channelling its water to feed the fertile region around Osiris' Lake. It's still three months until the inundation will replenish its dwindling stores, yet the Ha-Uar dams ensure there's water enough to feed all the fields around until the god Hapi releases his bounty to fill the lake with fresh water and fertilise the land with rich silt. Once again, however, fields that should be green and gold stand barren, empty and brown. The water has not failed, but the life it promises has been cut off at the root.

Between the lake and the main branch of the Nile rests the city of Itjtawy, seat of kings. From between the gleaming pillars of his temple, the cruel stone features of the crocodile god Sobek watch over the palace where six kings had taken his name and devoted themselves to his service. But he glowers in vain; his rage is impotent. The palace is empty; the occupants have gone northward with the Nile, to their doom.

Onward past towering pyramids the Nile wends, the resting places of kings long past. Along a wide straight past more ruined fields, it comes to Inebu-hedj and the ancient city of Ankh-Tawy, the Life of the Two Lands. But where is that Life now? The Sacred Tree stands charred to a stump by lightning, the great temple of Ptah crumbling to ruin. And through it all, the wailing continues.

Beyond Inebu-hedj the Nile fans out like the petals of a lotus flower, sending silver tendrils throughout the delta region – the fertile land that the Hebrews call Goshen. Here the fields are still golden, and small flocks of sheep and goats browse on green pastures beside the riverbanks. Yet many of the animals are in poor condition – old, sick, lame – and there is no herdsman to watch over them; they wander aimlessly, easy prey for jackals or the sly, basking crocodiles. And still the living are outnumbered by the dead; from time to time one of the beasts, straying too far, shies suddenly away as it comes face to face with a bleached skull, empty eye sockets gazing balefully at the sky.

To left and right the river splits, the easternmost branch dividing again only to rejoin as it rushes on toward the sea. Beyond the confluence, it meanders past the walled town of Rowaty. Here, too, the noise of mourning is heard, but from fewer throats: barely an eighth part of the people remain within the city walls. Houses stand empty, abandoned tools and half-threaded looms a testament to the hasty departure of the residents. Somewhere near the town's centre, a lone female voice wails; a few streets down it is joined by another and another, but not a man can be found unless one should ascend the hill at the north of the city to the palace district, where an extraordinary scene unfolds.

Groups of wild-eyed men in torn clothing, bare headed, their faces smeared with dirt and tears, are storming the pristine walls of the palace. Some beat upon the solid wooden gates, oblivious to their bruised and bleeding knuckles; some vent their fury on the walls themselves, kicking at them with bare or sandalled feet, taking a savage fury in the pain. Others, more rational in their rage and grief, have fastened ropes around one of the statues of the kings that line the entrance. They haul together, muscles straining, until the stone edifice topples with a crash, its regal features smashed and marred beyond recognition.

Seeing this, the group around the door find new purpose; they consult a moment and then disperse to find kindling and dry wood, returning to pile them around the door. Several of the men are armed with torches, which they thrust into the pile; soon flames leap and crackle, and the men draw back, waiting expectantly, until finally the timber gives with a crash, collapsing inward through the blackened, gaping opening. Water is thrown to douse the flames and then the men surge forward across the still-hot embers, clambering over the ruins of the door. With savage abandon they tear through the rooms, ripping and slashing with their knives at the extravagant wall hangings and spitting upon the images and frescoes. No guard is there to halt the destruction, no imperious voice orders them to stop. If any residents remain in the palace, they are sealed away in their chambers, lacking the power or the will to challenge the invading mob.

A man gives a shout; he's passed through the courtyard, slashing randomly at plants, and has come to the tomb complex of the officials who have administered from the palace through the centuries. Most of the tombs are sealed well against weather and robbers, but one stands open, the oldest and grandest of the limestone structures. Other men respond to the cry and gather around, one armed with a torch; there is a moment's hesitation, then the torch-bearer proceeds cautiously through the unsealed entrance, followed closely by the rest of the group.

After the sunlit courtyard, it takes a moment or two for the men's eyes to adjust to the dim torchlight. They look around, taking in the rich grave goods. Some of the men move to seize handfuls of gold rings and strings of beads, but most refrain: that isn't what they're here for. One, clearly a man of letters, steps forward and traces a finger over the colourful painted hieroglyphs that adorn the chamber walls.

"This is him," he says bitterly. "See! Here, and here. 'Yosef, son of Yaqob, of the land of Canaan.' This is the first of the Hebrews, the one who brought his family to settle here hundreds of years ago."

The torchlight reflects in the eyes of the group, a savage flame. With one accord, they look to the centre of the chamber, where a limestone sarcophagus rests. But the slab is already shifted from the top; the coffin within is missing.

"They took it," says one of the men. "That Moses, he entered the palace and came out with a body. They took it with them."

A rumble of anger surges through the group. Some pull out knives and begin to chip and scrape at the paint where the tomb owner's name is inscribed, as if to blot his existence from memory. Others raid the burial chamber, seizing jewellery, slashing at the richly ornamented robes that lie in musty piles, and urinating on the sarcophagus.

A low doorway at the other side of the chamber leads through to a chapel; some of the men spot it and pass on through. "It's him!" one cries, and the others leave their defacement of the burial chamber and come to see.

It is a colossal statue, made in the form of a seated man but twice human size. Painted in bright colours, it depicts a man with Asiatic features and red hair piled in a coif on his head. At the sight, the men seem to lose what little restraint they have left. Yelling a war cry, they set upon the statue with blades, chunks of rock, or their bare fists. Pushing against it all together, they succeed in toppling it, shattering the brittle stone into many fragments. Then they leave the desecrated tomb and continue their sacking of the palace, venting their bitterness and rage on royal and Hebrew property alike.

Away to the east, the red dirt of the Road of Atum lies compacted and furrowed from the passage of many feet. No stream flows through the wadi in this season, and the pastureland to either side is sparse and dry, but what little grazing remains has been ravaged and trampled as if by an army on the march. At Pithom, the well has been drained to a muddy trickle, and no guardsmen appear atop the watchtowers. Yet the trail continues, abandoning the wadi east of Pithom where an ancient trade route cuts across to the left and right, skirting the marshes to head north toward the coast, the land of the warlike Pilistim people, or south toward the Uatch-Ur, the Great Green Water, called Yam Suph by the Hebrews. At the junction, the easternmost frontier of Egypt, stands the fort of Etham, part of a string of fortifications built centuries before as the front line of defence against invasion. Yet once again the garrison stands empty, the well dry. All around are the signs of a vast camp: half-charred firewood and fragments of broken pottery attest to a great many cooking fires, while uprooted thornbushes are arranged in rings to form corrals for livestock. Yet this, too, is abandoned, and the trail turns southward down the Desert Road, along the edge of the wilderness.

To the right, the land now becomes increasingly barren the further south the road continues. To the left lie patches of greenish-brown vegetation interspersed with shallow pools; in a few months these will be filled with runoff from the Uatch-Ur and the Nile and will join together in a vast sapphire sheet, drowning the weeds and rushes that surround them, but for now the water level sits low beneath sloping banks crusted with cracked white salt deposits. These are the salt marshes of the Eastern Desert, and crossing them is perilous, even for one man alone; what looks like a firm white rock will suddenly give way beneath the feet, proving to be no more than a crust that cracks and breaks, sending one crashing through to the stinking mire beneath. No fresh water can be found there for man or beast; all is salt and would leave the drinker gasping like a landed fish to soon shrivel in the desert sun.

The pools get broader and deeper as they go along, and now there are signs that the host was hurrying: a broken sandal discarded by the wayside, a lame donkey left to wander, its pack unstrapped and the less necessary baggage items strewn about the ground. Further, we see indications as to why: another track joins the road from the north-west, and it is rutted and scored by the furrows of chariot wheels and the prints of hooves and sandals. Turning south, it follows the older trail, trampling and obscuring the marks beneath its own. This trail is quite fresh; an experienced tracker would put it as no more than a day old.

Ra's celestial barque has spanned the skies from east to west and is almost ready to begin its descent to the underworld. Egypt glows orange in the fading light, while to the east the marshes fall into purple shadow. As the trail wends ever southward, the pools morph and meld together while their waters darken to deep indigo. The patches of green between them grow sparser and cease altogether, leaving only an unbroken sheet of inky blue: the Uatch-Ur. The full moon, riding low in the east, reflects over its surface like a shimmering silver bridge.

It is here that both trails abruptly end. The road continues, lined with gnarled tamarisk and purple-flowering sea-lavender, but beyond this point they are untrampled, the red dust undisturbed. Anyone seeking to read this puzzle would find no clues to the west: it is eastward that they must turn their eyes, to the shores of the lake, where the vultures circle, their pale plumage ghostlike against the darkening sky. As the salty waters lap at the shore, they carry with them a horrible flotsam, the reason for the vultures' presence and at least part of the answer to the riddle.

Away beyond the eastern shore, the old woman glances back one final time as the topmost edge of the sun's burnished disc slips silently beneath the watery horizon. Only the far shore of the lake still glows red-orange;

the rest of its expanse is a serene indigo, lapping calmly at the darkened shore. Puah closes her eyes briefly, her breath drawn out in a single long sigh; then her shoulders drop and she turns, continuing her trudge eastward.

The moon rides higher now, partially obscured by the odd-shaped cloud that hangs in the east, flashes of red and orange flickering through its centre like the flame of a beacon. On the ground below, pinpricks of red indicate that the front of the column has halted for the night. The promise of the campfires is welcoming, but for those at the back there is still a weary distance to walk beneath the blossoming stars before they can cast themselves down and rest.

Echud still carries the little she-goat, and Puah now walks beside him, with Chenya, Reena, and the children a few paces ahead. Tomorrow Mosheh and Aharon will organise a proper marching column, with a rearguard to support the slower and weaker contingent, but today the pursuit and the crossing of the lake have put them into disarray and it's only the stragglers left at the back. The very old, the very young, the sick and the wounded are here, but there are also some more able-bodied people who have deliberately hung back from the main column, reluctant to join it. The clothing here is more diverse, many of the men clothed only below the waist while not a few women are bareheaded, in contrast to the more conservative dress of the main throng further ahead. While a few are adorned with jewellery, all have a lean, hungry look to them, ribs protruding through sallow, pockmarked skin. But they are here; they are alive. While little about the future is certain, save for the promise of a long, hard trek through barren lands, at least there is a future to look to. For most, this is preferable to the alternative.

Puah's group are hurrying now, eager to reach the security of the camp before the last orange glow of the horizon fades to blue-black night. As they pass up through the disparate rear ranks of the column, Puah pauses occasionally to greet a familiar face. A fine-clothed young woman with a royal hairpiece, cradling a tiny baby and supported by an older woman whose wrinkled face is lined with tear tracks. A dark-skinned woman in her fifties, with whom Puah exchanges a few words: she could be with her husband at the front of the column, but somehow she's ended up here at the back, among the other misfits. Perhaps the most surprising figure of all is that of a young man barely out of boyhood, clad only in a white shendyt skirt and clutching a bronze-headed spear. The rest of the exiles give him a wide berth, but Puah lets out a little exclamation and hurries forward to greet him. Echud hangs back, his brow dark, but the young man's eyes light with recognition at the sight of the old lady, and he hastens toward her and clasps both her hands warmly in his.

The last of the day's rays have faded by the time the stragglers reach camp, but the flashes of fire from within the cloud give enough light to keep their feet from stumbling. Puah and her family approach a group gathered around a campfire, who shuffle over to make room for them. Slowly and wearily, Puah lowers herself to the ground, exhaling as she unbinds her pack from her shoulders and stretches out her protesting limbs. A cake of unleavened flatbread is passed to her, hot from the flames, and she takes it gratefully.

Beside her, Echud lifts the lame she-goat from his shoulders and sets it down. He raises a hand to slap it on the rump and send it off with the rest of the herds to forage what it can from the scattered acacias and tamarinds that are dotted here and there across the dusty landscape, but his mother stops him with a word. Instead, she reaches into her bundle and withdraws a handful of barley, the goat's velvety lips brushing her skin as it eagerly accepts it. Next, she pulls out a wooden bowl and pours in a little water from her own waterskin, holding it out for the goat to lap. Many eyes around the campfire watch this performance, and not a few eyebrows are raised; yet, maybe because of the honour due her years, no remonstrations are voiced.

On finishing the water, the little goat lays its head in Puah's lap and closes its eyes. Tomorrow, there will be another long trek. Tomorrow, their camp will be further from the water's shores, and grazing will be even sparser. Tomorrow, the stores of grain will be depleted, and not even the most careful rationing can keep the leather skins of wine and water from running dry. But the goat knows nothing of this. Free from anxiety, it sleeps secure in the old lady's encircling arms.

Historical Note

There have been many attempts to date the Exodus and to determine Moses' place in Egyptian chronology. As I read up on the different theories and the evidence for and against each, one thing stood out in my mind: the need to start with the *effects*. As the Bible tells it, the Exodus cost Egypt not only the vast bulk of its labour force, but also its army, drowned in the Red Sea. We're told that "many other people" joined the Israelites in leaving Egypt (Exodus 12:38), and those who remained were in a bad way, ravaged by famine and disease. It seems inconceivable, then, that Egyptian history could have carried on unchanged. We'd expect to see, at the very least, a cessation of all building projects, and most likely a major invasion by Egypt's enemies, who would be sure to take advantage of the fact that the Egyptians were in no state to resist them.

All these conditions can be seen at the end of the Middle Kingdom period. Egypt's Thirteenth Dynasty petered out and died, and the country was overrun by Hyksos invaders. According to Egyptian historian Manetho, the Hyksos were able to conquer Egypt "without striking a blow", which indicates that some terrible disaster had overtaken Egypt and left them entirely devoid of military strength.

As their capital, the Hyksos took the city of Avaris, which before that point had been known as Rowaty. In later years, its name was changed again to Pi-Ramesses – the city named in Genesis 47:11 and Exodus 1:11 as the centre of the Israelites' residence in Egypt, and in Exodus 12:37 as the starting-point of the Exodus. Archaeologist Manfred Bietak, excavating this site in the 1990s, made an amazing discovery. Beneath the Thirteenth Dynasty palace was an older building, a mansion built in the Asiatic style. In one of the tombs belonging to this older mansion was a colossal gold statue. The figure it depicted held all the regalia of high office, but he was not Egyptian – the features and styling showed him to be Semitic. The sarcophagus in this particular tomb had been emptied.

Could this be the tomb of Joseph, his body removed by Moses as described in Exodus 13:19?

There's other evidence, too. The Ipuwer Papyrus, dated to the late Middle Kingdom, which speaks of the river running with blood and of gold and jewels being placed around the necks of slaves. The workers' village of El-Lahun, where the hastily abandoned homes of Semitic workers indicate that they downed tools and left en masse during the late Thirteenth Dynasty. Equally, there are objections that can be raised. There's the anachronistic use of the name "Ramesses" and even "Pharaoh" in the Exodus account (the term "Pharaoh" was not used until the Nineteenth Dynasty, hence why I've used "King" instead in this book); maybe these were "translated" by later scribes who wanted their audiences to recognise the names and places mentioned. Another oft-cited objection is the mention of chariots and horses; there's little to no evidence of these in the Middle Kingdom, and it's widely believed that they were introduced by the Hyksos. If they did exist as brand-new technology in the Thirteenth Dynasty, however, and if the entire fleet ended up at the bottom of the Red Sea, this could explain the lack of evidence! The traditional Egyptian chronology also presents a problem, as it does not align with the biblical timespans. David Rohl addresses this in his excellent book *A Test of Time*, which also discusses many of the points I've raised here in more detail. For anyone interested in the evidence for and against a Middle Kingdom exodus, this book is a great place to start, along with Tim Mahoney's book and film *Patterns of Evidence: Exodus*.

Both an advantage and a disadvantage of writing about such ancient history is that we can never fully know all the detail. It's a disadvantage because I've inevitably got things wrong; the advantage, however, is that I can let my imagination run wild to fill in the missing detail! The political situation described by Hasina and Aahotep in chapters 2 and 13 is purely conjectural, though not out of the question considering what is known of the period. Likewise, the history and physical description of Pithom in chapter 4 is my own invention based on the little we know from the Bible. The descriptions of Rowaty, and particularly the Palace, however, are founded in archaeology – Manfred Bietak's *Avaris: The Capital of the Hyksos* is an excellent source filled with descriptions and diagrams.

Meanwhile, the naming of Khaneferre Sobekhotep as the Pharaoh at the time of Moses' birth, and Queen Merris as his wife and Moses' adopted mother, comes from Jewish historian Artapanus (again covered in Rohl's *A Test of Time*).

I drew on many other sources as well, to fill in details such as the seasons, diet, housing, clothing, travel, gods, and medicines. Some of these sources are named in the bibliography on the next page. However, time and time again, my research came up with unanswered questions and uncertainties, on everything from the order of the kings to the colour of their skin (see https://en.wikipedia.org/wiki/Ancient_Egyptian_race_controversy). This is all part of what makes the period so intriguing, and it is why I have attempted to reach through the millennia and give form and voice to these shadowy, mysterious, unknowable characters!

Selected Bibliography

First and foremost of my sources is the book of Exodus in the Bible, in particular chapters 1–14. I also drew on other books of the Bible – for example, the character of Batyah and her son Yisbah are taken from 1 Chronicles 4:17–18 (where most English versions transliterate them as Bithiah and Ishbah).

My main source for the chronology and the evidence for a Middle Kingdom exodus was David Rohl, *A Test of Time, Volume 1: The Bible – From Myth to History* (Arrow, UK ed., 2001). These ideas are further explored by the film documentary *Patterns of Evidence: Exodus*, directed by Tim Mahoney (2015).

Manfred Bietak's *Avaris: The Capital of the Hyksos* was the main source for my descriptions of Rowaty, in particular the Palace.

Ancient History magazine, Issue 36 (Nov/Dec 2021) focuses on Egypt in the Middle Kingdom and helped supply many of the incidental details.

Other sources for details of Middle Kingdom culture, politics, dress, diet, travel and many other details that helped build the setting are listed below. There are too many to list them all individually, but the following were some of the most helpful:

- Ahrens, Alexander. "A Hyksos Connection? Thoughts on the Date of Dispatch of Some of the Middle Kingdom Objects Found in the Northern Levant." In: J. Mynářová (ed.), *Egypt and the Near East – the Crossroads* (Czech Institute of Egyptology, 2011), pp. 21–40.

- "Ancient Egyptian boat-building." *Solar Navigator*, © 2012, www.solarnavigator.net/ancient_egyptian_boat_building.htm.

- "Egyptian Farming: Agriculture in the Old, Middle, and New Kingdoms." *History on the Net*, © 2000–2022, Salem Media. https://www.historyonthenet.com/egyptian-farming.

- Fordham University, New York. *Internet Ancient History Sourcebook: Egypt* (2021), https://sourcebooks.fordham.edu/ancient/asbook04.asp.

- Millmore, Mark. *Discovering Ancient Egypt*, © 2021, https://discoveringegypt.com.

- Shehab, Naglaa. "Lights on the Royal Guard through the Significance of Two Titles Ḫnty-š and Šmsw." In *Journal of the General Union of Arab Archaeologists*, vol. 4, no. 2 (2019), pp. 90–123. https://jguaa2.journals.ekb.eg/article_30930.html.

- Spalinger, Anthony. "Nut and the Egyptologists." In *Studien zur Altägyptischen Kultur*, vol. 41 (2012), pp. 353–377. https://www.academia.edu/36332073/Nut_and_the_Egyptologists

- University of California. *UCLA Encyclopedia of Egyptology*, Open Version, © 2021, https://escholarship.org/uc/nelc_uee.

- Ziadeh, Nicola Abdo, et al. "The Egyptian calendar." *Encyclopedia Britannica*, © 2021, www.britannica.com.

Note from the Author

I hope you have enjoyed this book. I would love to hear any feedback or comments you may have; please feel free to contact me at nmunts@yahoo.co.uk.

Reviews mean the world to me as an author, so if you could take the time to leave one on Amazon, I would be immensely grateful!

Finally, I would like to acknowledge the invaluable contributions of my beta readers, Julia, Heather, and Kathryn. Kathryn in particular provided expert advice on the midwifery aspects of the book, keeping me from writing about impossible or unrealistic gynaecological situations! Heather and Julia likewise helped me avoid several errors and inconsistencies. Any errors that remain are mine and mine alone!

Printed in Great Britain
by Amazon

44065440R00138